"SHH."
She put her finger to his lips, and he kissed it.

Ashley moved her hand and touched his face, running her index finger over the hard line of his jaw.

"It's like a miracle to be able to touch you, after wanting it for so long," she whispered.

"You could always touch me," Tim said. "Anytime."

"If only it were that easy," she murmured, her eyes filling. "You'll lose your job if your captain finds out you were doing anything more than guarding me."

"What have I done?"

"Oh, Tim, don't be naive. This wasn't supposed to happen, and you know it." She bit her lip, her eyes searching his.

He reached for her and pulled her into his arms. When he kissed her, the satisfaction was so intense for both of them that they remained for a long time locked in a fierce embrace, like teenagers who are loath to lose contact for fear the magic may never happen again.

Then Tim finally lifted his head and Ashley buried her face against his shoulder.

"Come down to my room with me," he said huskily.

♦♦♦♦

"An extremely talented author...writing with conviction and power. Ms. Malek excels in detailing human relationships under fire."

—*Rave Reviews*

Doreen Owens Malek
Fair Game

POPULAR LIBRARY

An Imprint of Warner Books, Inc.

A Warner Communications Company

CHAPTER
One

ASHLEY FAIR glanced into the gilt-edged mirror over the hotel dresser and automatically straightened the bodice of her silk dress. It was going to be a long day, like many others before it. She knew she had to look flawless because of her position, and she accepted the burdens along with the perks.

She lifted a few errant strands of ash-blond hair out of her collar and surveyed herself with wide gray eyes. Good enough. Then she reached for the cup of coffee that sat steaming on the room-service tray and took a sip, mentally running through the morning's schedule. Ashley grimaced at the coffee's bitterness and began to add more cream, when a knock sounded on her bedroom door.

"Come in," she called. It was very early, but everybody she knew got up in the dark these days.

Meg Drummond, her father's assistant, walked in through the adjoining sitting room and said, "My, don't you look nice. New dress?"

Ashley nodded. "Giancarlo contributed it to the cause."

"What cause?" Meg asked dryly. "Your father's election campaign or Carlo's design career?"

"Both," Ashley replied, smiling. "I want to look my best for Dad, and when Carlo sends me things I don't have to waste time searching for clothes. But I told him we're paying full price, no freebies, no discounts. Got it?"

"Got it," Meg replied crisply.

"Don't let him talk you into anything else. He wants me to be indebted to him so he can collect later, and that's exactly what I want to avoid. He'll go along in the end. What he wants more than anything is to get his creations before the public eye, and I serve that purpose very well."

"Speaking of eyes," Meg said. "Jim thinks Carlo's got his on you."

"Don't be silly. The only figure Carlo's got his eye on is his future sales total. Did I mention that he's hired a team of chemists to create a new perfume? He's going to sell me an advance sample as soon as it's ready."

"What's it called? 'Avarice'? That guy is a bandwagon jumper; if your father loses the presidential election, Carlo will disappear like a mist at sunrise."

Ashley gazed at her friend levelly. "I know that," she said quietly. "But you're the political animal, Meg. I don't have to tell you that it pays to deal with people like him. For the moment, we can help each other, and that's what counts."

"Yeah, well, I still don't like him," Meg said darkly.

"All that oily charm. After I shake hands with him, I always want to take a shower."

Meg grinned. "One hand washes the other. Now, what's on the agenda for today?"

"This just arrived by messenger," Meg said, handing Ashly a thick manila envelope with the Justice Department seal on its cover.

Ashley slit the flap with a fingernail and glanced inside the parcel. "Oh, this is the case Harry called me about yesterday, remember? He wants me to read the briefs and give him some suggestions."

"I don't know why the Department felt they had to give you a leave to work on your father's campaign when they know they can continue to send you mounds of papers," Meg grumbled. "You have enough to do as it is."

"I told Harry when I left that I would continue working in an advisory capacity," Ashly replied, draining her cup and setting it down.

"Well, the way things are going you'll be reading that file in the bathtub," Meg said. "I don't see how you'll find any other free time. You have the regional Bar Association meeting at ten o'clock and then the League of Women Voters luncheon at twelve-thirty, with your father and stepmother in attendance."

Ashley didn't quite make a face, but her mien altered slightly. Her stepmother meant well, but her main interests in life were shopping and redecorating the Harrisburg mansion she shared with Ashley's father. Ashley didn't have an hour to waste making mealtime conversation about the deplorable lack of variety in the spring collections or the shades of color in fabric samples. But the image of solidarity must be preserved, so she resigned herself to the lunch. She hoped she would be seated near somebody more lively.

"And Jim is picking you up at eight for the Democratic dinner. It's at Congressman Marshall's house," Meg was saying.

Ashley nodded.

"And, oh, I almost forgot," Meg concluded. She snapped into a salute. "The boys in blue are arriving this afternoon."

"The boys in blue?" Ashley asked, staring.

"The police bodyguards the commissioner is sending over to stay with us during the Pennsylvania tour. Don't you remember?"

Ashley remembered. The senator was launching an eight-week tour of his home constituency to build grassroots support before widening out to canvass the nation. He had his own security force, of course, but his advisers had insisted on taking a couple of local professionals along for high-visibility protection.

"What time?" she asked Meg.

Meg looked at her notes. "After lunch."

"Do I have to see them?" Ashley inquired.

"You know better than to ask me that. Your father will be rushed; he'll just meet them quickly and pass them on to you. You'll have to do the official welcome."

Ashley sighed. As a civil rights lawyer, her impression of cops was a somewhat jaded one, and she was not looking forward to making nice with a couple of flatfeet when she could be preparing for the congressman's dinner, which was important. Her father was a prominent senator with a healthy groundswell behind him, but he still needed the wealth and influence of the Philadelphia contingency to launch him into the national spotlight.

"Okay, I'll come right back here after the lunch. By the way, what are we going to do with them?"

"I've booked suites all along the route. The plan is for them to sleep on convertible couches in the adjoining sitting rooms."

Ashley closed her eyes, then opened them. "Can't they stay in separate accommodations? We'll be tripping over them, for God's sake."

"Be reasonable, Ashley. How can they guard you if they're off somewhere down the hall? You could be dead before they realized anything was wrong. I'm booking rooms for them to shower and change and store their clothes, but they're sleeping with you and your father. In a manner of speaking."

"How many?" Ashley asked, picturing the Assyrian horde camped out in her anteroom.

"Only two."

"Thank God for that."

The telephone rang, and Meg picked it up. She listened for a moment, said, "All right," and replaced the receiver in its cradle.

"Our master's voice," she said briefly to Ashley. "Gotta go. I'll be in your dad's room if you need me. See you later."

Ashley lifted her hand as Meg left and then turned to the window to look down at the street. Her beloved Philadelphia was waking up below her. She thought of the town house her maternal grandmother once had only a few blocks away, in what was now Society Hill. But her grandmother had been dead for ten years, the brownstone long sold, and the happy Christmases she'd spent there now only a cherished memory.

Her mother, an only child, had died in an auto accident when Ashley was a year old, and her father had remarried four years later. He and his new wife raised three other children, and despite his efforts to include Ashley in everything, she had always felt like an outsider with his second family. She knew her decision to work with him on his presidential campaign, a position her stepmother was too unskilled to fill and her stepsiblings too young to assay, resulted in part from a desire to fit into his life, in some essential way, at last.

Dad, she thought, gazing unseeingly at the increasing traffic. Joseph Randall Fair III, senior senator from the state of Pennsylvania. She had watched his rise from state representative to lieutenant governor to his current pursuit of the highest office in the land. And in many respects he was still a stranger, a smiling, competent, charming stranger.

Fair was a liberal democrat, like his parents before him, bastions of the Main Line for many years. Joseph Fair II had been Ambassador to the Court of Saint James, and his widow, the candidate's mother, was even now a dowager socialite active in local and national charities. The candidate's younger brother, Ashley's uncle Will, ran the family business, a real-estate conglomerate, and his sister was a prominent clinical psychologist with a hospital practice. Achievers, all of them. Ashley thought it was as if their collective liberal conscience forced them to work like demons and to contribute disproportionately in order to justify inheriting all those millions.

And I'm carrying on the tradition, she thought wryly. Dean's List, Law Review, shunning private practice for the less lucrative but sociologically correct Justice Department. There she was able to prosecute white-collar criminals who took unfair advantage of the system she and her family believed in so strongly. Yes, she had done everything right, all down the line. Then why, when Ashley had five minutes alone to think about it, did she feel so empty? She filled her days with frenetic activity and fell into her bed exhausted so those reflective intervals didn't come too often.

The phone rang again, and she roused herself from her reverie to answer it.

Timothy Martin strolled into his office and set his Styrofoam cup of muddy coffee on the scarred desk. Thin spring sunlight filtered through the film of dirt on the leaded windows of the precinct house as he loosened his tie and tossed his coat on a chair. The walls of his office were painted institutional green and everything within them was made of metal: the desk, the chair, the filing cabinets, the trash can, even the arc lamp positioned to shine its light over his shoulder. The police force was utilitarian in its approach. Metal didn't crack and it didn't burn, and if treated with sealant it didn't even rust. The room resembled its counterpart on the other side of the law, a prison cell, similarly appointed and just as practical.

Martin was so used to the cheerless surroundings, however, that he didn't see them, concentrating instead on the pile of paperwork waiting for his attention. He was staring at it morosely, debating where to begin, when his frosted-glass door popped open and a head of red-gray hair appeared. The face below it was grinning wickedly.

"Well?" Martin said, eyeing his boss warily. Experience had taught him that Captain Rourke wearing this impish expression was never delivering good news.

"Got a job for you, Timmo," Rourke said happily.

Martin waited. Rourke explained himself in his own good time.

"Special assignment," Rourke announced, handing him a typewritten sheet of paper. "They practically requested you by name." He stood back, rubbing his hands together, savoring the younger man's response as he scanned the letter.

Martin perused a few lines and then looked up from the page. "Gerry, what is this?" he demanded.

"You can still read, I hope," Rourke replied. "They need two men to act as bodyguards to the good senator while he's on the campaign trail in his home state. He'll be on this tour for a couple of months, and the Philadelphia Metropolitan Police Force has been selected, for its outstanding record of service, to give up a couple of its own for the effort."

"Gerry..." Martin said slowly, aware of what was coming.

"You're elected," Rourke said triumphantly. "So to speak."

"Like hell I am," Martin said flatly, tossing the letter in his wastebasket with a flick of his wrist.

"Didn't you see what it said?" Rourke inquired,

wide-eyed, his lips twitching. He retrieved the paper from the trash and read aloud—" 'The officers should be between five-ten and six-two and between 170 and 200 pounds.' They're describing you, boyo." He reached up and patted Martin's cheek. "They want you should look nice on TV."

"You're not serious."

"I am. Pack a suitcase and take an unmarked car. You're attached to the senator like lint on his suit for the next two months."

"I won't do it," Martin said, meeting his superior's amused gaze.

"Oh, yes, you will. Orders from the top. Go on, take Capo with you. It'll be like a vacation."

"Come on, Gerry. It's baby-sitting."

"Sure it is. So go sit with the baby. Is this place gonna fall down while you're gone?"

"I've got the Carson murder cooking. The stakeout starts tonight."

"Jensen can handle that for you. I'll have him take over your cases while you're away."

"Jensen!" Martin snorted. "He couldn't supervise a Girl Scout Jamboree. By the time I get back, everything will be in chaos."

"Timmo, get used to it. You're the man for this job." Rourke grinned. "The senator's daughter is traveling with him, heading up his campaign staff. She's a civil rights lawyer. You can have a nice discussion with her about how hard she works to spring the criminals we take off the streets."

Martin threw him a dirty look.

"Now, don't pout," Rourke said cheerfully. "I hear

the daughter isn't bad looking. Great legs, Carmino says."

"What does he know?" Martin said scornfully.

"He saw her at the hotel when they arrived yesterday."

"Then send Carmino," Martin shot back.

"But Timmy, he's a little too short and a little too fat to match the stated requirements," Rourke observed, batting his lashes. "They want a couple of pretty boys. Like you and Capo."

"Capo will go nuts when he hears this," Martin warned.

"He'll do what he's told," Rourke said gruffly, sending the message to Martin as well.

"What's it matter what we look like, anyway?" Martin asked, irritated, certain that he was doomed but still trying, out of habit.

"Photo opportunities, Tim. Don't you read the papers? They want a couple of clones for the senator. If you're too tall you make him look like a dwarf, very bad for image. If you're too short, he's the jolly green giant by comparison. You just don't understand politics, son."

"I don't understand *you*, sending me on this . . . this . . ."

"Modeling assignment?" Rourke suggested, deadpan.

"Go on, yuk it up, old man," Martin said bitterly.

Rourke chuckled agreeably. "You'll have a ball, hobnobbing with all those high-tone, ritzy types."

"The only person I'll be hobnobbing with is Capo, and we're already sick of each other." Martin tried a final, desperation measure. "Look, can't you send a couple of rookies? They'd be easier to spare than Capo and me."

"Oh, but they wouldn't have the polish, the finesse, that refined quality you experienced officers project so beautifully," Rourke replied solemnly. "Good public relations is my life."

"I'm glad you're getting such a charge our of this," Martin said. "Why does Fair need bodyguards, anyway?"

"Standard operating procedure. Every candidate attracts a few wackos. This one is no exception. Fair has his own people, but they like to remain in the background. They need a couple of blues around to boost confidence. The commissioner wants us to 'cooperate fully.'"

"So what does that involve?" Martin said, sighing resignedly.

"You hang around and watch him, go where he goes, no big deal. They've sent us the file on the great man, and I'm having it Xeroxed right now. There are copies of questionable letters, transcripts of nut phone calls. No death threats yet, but some nasty messages. The senator is a flaming liberal, as you may know, and he attracts the sort of lunatic fringe who think his fondness for social programs is going to sell this great country of ours down the river. In other words, the usual political stuff."

"Isn't this a job for the feds?"

"Not unless something actually happens. And nothing will. Don't sweat this one; it'll be a walk in the park."

Martin was still wearing a remarkably unfestive expression.

"Look, Tim," Rourke said in a serious tone, "you could use a rest. You practically lived here during that Donelly case, and your vacation isn't coming up until August. You can't breathe this job twenty-four hours a day. You need some relaxation. A hobby, an outside interest. A woman."

"I had a woman. She left me," Martin said quietly.

Rourke skirted that delicate subject, wishing he hadn't brought it up, and said instead, "My point is, this is an opportunity for you to take it easy for a while. Go hold the senator's hand, stand on the sidelines and scare off the crazies, play poker with Capo while Fair catches forty winks. What have you got to lose?"

"Am I to understand that I'm being selected for other than cosmetic reasons?" Martin asked directly.

"Let's just say that you fit the bill in more ways than one. You're the right size and shape, and you need the down time." Rourke raised his bushy ginger brows. "Who breaks this to Capo, me or you?"

"I'll tell him," Martin said.

"Fine. He follows you around like a puppy anyway. This will give him an excuse to do it. He's out on a call now, so you can go home and get your stuff, then catch him later."

"Right. When does it start?" Martin asked, as if anticipating a death sentence.

"Today."

"Today?" Martin repeated, staring.

"You're scheduled to meet Senator Fair and his daughter this afternoon at two."

"Thanks for giving me advance notice, Gerry," Martin said dryly.

"What do you need notice for? To pack some under-wear and socks? Now, here's the address of his hotel," Rourke said, handing Martin a slip of paper. "You just stick with Fair and the girl wherever they go. They'll have a printed itinerary ready. There's a woman named Drummond on the staff; she'll handle all the hotel ar-rangements. She said that the senator wants the senior man with his daughter, so when they split up, you go with her and Capo can take Fair."

Martin nodded sourly.

"And Tim, be on your best behavior. No swearing, no spitting, no gum on the shoes. Pretend you're on a SEPTA bus."

Martin smiled thinly. "I'm going to get you for this."

"Yeah, yeah, I know," Rourke replied, laughing. "Don't be a stranger. Keep in touch." He waved and left, pulling the door closed behind him.

Martin looked after him for a moment, then sighed heavily, picking up his coat again.

He'd better go back to his apartment and pack.

Peter Ransom gazed up at the conference-room win-dow from the safety of his rented car. There was nothing unusual about it; the window looked like every other window in the Pittsburgh hotel. It was still as ordinary as it had been when he first checked it, before dawn several hours earlier. He got out of the car, strolled through the parking lot around to the front of the hotel. The doorman, busy flagging cabs in the morning rush-hour traffic, didn't notice him as he examined the brick facade closely, hands in pockets in a casual posture. When the doorman paused in his labors and glanced

around, Ransom drifted past him, ascending the stone
steps and passing through the revolving door into the
lobby.

He noticed everything, fading into the wallpaper himself, passing through the flow of hotel guests like a
wraith. He was dressed for obscurity in light gray slacks
and a dark gray jacket. His blond hair was short, neatly
and conservatively styled, and he wore dark sunglasses
that hid his eyes and disguised his expression.

No one paid any attention to him.

Peter Ransom was not his real name. He remembered
his real name, which had been made up by the nurse
who found him, but he rarely thought about it, the way
he rarely thought about old weapons he had discarded
for newer, more useful ones.

Ransom stopped at the foot of the main staircase and
pretended to peruse one of the magazines left for the
entertainment of the guests. He checked out the bank of
elevators and the activity at the registration desk, then
dropped the magazine and walked up the curving main
staircase.

He avoided elevators as a matter of practice.

Ransom turned the corner to the second-floor corridor, then fell back and glanced around it, his hand going
to the pistol nestled in the small of his back.

It probably wasn't a setup, but his almost supernatural
caution had kept him alive more than once.

The hushed, carpeted hallway was empty.

The conference room was at the end of the hall. He
walked toward it slowly, checking out the closed doors
all along the way, trying the handle of a service closet as
he passed. He finally paused before the conference-

room door, listening, and then knocked on it, his hand still in position to draw his gun if necessary.

"Come in," a male voice called.

Ransom accepted the invitation. He opened the door halfway and looked inside, then entered the room.

There were three men, dressed in suits, seated at a large oval table. The man in the middle had a stack of manila folders at his place, and his heavily veined hands were folded on top of them. The men on either side of him, one short, one portly, wore identical sober expressions.

Ransom glanced at his hosts, then around the room. He had checked it out before they arrived, going back to his car to watch each of the men come to the hotel separately.

Everything seemed to be in order. He relaxed marginally, eyeing the leader.

"Please be seated," the spokesman said.

Ransom hiked one leg up onto the edge of the table and waited.

The leader cleared his throat. "You know the purpose of this meeting," he said in a soft, modulated voice. "It was explained to you when this was arranged that we represent a group with quite a large stake in preventing Senator Fair from coming to power. We feel that we are unable to run the risk of the forthcoming election. . . ."

Ransom raised his hand, interrupting the speaker. "I don't care why you want it done," he said flatly. "Your politics and your motivations are of no interest to me."

The leader fell silent, watching him.

"I think you are familiar with my terms, but I'll go over them again just so there is no misunderstanding,"

Ransom continued. "These terms are not negotiable. They will be met or I will not take the job."

The men waited.

"First, I'll require half of the stated fee up front, and the second half on completion of the assignment. You will not contact me at all after today, and you will not discuss me or my assignment with each other or anyone else outside of this room. If I discover during the course of preparation that you have not complied with these terms, I'll keep the money I have and consider the order terminated. If I complete the job and the second half of the fee is not deposited in the numbered account I have indicated within three business days of completion, I will come after each of you. Personally. Right now I know you only as nameless customers, through my contact, but I'll find you. Believe me."

The three men exchanged nervous glances. They believed him.

Ransom pulled out a pack of cigarettes and lit one, inhaling luxuriously as he relaxed. These men were afraid of him; there was no threat here.

"Second," he went on, "I pick the place and time of the hit, and the method. I'm the professional; I'll make the professional decisions. You supply me with the information I require, and I'll formulate the plan."

The leader shifted in his seat. Ransom waited, but the man didn't speak.

"Third," Ransom continued, "the identity you manufacture for me will be discarded as soon as the job is done. All papers, pictures, and other items will be destroyed immediately, and the name and occupation never re-used."

Ransom looked at each man in turn. He was met with expressionless stares.

"Fine," he said, aware that this lack of protest was assent. "What do you have for me?"

The leader passed the stack of folders down the table to him. "All the background information you requested on the senator, his family, and close associates. His itinerary for the eight-week campaign tour of Pennsylvania, including what details we could obtain. Security is already tight. Not a lot was available."

"I'll get what I need," Ransom replied shortly, riffling through the papers. He examined the contents of two packets and put them aside. "Is this my identity?" he asked, opening another folder.

The leader nodded. "Social security card, employment ID card, driver's license, credit cards, all made out to the name Peter Ransom. The photo you gave the contact was used for the pictures."

"Where am I working and what am I doing?" Ransom asked, picking up the ID card.

"You lease office space for a real-estate concern," the leader informed him. "Real estate was one of the areas of expertise that you indicated to your contact."

Ransom smiled slightly. He had worked in real estate for a short time after the army, until he determined that killing people for a living, as opposed to killing them for his country, was a distinctly more lucrative field.

"Do you have a monitor on this number?" Ransom asked, indicating the telephone exchange on the ID card.

"Monday through Friday, nine to five," the leader replied. "She'll answer with the indicated company name, say you're out for the day or away from your desk, and take any messages for you."

Random nodded. The company had to seem real if anyone checked.

"There's a stack of business cards there, too, and stationery," the leader added.

"How about the location?" Ransom asked.

"It's an office building. We took a suite and put the name on the door. The girl monitoring the phone will be at the reception desk."

"What did you tell her?" Ransom asked.

"She thinks that we're opening a new branch of the business and won't be moving in for a while, so we need an advance guard to make sure we don't miss any calls. The girl's an evening college student; she doesn't care what's going on there. She's just collecting her pay while she reads her textbooks and hopes the phone doesn't interrupt her."

"Okay. What about after hours?"

"The door will be padlocked from the inside, and we'll have a guard on duty there at night. If somebody got curious, they'd have to break down the door, and then have a lot of explaining to do."

"Good," Ransom said. The deception would hold up short term, time enough for him to get the job done; he was never around long term.

"Here are the keys you'll need," the leader said, indicating a thick envelope. "This one is for the apartment we rented, and there's a copy of the lease. It's rented in the company name, furnished, in a luxury high rise in Philadelphia. The address is there. Wardrobe has also been supplied, as requested. The car is leased in the company name, like the apartment. Any questions?"

Ransom opened the envelope, looked at the contents briefly, then shook his head.

"The rest of it is miscellaneous," the leader said. "The senator's quirks and habits, hobbies, favorite restaurants, anything we could find. We didn't know what might be helpful, so we put it all in there."

Ransom looked up. "Where's my money?" he said.

The short man to the left of the leader spoke up for the first time. "Wait a minute," he said stiffly. "So far we've made a substantial investment in you merely on the recommendation of your contact. How do we know you'll perform as expected?"

Ransom stubbed out his cigarette in the hotel ashtray, not bothering to answer.

"How do we know Fair will be eliminated in accordance with our timetable?" the short man insisted.

Ransom directed his hazel gaze to the speaker, and the man held it for only a moment before looking down.

"The senator will not survive this tour of Pennsylvania," Ransom replied flatly. "That's all you need to know."

The short man looked up again. "I don't like it," he said defiantly, looking at each of his companions in turn. "We don't know this guy that well."

The leader, who had heard this from him before, moved to silence him, but Ransom intervened.

"Do *you* want to kill the senator, little man?" Ransom said to him scornfully.

The short man flushed, his hands gripping the table.

"No?" Ransom persisted, his lips twisting with disdain. "Too much at risk? Career, kiddies, sterling reputation?"

The short man looked away.

Ransom nodded. "Well, that's the difference between me and you, junior. I got nobody, and I got nothing to lose."

The leader sighed heavily, shaking his head. He wanted to secure this deal as bloodlessly as possible; it was a mistake to get into personalities.

"So I guess you'll have to rely on me to get the job done, won't you?" Ransom concluded sarcastically.

There was no reply.

"Look," Ransom said, standing, "I don't have to prove myself to you people. If I made a practice of stiffing my clients, I'd be out of business. I realize that it's upsetting for solid citizens like yourselves to talk to me, but I insist on an initial meeting with the paying customers, and we've had it. You won't see me again, so you can forget this ever happened and just look forward to the result." He shrugged with an air of finality. "The contact knows my track record. He discussed it with you. Now, if that's not enough, just say so, and I'm gone."

The leader held up a placating hand, drawing a final envelope from his inside breast pocket.

"We're satisfied," he said. "Here's your retainer. Good luck."

Ransom took the money and counted it before stowing it inside his jacket.

"Gentlemen," he said with a faint, sneering emphasis on the word that did not escape his audience, "it was a pleasure doing business with you."

He walked around the table and left the room.

"Bastard," the short man said when Ransom was safely gone.

"You don't have to love him, Charlie. You're not getting married," the leader said. "He can be as arrogant as he likes as long as he gets the job done."

"He's charging a fortune," Charlie said furiously.

"Murder comes high," the leader said. "And he's the best. Twelve hits in the last five years. Only one of the targets survived, and he's now a vegetable, due to extraordinary medical intervention. Ransom uses the mob method: two shots, head and heart. He never misses."

"I still don't like it," the short man complained.

"Do you want Joseph Fair to become the next President of the United States?" the fat man asked rhetorically, speaking for the first time.

The short man didn't answer.

"Then we have to make sure he isn't alive to run. Stop being such a chickenshit, Charlie, and face up to what must be done," the fat man said.

The leader stood, closing the hasps of his briefcase. "I think our business here is completed," he said, and his colleagues rose to follow him as he left the room.

When Martin got back to the precinct house, Capo was seated behind a desk in the open booking area, typing with two fingers on an old portable. He was wearing an intense, pained expression.

"Hey," Martin greeted him, sitting on the edge of the desk.

"Don't interrupt me. I'm concentrating," Capo said. "Why don't they get us one of those computers like they

have in Burglary? I feel like George Washington writing
the Declaration of Independence with a quill pen."

"George Washington didn't write the Declaration of
Independence. Thomas Jefferson did."

"Excuse me, Joe College, I stand corrected."

"You don't have to go to college to know that, Capo.
Fourth-graders know that. My nephew is in *second*
grade and he knows that."

Capo ignored the razzing, searching out another key
and stabbing it with his forefinger. Then he said, "Damn
it."

"What?"

"Made another mistake." He yanked open the desk
drawer to get the bottle of correcting fluid.

"Didn't you take typing in high school like everybody
else?" Martin asked, smiling.

"I barely took high school," Capo replied absently,
unscrewing the plastic cap.

"What is that, anyway?"

"Interview report. This woman listed her husband officially missing this morning. Seems he was a gym
teacher and he got suspended by the Board of Education
for taking weird things from the kids' gym lockers. Jock
straps, baseball gloves, track shoes. She says he was so
humiliated he may have killed himself. Or somebody
else killed him. Anyway, he's disappeared and she
thinks he's dead, which is why she was talking to me.
She wants a homicide investigation, and he's been gone
long enough."

"You sure do catch the garbage, don't you?"

"That's because whenever somebody calls in and they

sound like they're one step away from a psychiatric ward, Rourke sends me to talk to them."

"Maybe he thinks you're on the same wavelength."

"Thanks a lot," Capo said, unoffended.

"Well, forget that. You can give it to somebody else to finish. We're got something more important going."

Capo looked up at him. "What could be more important than this?" he asked sarcastically.

"Senator Fair."

Capo looked interested. "Oh, yeah? Are we escorting a motorcade or something? I saw on the news that he was in town."

"It's more than a motorcade."

Capo waited.

"We've been assigned to guard him and his daughter for the next couple of months."

Capo's mouth fell open. "Are you kidding me?"

"Do I look like I'm kidding?" Martin countered.

Capo sat back in the swivel chair and said slowly, "I always knew Rourke hated me."

"Come on, it won't be that bad," Martin said, trying to sound convincing.

"Two months of wetnursing some gladhanding politico?" Capo said. "Geez, I thought filling out reports was bad."

"You have to go home and get some clothes," Martin said. "We're going to be staying in the hotels with them as they travel."

"Why is Rourke sending you on this?" Capo asked. "You're his boy, he's your rabbi. Everybody knows he and your dad were tight in the good old days."

"He thinks it will be an easy tour," Martin said

lightly. "And we both fit the physical description they sent."

"Physical description? Oh, God, I don't think I want to hear this."

"They requested people of a certain height and weight to match the senator so he doesn't look out of place with us."

"Great. I wish I was a midget."

"Stop complaining and go home. Kiss the wife and bambinos. You won't be seeing them for a while."

"Lorraine isn't going to like this."

"Sic her on Rourke. He deserves it."

"Maybe I will. What do I do with this?" Capo indicated the report he was still holding.

"Put it on Hadley's desk. Just leave him your notes to fill in on it. It'll take him five minutes. He can type."

"Ha." Capo did as Martin advised, and then picked up his jacket, slinging it over his shoulder.

"Are you coming with me?" Capo asked as Martin followed him between the rows of desks.

"Looks like it."

"You just want to see Lorraine again. I know you like her legs."

"I don't deny it."

"Why don't you get married, Tim?"

"You got somebody for me to marry?"

"Lorraine has a sister."

"Oh, yeah?"

"She's twelve."

"Very funny.

"She's got her junior-high spring dance coming up soon."

"I just bought a new suit."

They passed through the lobby and out into the spring day.

Meg Drummond sidled up to Ashley and whispered, "The policemen are here. They're waiting out in the sitting room."

"What do they look like?"

Meg grinned. "Cutest cops you ever saw. I think they sent us the PBA poster boys."

Ashley laughed. "How do they seem?"

"Like cops," Meg replied, rolling her eyes. "'Just the facts, ma'am,'"

"Has my father seen them?"

"He met them and passed them on to you."

"I guess I'd better get to it, then," Ashley said, putting aside the brief she was reading and standing up. She followed Meg out of the bedroom and into the adjoining sitting area, which had been fitted with a sofa bed. Her father's quarters had a like arrangement.

The two men stood when Ashley entered. They were almost the same height, dressed similarly in dark pinstriped suits. The slightly taller one had thick black hair and startlingly blue eyes, framed by long jet lashes. He was saved from a feminine prettiness by the hard, masculine planes of his face and the lean muscularity of his body, which the tailored lines of his clothes did nothing to disguise.

He stepped forward, extending his hand, which Ashley shook. "Miss Fair, I'm Lieutenant Martin," he said, his gaze level and direct. Ashley was conscious of the strength of his grip, the shoulder holster partially revealed when his jacket pulled back as he moved his arm. She looked up at him, saying nothing. In some subtle way he was not exactly what she'd expected.

Martin nodded to indicate his companion. "This is Sergeant Capo."

Ashley shook hands with the second cop, who was also handsome, but in swarthy Mediterranean style, with dusky skin, wavy hair, and eyes like onyx gemstones. He was staring at her.

"Gentlemen, welcome," Ashley said easily. "My father and I appreciate your presence, as I'm sure he told you. We're aware that a political candidate can never be popular with everyone, so we're grateful for the protection."

She's as smooth as her old man, Martin thought. The candidate was all iron-gray hair and Bar Harbor tan, and his daughter bore hardly any resemblance to him, but the infectious, intimate directness was the same. She had obviously been well trained.

"I hope you have everything you need," she was saying graciously.

Capo was eyeing her as if she were dessert.

Martin nudged him unobtrusively, and he started slightly.

"We're very comfortable, thank you," Martin replied flatly.

She had a polished porcelain beauty that she must have inherited from her dead mother. The taupe dress she was wearing flattered her light coloring, the appealing lines of her petite, slender frame. Jasmine perfume, no doubt ruinously expensive, floated between them, seeming to emanate from her ivory skin. A heartbreaker, Martin suspected. But in appearance and manner, a lady.

"I assume there isn't any reason to anticipate trouble," she said pleasantly.

"There's no cause for alarm, Miss Fair," Martin replied, his tone professional, disguising his reaction. "We expect this to be a routine assignment, but we'll take every necessary precaution."

Ashley nodded, thinking that she could understand why he had been selected for this job. He certainly was no strong-armed type; his demeanor was more that of a business executive or a middle manager. Though she strongly suspected he could be very tough if the necessity arose.

"Well, Lieutenant, I have things to do, and I'm sure you do too. Make yourselves at home, feel free to use the bar or room service. We won't be going out until this evening, and then my father and I will be attending separate events. I assume one of you will be accompanying each of us."

"Yes."

"Good. Until then." Ashley turned and disappeared into the bedroom, followed by Meg Drummond, who cast one curious glance over her shoulder before she pulled the door closed behind them.

"Give me some air. I'm dying," Capo said in a loud stage whisper, closing his eyes and leaning against the wall, feigning weakness.

"Knock it off," Martin said tersely.

"Did you see that skin, that hair? Jesus, help me, I'm a dead man."

"Will you shut up, for Christ's sake? They'll hear you," Martin said savagely under his breath.

Capo stared at him incredulously. "What's the matter with you, man? You had a hormone transplant or something? That is one good-looking woman."

"You'd look good too if you had a team of servants waiting on you hand and foot the way she does," Martin said darkly.

"A team of servants didn't give her that figure. Come on, Timmy, the privileges of rank irritating you again?"

"She was talking to us like we were a couple of waiters sent by some caterer she'd ordered up on the phone."

"I don't feel that way. I thought she was very nice. You're too sensitive."

Martin shot him a skeptical glance.

"Oh, I get it," Capo said. "Everyone else may be taken in by her, but not you, Timmy. You're too smart for that, right?"

"I just don't think it's a good idea to make fools of ourselves the first day on this job, so will you can the discussion of her assets?"

"The other one's not bad either," Capo observed, ignoring him. "Not in the same league with the candidate's kid, but not bad. I think she probably bites, though. She looks awfully efficient."

"Capo, this may come as news to you, but we are not here to rate the female members of the senator's entourage," Martin said testily.

"Ah, so she did get to you," Capo said, smiling slightly. "Which one of them do you want to go with tonight?"

"The senator requested you," Martin replied shortly.
"He wants the higher-ranking body with his daughter."

"I guess chivalry isn't dead."

"Guess not."

"I'd love to escort Lady Ashley," Capo said, sighing,
"but if my wife sees a newspaper picture of me within
five feet of that delicate dish, I'm going to wind up
divorced. I'm safer going with the senator." He walked
to the portable bar in the corner and got himself a soft
drink. "Want one?" he said to Martin, unscrewing the
cap.

Martin shook his head.

"Well, now we know how the other half lives," Capo
said, taking a deep swallow.

"You've been here five minutes," Martin replied
dryly. "I don't think that's long enough to learn much."

"I got a look at her ladyship. That's enough. She be-
longs in one of those magazine ads, wrapped in a mink.
If I weren't a happily married man . . . *madonna mia, o
sole mio*." He downed another swallow of his soda.

When Capo lapsed into Italian it was always a bad
sign. "She's got a boyfriend, Romeo," Martin reminded
him. "James Dillon. His name was on the list they gave
us of people allowed free access to the Fairs."

"Oh, I haven't read all that stuff yet."

"Well, do it. Dillon is some lawyer type whose daddy
has a big-deal firm down in D.C. She met him at
Georgetown."

"You remembered all that, did you?" Capo said
mildly.

"We're supposed to remember all of it. That's why
they gave us the information, Tony. Now, stop trying to

be cute, because I've seen that act before and it's wearing thin, okay?"

Capo surveyed him for several seconds in silence and then said easily, "Settle down, Tim. I was just kidding about the girl. I thought as long as we were on this joke assignment we might as well have a little fun. But if you're going to turn into Sergeant Friday, I can play that game too. Any way you want it."

Martin met his friend's gaze, and then shrugged.

"I must be a little more ticked off about this thing than I realized," he said.

"Something's bugging you, buddy," Capo agreed.

Martin dropped into one of the needlepoint chairs and stretched his long legs in front of him. He sighed and ran his hands through his hair.

"Two months of following her and her father around the state, watching the senator shake hands and kiss babies," he muttered. "Rourke's idea of a rest."

"I guess it beats staking out your average murder suspect," Capo said philosophically.

"We'll meet a better class of people on this tour," Martin said with a wry smile.

"Oh, I don't know. Remember that baroness who poisoned her husband with prussic acid in his tea? She was pretty classy."

Martin laughed.

"And the senator's politics are just a little to the left of 'Yippie! Hooray!' Maybe some of the opposition richies will get stirred up enough to make things colorful."

"Not too colorful, I hope," Martin said fervently.

"What time are they going out tonight?"

"Eight."

"Come on. We're off duty until then. Let's go get some lunch. The restaurant downstairs is supposed to be the best in town."

Martin rose and followed Capo into the hall.

CHAPTER
Two

T HAT NIGHT, as Ashley dressed, she tried to imagine what the evening would be like with the constant presence of the policemen. She wondered which one would go with her, and how Jim would react to him.

She smoothed the hem of her black crepe sheath and tried on two pairs of heels, one open at the toe and the other closed pumps. She settled on the pumps and added a string of mobe pearls with a diamond-and-sapphire clasp. She studied the effect, and then tried on the matching earrings, wondering if it was too much. She decided it wasn't, and looked around for her makeup case to select the right shade of powder and lipstick.

Her mind was occupied as she went about her toilette. She hadn't seen Jim in a couple of weeks; he'd been busy at the firm and unable to get away, even for a quick trip on the shuttle. Dillon and Hunley was one of the most prosperous commercial firms in Washington, where there were quite a few, and Jim was the heir apparent. He had been courting Ashley since their final days at Georgetown Law School. Five years later, she still hadn't agreed to marry him.

He was nothing if not persistent. She'd turned down an offer from D & H to take the Justice Department job when she graduated, but that had not discouraged him. He pursued her relentlessly, and they were now an item on the D.C. social scene, drifting along in a quasi-engaged status that she was somehow too enervated to disturb. Jim offered social protection, he was an acceptable escort, he knew all the same people, and she needed someone to accompany her through the campaign. She kept telling herself that she would do something definitive after the election. That was far enough off not to be an immediate concern.

She traced her lips with vivid red, studied the effect, and then wiped them clean with a tissue. That shade, combined with her white skin, always made her look like a performer in Kabuki theater. She settled on a pinker tone and then brushed her hair briskly, her thoughts returning to Jim.

He said he loved her, and she believed that he thought he did. She was afraid, however, that what he really loved was the image: an attractive, educated senator's —perhaps president's—daughter to pose before the family hearth with the next generation for the Christmas cards. Raised in a political family, she was very aware of appearances, and she could understand why he wanted her so badly. But she always had the feeling that anyone else with her background would have done as well; he had settled on her because she was the one he happened to meet. He was ardent and dutiful and even endearing in his way, but for her there was no fire.

Was she wrong to miss it, to want it so? Was she selfish to look for more, when she already had so much? Was there really anything else out there, or had she just seen *Wuthering Heights* too many times?

She didn't have the answers to these questions.

She put down her hairbrush and transferred her wallet and cosmetics to a beaded black evening bag, picking up a silk knit shawl from the back of a chair as she passed.

She was ready.

When she stepped through the door into the sitting room, Martin was waiting for her. He was wearing the same suit with a fresh shirt. He straightened as she entered and hastily stubbed out the cigarette he was smoking.

"Hello," Ashley said.

He nodded, his eyes traveling over her from head to foot, then moving away.

"Have the others gone already?" she asked.

He nodded again. "Your father and Miss Drummond left with Sergeant Capo about ten minutes ago."

"I see." So Martin was going with her. "Mr. Dillon hasn't called up, has he?"

"No."

"He must be running a little late."

As if in response to her statement, the outer door opened and Ashley exclaimed, "Jim! I was just looking for you."

Dillon crossed the room in three strides, ignoring Martin, and took both of Ashley's hands, kissing her on the cheek. He was about what Martin had anticipated. He looked as though he had stepped from the pages of a menswear catalog, with carefully streaked chestnut hair, expensively understated clothes, and a "tennis anyone?" physique.

"I missed you," he said warmly to Ashley.

She smiled. "Jim, it's good to see you." She turned and indicated their companion. "Jim, I'd like you to meet Lieutenant Martin of the Philadelphia Police Department."

Martin stepped forward, and Dillon shook hands with him.

"He's been assigned to us for the state tour," Ashley added. "He'll be going with us tonight."

It was clear that this was an unwelcome bulletin.

"I thought the cops were for your father," Dillon said in a low tone, but loud enough for Martin to hear.

"For both of us," Ashley said shortly, putting on her gloves.

"Can't he just meet us there?" Dillon asked. He obviously wanted to get Ashley alone.

"He's supposed to travel with me, Jim. Please cooperate," Ashley said with a note of suppressed impatience.

Martin felt ridiculous letting her speak for him. But since he was not a party to the conversation, he could do nothing but stand by and listen to them discuss him as if he weren't there.

"Ashley," Dillon said in a wheedling tone.

"We're late," she said, and turned to Martin. "I'm ready, Lieutenant."

"Do you have to wear that?" Dillon asked, addressing Martin for the first time. Having lost the argument, Dillon turned his irritation on its cause, pointing to Martin's gun, visible as he adjusted his coat.

"Yes," Martin replied tersely.

"I really don't think that's necessary," Dillon complained, his fine features mirroring refined distaste.

"Let the man do his job, Jim," Ashley said briskly, and strode from the room.

The two men had no choice but to follow her.

It was a silent ride down in the elevator, and when they got to the waiting limousine, Dillon said to Martin, "Can't you follow us in another car?"

Martin felt his patience waning, but he managed to say levelly, "No, I'm sorry."

He got in front with the driver. As soon as Dillon and Ashley were settled in the back, Dillon pushed the button to raise the window between the seats.

"Jim, what's the matter with you?" Ashley demanded of him immediately. "You're doing everything you possibly can to make that man uncomfortable."

Dillon was silent a long moment and then said, "I'm sorry, Ash, but I was looking forward to spending the evening alone with you. I haven't seen you in quite a while, and I didn't expect to be sharing you with some . . . bodyguard."

"I told you they were being assigned to us."

"I know, I know. I guess I forgot. Or I didn't realize they'd be showing up so soon."

"Well, they're here, and we have to make the best of it," Ashley said shortly.

Dillon took her chin in his hand and kissed the tip of her nose. "I promise, I will. Now, can't we talk about something else?"

The conversation shifted to the campaign and Dillon's practice. In the front seat, cut off by the glass partition,

Martin could hear nothing of what they were saying. He suspected that Dillon was deliberately trying to make him feel déclassé, and then realized that Dillon wouldn't consider a cop important enough to snub. To him Martin was just another type of servant, and he'd treated him exactly as he would one of the help, as Ashley Fair had done.

Martin stared out the side window at the passing scenery. It changed from city to highway to blooming suburbs as they headed out the Main Line. They were going to the home of one of Senator Fair's staunchest supporters, Congressman Matthew Marshall, heir to a newspaper fortune. The senator had to speak at a fundraiser first, so his daughter was making an early appearance to smooth any ruffled feathers until the man himself could arrive.

The trip to Gladwyne was short, without traffic, and they arrived in about twenty minutes. Martin looked around as they pulled up to an electronically controlled gate manned by a uniformed security guard. He examined the car from the safety of his little house and then picked up the telephone, waving them through the wrought-iron barrier, which sprang open like Aladdin's cave to let them pass.

The guard had evidently recognized Ashley.

The house was visible as a blaze of light through the trees as they drove up a long lane lined with elms and maples. At its end the driveway widened to a circle with a marble fountain splashing in its center. The stucco Georgian colonial rose behind it, with double oak doors hung with brass, and quoined corners and crenellated windows, evidence of a stonemason's artistry. Lush landscaping crowded the brick walk as Ashley and Dillon made their way to the entrance, Martin trailing them while the chauffeur parked the car.

The door was opened by a uniformed maid who showed them into the largest entry hall Martin had ever seen. An immense crystal chandelier sparkled overhead, its light reflected from the gleaming surface of the polished parquet floor and the delicate cherry antiques. An ivory Kirman rug cushioned their footsteps as the maid took Ashley's wrap and showed them into a large parlor where people were milling about with drinks in hand. Martin could hear dance music coming from somewhere else in the house as he followed the moving couple.

Their hosts greeted them, the smiling congressman with his bluff, hearty good looks—why did these politicians all seem like doppelgängers of one another? Martin wondered—and his slim, blond wife in a chic ice-blue dress. Marshall kissed Ashley, shook hands with Dillon, and nodded to Martin when his presence was explained. Then he guided them into the throng, making sure they blended in effortlessly.

Martin kept well back, observing Ashley work the room.

She seemed to know everybody, and Martin had to admire her panache. She appeared born for the performance she was giving, moving through the crowd as naturally as a dancer on the boards. He began to unwind as she bussed cheeks and shook hands and exchanged pleasantries with the guests. These people were all supporters of the senator; it was unlikely he would find any assassins here. He took up a position next to the ornate fireplace and leaned on the carved pine mantel. He took a drink from a passing server, standing with the fluted glass in his hand, not sipping it but trying to blend in with the festive crowd. The burning logs in the grate lent a cheerful warmth to the room, which was exposed to the cool spring night, French doors open to a flagstone patio beyond the house.

The beautiful people, Martin thought. And they certainly were. He had never seen so many stunning women together in one place in his life, the young ones fresh and brimming with juice, the older ones well tended and carefully preserved, all of them groomed and outfitted like thoroughbreds. And yet even among them Ashley stood out, or so it seemed to him as his eyes followed her through the crush of people.

He was supposed to be watching her, so he did. His gaze was cynical, recognizing her act for what it was, and yet he felt the pull of her beauty and her charm, even so. Dillon remained at Ashley's side, smiling and playing the hail-fellow-well-met role to the teeth. He was obviously an asset, moving as easily through the crowd as Ashley did, greeting many of the partygoers by name. Martin's gaze passed over the elegant furnishings, the silk draperies and lighted curio cabinets and Aubusson carpet, looking instead for hiding places and suspicious characters. It appeared impossible that any uninvited guests could have gotten through the security system, or approached on foot through the surrounding acreage of the estate, but Martin had seen too much in his years on the force to take anything for granted.

He was so absorbed in his scrutiny that he started when Ashley said at his elbow, "Are you holding up the fireplace, Lieutenant?"

Her tone was light, her expression teasing.

"Uh, no. Just trying to stay out of the way," Martin replied shortly.

"Do you like it?" she asked.

"The fireplace?"

"Yes. It's very unusual, don't you think?"

He nodded. Since she had brought it up, he asked bluntly, "Why is it green?"

She smiled. "That's Connemara marble, quarried in Ireland. The chandelier and the glassware are Waterford. The rococo gilt mirror over there is from the estate of Lord Cadoghan of Kerry. Sean Marshall is very proud of his heritage."

Martin said nothing. He didn't know what rococo was, and he'd never heard of Lord Cadoghan.

"You're Irish, aren't you?" she asked, smiling.

"My father was," he replied stiffly, consciously resisting what he saw as a transparent attempt to disarm him. Then he added curiously, "How did you know?"

"From looking at you," she said, and he almost smiled back at her.

"Relax, Lieutenant," she said in an undertone. "No one has a gun to my head."

"It's my job to make sure that doesn't happen."

"So of course you can't enjoy yourself."

"I'm not here in a social capacity, Miss Fair," Martin answered.

"I know that, but you don't have to look so . . ."

Martin waited.

"Grim," she finished.

Dillon appeared behind her. "Are we moving on, Ash?" he said, glancing at Martin.

She nodded. "There's another crowd in the ballroom, Lieutenant, and I want to get in there before my father arrives. All right?"

"Fine."

Martin trailed after them through the central hall, passing a dining room with another elaborate chandelier, where the staff was setting up a cold buffet, and a paneled study lined with books. At the back of the house a set of sliding doors parted to reveal a cavernous room with a strip hardwood dance floor and a raised musician's dais at the back. It was occupied by a five-piece band playing retrospective tunes; "Moonglow" was currently floating through the air. About forty couples were dancing to its strains.

They stood waiting for the number to end as Martin scanned the entrance and exits. When the music stopped, the band took a break and the people eddied around Ashley. Dillon excused himself and left the room with an older man as Ashley fell into conversation with the man's wife. Martin moved off to a discreet distance, always keeping Ashley well in sight.

"My dear, wherever did you find him?" Mrs. Clinton said to Ashley, nodding unobtrusively to Martin. "He's absolutely delicious. Those mesmerizing eyes. 'Put in with a sooty finger,' as we used to say in my day."

Ashley smiled dryly. "That's the police escort your husband encouraged Commissioner Reardon to provide, Mrs. Clinton. Lieutenant Martin."

Mrs. Clinton looked shocked. "Darling, he can't be a policeman. They carry those big sticks and walk around with handcuffs dangling from their belts."

"I assure you, he's a cop," Ashley replied, suppressing a smile.

"Well, if that's what they look like, I'll have to speak to Harold about getting me one," Mrs. Clinton replied wickedly, and went off into a peal of laughter.

Ashley couldn't help but join in, and was soon in a ribald discussion with the delightful old lady, who was secure enough in her position to say startling things without worrying about the consequences. The band returned, but Dillon didn't, and a ward leader Ashley knew casually asked her to dance.

It wasn't until they got out on the dance floor that Ashley realized how intoxicated the man was. The champagne had been flowing freely for a couple of hours, and he had obviously drunk too deeply from the well. He trampled her feet and held her too close and breathed alcohol fumes in her face. The band was unfortunately playing the long version of "As Long as I Have You," and showed no sign of stopping. She stumbled along clumsily with her partner, looking around anxiously for Dillon, who had not reappeared.

It was some moments before Martin realized that Ashley was in trouble. She was so good at playing her role that he didn't realize her partner was smashed until they practically collided with another couple dancing next to them. Then he noticed the white lines of strain bracketing Ashley's mouth, her fixed smile, and he glanced about quickly for Dillon, who was nowhere in sight. Making a quick decision, he strode purposefully to the lumbering couple and tapped the man on the shoulder.

For an instant he thought he had made a mistake. The

drunk looked around at him querulously, and Martin hoped he hadn't precipitated a fight. But the man wasn't too plastered to notice that Martin was four inches taller than he was, years younger, and superbly fit, so he surrendered Ashley reluctantly, but without a word.

"Thank you," Ashley said fervently as she stepped into Martin's arms and they began to dance. "I wasn't sure how much longer I could go on with that."

"Why didn't you just tell him to get lost?"

"He's important to my father's campaign. I couldn't risk offending him," she replied.

"I guess your job isn't always as easy it looks," Martin conceded grudgingly.

"It isn't an easy life at all, Lieutenant," she said seriously, looking up to meet his eyes.

Martin must have appeared doubtful, because she added, "I sense that you find that difficult to believe."

Martin said nothing.

"Too professional to reply to that comment, Lieutenant?" Ashley inquired.

He felt that she was baiting him, so he answered shortly, "Money like yours can generally solve a lot of problems the rest of us have to handle, Miss Fair."

"I wasn't talking about money, Lieutenant. But I suppose, like most people, when you first meet us that's all you can see."

There was a testiness in her tone, and Martin knew that the conversation was taking a dangerously personal turn. He gazed down at her, hearing the music at a remote distance. He was holding her loosely on purpose, hardly touching her, but her waist still felt like a handspan, and her small fingers were lost in his other palm.

Her perfume drifted around them and her hair brushed his cheek.

"I try to be objective in any situation," he said neutrally.

Ashley let that pass, but her mouth set unhappily.

He was relieved when the music ended.

They turned to find that Dillon was watching them. Martin walked away and Ashley returned to her date.

"What were you doing dancing with that guy?" Dillon demanded.

"Phil Kennedy was drunk and he asked me to dance. I couldn't get away from him, and he was practically maiming me on the dance floor. Lieutenant Martin saw what was going on and rescued me. What happened to you?"

"Oh, Dave Clinton got my ear about some legal problem he's having. I don't know why people always think I'm conducting office hours at these parties."

"Occupational hazard," Ashley said.

"I think it's going very well, don't you?" Dillon asked, referring to the party.

"Yes, very well."

"When is Joe arriving?"

"He should be here any time."

They mingled for a few more minutes until a stir of excitement at the door indicated that the senator had arrived. He passed through the backslapping crowd and ascended the musicians' dais, adjusting the central microphone to his height as the rest of the guests filed into the ballroom. Martin saw Capo standing off to the side as the candidate made his speech, which was punctuated by enthusiastic cheering at various points and wild applause at its conclusion. As if by some unseen command, the throng, led by the senator and his wife, filed out of the ballroom and back to the buffet.

"Some circus, huh?" Capo said, moving next to Martin as the crowd passed.

"What did you make of the speech?" Martin asked, grinning.

"Rah-rah," Capo replied. He nodded to Dillon, walking with his arm around Ashley. "You think that guy dyes his hair?"

Martin laughed.

"Barbie and Ken," Capo observed. "They ought to come as a matched set, with a little wardrobe for each of them in the box."

"The girl's a good actress, anyway. I don't think she's having a much better time than we are."

"What gives you that idea?"

"Something she said."

"Then why is she here? She took a leave of absence from her job to do this."

"Capo, the guy's her father."

"He has other kids. Where are they?"

"They're young, still in school."

"Did you see the wife?" Capo asked. "She's only about ten years older than his daughter."

"Yeah, Ashley's mother died when she was a kid."

"Ashley, is it?"

"That's her name."

"You'd better not let her hear you calling her that. It's 'Miss Fair' to you, bub."

Martin made no reply, following Capo back to the dining room.

Two hours later, everyone had eaten and the party was winding down rapidly. Senator Fair came up to Ashley and Meg where they were talking in a corner and slipped his arm around his daughter's waist.

"How's my girl?" he said.

"Fine, Dad," Ashley replied.

"You look tired, honey. Maybe you should skip the meeting tomorrow morning and sleep in, let Meg fill in for you."

"Meg is just as tired as I am, and she doesn't know the fund-raising roster as well as I do. I'll be there."

"Do you have all the major events lined up?" Fair asked.

Ashley nodded. "I just have to work out a few minor details and we'll be ready to roll. I'll have the calendar fixed by the end of the week."

"All right, baby. Oh, there's Bill Sanders. I'd better go and talk to him. I haven't seen him all night."

The senator moved away and left the two women standing alone.

"How did Sylvia hold up tonight?" Ashley asked, nodding to her stepmother, who had joined her husband and was visibly wilting.

"All right," the senator's assistant said. "We had a long, stimulating conversation on whether Choate or Wilbraham Academy would be more appropriate for little Joe."

Ashley shook her head wearily.

"At least it kept her from talking to anybody else," Meg said. "Last week I heard her ask Judith Clinton if the Bay of Pigs was a Mediterranean resort."

"Oh, God."

"I got her away from Judith as quickly as possible, but I'm trying not to take any more chances."

"Can't we give her some more books to read?"

"I've given her the contents of a library already. Either she's not reading them or nothing stays with her. I don't know."

"I've tried to talk to my father, but you know how he is about her. He says things like 'she's a wonderful mother,' which is not in dispute. Plus I'm not the best person to undertake that mission. He still thinks I resent her for sending me away to boarding school."

"Do you?" Meg asked, turning to look at her.

Ashley shrugged. "It's all water under the bridge now. I can see how I would be in the way when she wanted to have her own kids and her own little family. I was a living, breathing reminder of the previous marriage, of the paragon first wife everyone, including my father, remembered so fondly."

Meg nodded as her eyes roamed the room. They stopped moving as she said, "Look at that cop." She was staring at Martin, who was gazing past them with a fixed, intent expression.

"Every woman here has been looking at him. He's causing something of a stir."

"Have you seen him smile yet?" Meg asked.

"He almost smiled once tonight. I should have taken a picture."

"Well, he may not be jolly, but he does radiate confidence. I have a suspicion he can handle whatever comes his way."

"I wish Jim felt that way. He's not exactly thrilled with the police presence, if you know what I mean."

"That doesn't surprise me," Meg said.

Ashley looked at her.

Meg shrugged. "You've been turning down his proposals regularly, and all of a sudden *that*"—she stabbed her finger at Martin—"shows up to become your shadow day in and day out? If I were Jim, I wouldn't be too happy either."

"Lieutenant Martin is on assignment. Jim's reacting completely irrationally."

"He's reacting emotionally. He's in *love* with you."

Ashley took another sip of her drink, which was now melted ice, and watched her father laughing at a crony's joke.

"So when are you getting married?" Meg said brightly.

"Meg, don't start that. I'm tired."

"Is that what you say to Jim?"

Ashley shot Meg an exasperated glance.

"Okay, okay, enough said. I think we'd better get out of here. You have a tour of Ardmore Elementary School scheduled for eleven A.M., right after the staff meeting."

Ashley groaned. "You didn't tell me about that."

"I certainly did."

"An elementary school?"

"Roger's idea." Roger Damico was the senator's press agent.

"I don't think I can handle it after this."

"You'll handle it."

Dillon approached on Ashley's left. "Ready to go?"

Ashley glanced at her father.

"He's leaving too," Dillon said. "None of them will go home until we do."

"That's my cue," Meg said. She put down her drink and left, going to stand with the senator and his wife.

"I'll get your wrap and call for the car," Dillon said to Ashley. She saw him signal to Martin as he passed, and the policeman began to drift unobtrusively in her direction.

"Everything okay?" Ashley said to him when he arrived.

"Seems to be," he replied.

"No subversives lurking in corners?"

He examined her, suspecting sarcasm, not answering.

"Sorry," she said. "I guess that isn't very funny, is it? I must be getting punchy. It's been a long day."

"You'll be home soon," Martin observed neutrally.

"Home? If you call a hotel home. I haven't seen my apartment in Georgetown since January."

Dillon returned with her shawl and they made their way to the Marshalls to say good-night. Once they were outside, the crisp evening air began to revive Ashley, and she said to Martin, "I hope I didn't sound like I was complaining back there, Lieutenant."

"No, ma'am, not at all," he replied, avoiding her eyes.

"Lieutenant, I promise that if you look at me you will not turn to stone," she murmured in an aside as she passed him to take Dillon's arm.

Martin stopped, startled, and then walked on as if he hadn't heard.

Ashley got into the car. Dillon slid in beside her, and Martin climbed in with the driver. They waited until the senator's car pulled up behind them, and then both limos pulled away at once.

It was after one in the morning when they got back to the hotel. The senator and his daughter retired to their respective rooms, and the two cops were left alone.

"Not so bad," Capo said, yawning. "A snore, more than anything."

Martin lit a cigarette. "Did your car go on to take the wife back to Harrisburg?"

Capo nodded.

"Odd setup, don't you think?"

Capo shrugged. "Who knows, with this outfit? I'm just going to put in my time and go home, hope nothing happens to the senator in the meanwhile."

"I think they try to keep the wife under wraps as much as possible. She's a little light in the brains department."

"Yeah, well none of 'em are Rhodes scholars, if you ask me. Who says you have to have smarts to have money?"

"Not I," Martin answered softly.

"And how do you know about the wife? You didn't even talk to her, did you?"

"No, but I can tell. The daughter is filling in for her. What I can't understand is why. There appears to be no love lost between them."

"The kid's doing it for her father; you said so yourself. What's the difference, anyway?"

Martin shrugged.

Capo peered at him. "Did something happen to-night?"

Martin shook his head.

"Speak to me, Timmy. You've got that look."

"What look?"

"That look that means something is on your mind. I can recognize it by now."

"It's just . . ."

"What?"

"The Fair girl. She was different tonight, different from this afternoon, I mean. Tense, a bit edgy. Like the mask of perfection was slipping a little."

"Maybe she was nervous about the evening. It was big deal for her father."

"I don't think she's too crazy about me, to tell you the truth," Martin sighed.

"So then you're even. I wouldn't worry about it. Hey, I'd better get next door; I'm out on my feet. See you in the morning."

"Yeah, good night," Martin replied, exhaling a stream of smoke as Capo went through the connecting door to the senator's suite.

Martin kicked off his shoes and loosened his tie, stretching out on the sitting room's convertible couch without opening it. He switched off the light and lay staring at the ceiling, smoking methodically.

He was too keyed up to sleep; the evening spent in the company of the glitterati had been unexpectedly stimulating. The relationships in the Fair clan alone would be enough to keep him from boredom. The daughter was the true enigma; she was giving up a year of her life to campaign for a father she treated with a deference that hardly seemed familial, and was keeping steady company with a man she didn't love.

It was none of his business, of course, and by summer he wouldn't be seeing any of them again. But he'd had nothing to do all evening but study the girl and her behavior, and he couldn't understand why she was with Dillon.

Or maybe Martin was mistaken about her feelings. Perhaps he had a bourgeois idea of emotional involvements, informed by his experience with Maryann. In their courting days, they hadn't been able to keep their hands off each other. But then, they were younger, and entirely without aristocratic restraint.

His father had liked Maryann, Martin remembered. His dad had been a precinct captain during the fifties and turbulent sixties, a close companion of Gerald Rourke. And his immigrant grandfather had walked a Mayfair beat in the twenties. Martin was third generation in a police family, and he didn't pretend to grasp the vagaries of the idle rich.

He lit a second Camel from the stub of the first one and inhaled deeply. His only previous experience with wealth was meeting the son of a Connecticut tobacco heir who had served in his unit in Vietnam. Martin was astonished to find the kid there in the first place, since the upper classes always managed to get college or medical deferments for their draft-age sons. But he later found out that the boy had volunteered to get back at his old man, and they became quite friendly, being the same age, eighteen, and equally terrified. But Jack had caught a sniper's bullet during the Tet offensive, ending the friendship as well as his life. Martin had always remembered his stories of prep schools and skiing at Kitzbuehl and summer houses on Hobe Sound. Now that he found himself in the milieu he'd once heard described, he was remembering Jack, and the war, once again.

He shook his head and sat up abruptly. It wasn't a good idea to dwell on 'Nam before retiring. It led to nightmares. And reminiscing about Maryann wasn't much better.

She had left him after two years of marriage, tired of sharing him with a schedule that included full-time police work and part-time college on the GI bill. But more than that, she was tired of living a life of constant tension, wondering whether she would ever see him again when he left for each shift.

So now he was a big success, he thought ironically, stubbing out his second smoke. No wife, no kids, but rising steadily through the ranks like an inexorable force. And why not? He spent every waking minute either at work or preparing for it, not subject to the sort of family and personal considerations that "distracted" other men.

He stood abruptly, yanking off his jacket and unbuttoning his shirt. What the hell. Nobody had a perfect life. You made your choices, your mistakes, and then you lived with them.

He looked around for a pillow, realized that it was probably in a closet somewhere, and settled for folding his shirt under his head as he lay back down on the couch.

But it was still a long time before he fell asleep.

* * *

Ashley undressed by the light of her bedside lamp and put her jewelry in the wall safe behind the bed. Then she slipped into a robe and lay down on the bed, not bothering to remove the coverlet.

The policeman was on her mind. She prided herself on her ability to read people, but he was sending out confusing signals. In the space of one day, Martin had succeeded in confusing her completely. At times she felt waves of hostility coming off him, and yet she had caught him watching her on several occasions that night with a look of such intensity that she had felt it, wrenchingly, in her gut.

Why such dislike for someone he barely even knew? And was it dislike, or something more potent, some combination of feelings that she hesitated to identify even to herself?

There was a real person beneath that iron facade; she felt it. But she also knew that trying to reach him would be like trying to break through a brick wall. And did she even want to get through? He was her bodyguard, after all, and he didn't have to be fond of her in order to protect her.

Ashley punched the pillow under her head and closed her eyes.

Ransom drove through the night and arrived in Philadelphia the next morning. It didn't take him long to locate the address he'd been given. It turned out to be a modern building designed so that all the units had a balcony overlooking a central pool and tennis complex, complete with sauna and gym. His apartment was on the third floor, furnished in neutrals with blond woods and glass, and the double closet in the bedroom contained a complete wardrobe in sizes selected to fit him.

He went through the closet quickly: suits in dark blue and charcoal gray, a stack of dress shirts in white and cream and pale blue, cotton polos in a rainbow of soft, preppie shades, casual slacks and jeans. Fine. He would be striving for a successful but conservative image, and the threads had to fit the picture.

He dropped to one knee. Shoes were lined up on the floor, with the tissue paper still intact: weejuns, dingo boots, topsiders, cordovan wingtips, dressy black loafers. The drawers contained socks and underwear, jogging clothes, and a windbreaker. There was even a tuxedo in a plastic bag, complete with boiled shirt and cummerbund. Everything he had requested. The only problem was that it all looked too new, but he could take care of that, run the clothes through the washer a couple of times, clean the suits, scuff the shoes. He would be leaving it all behind when the job was finished, but he wanted to be prepared at a moment's notice for anything.

He pursed his lips, turning around to look at the precisely decorated rooms. It looked like a dentist's office, but no matter. He'd buy a few things, throw some junk around; he'd done it before and achieved the desired result.

So far, so good. The clients seemed prepared to meet his terms. The little man with the big mouth had irritated him, but he was used to the type. They wanted the dirty deed done, but of course they were above doing it themselves. The intercessor was money, and that was all right with Ransom. He was prepared to take it, and he didn't have any illusions about himself that he needed to preserve.

He sat on the linen sofa and set the folders he'd been given on the glass coffee table, pulling the pack of cigarettes from his pocket. He lit up and began to read, going from one stack of papers to another as he smoked steadily, filling the marble ashtray with butts. Finally, after two hours, he sat back and folded his arms behind his head, staring at the hexagonal light fixture in the ceiling.

His target had to be the senator's assistant, Margaret Drummond. The daughter might have been a possibility, but she was too obvious, too well protected, and she had a boyfriend. The Drummond woman would do. She was single and the right age, and she lived alone.

He sat up and flipped through the material he had until he came to the specifics on Drummond, thirty-one, born in Doylestown, Pennsylvania, and known as "Meg." She'd been with the senator nine years, since her graduation from Penn State, moving up rapidly from campaign worker to her present position at his right hand. She was tight with the daughter and apparently was trusted implicitly by the senator and his staff. She handled the senator's correspondence and appointments, which was ideal for Ransom's purposes. Best of all, she was a dedicated career woman and not dating anyone steadily. That would make his entry into her life so much smoother.

He studied the facsimile picture of Drummond at the top of the bio sheet. Dark hair, dark eyes, even features. Not bad. Of course, that was immaterial; it was his job to pursue her if she looked like the Medusa. But the fact that she was attractive would make it easier for her to believe he was interested.

Ransom had no doubt that he would be able to use her. He was notoriously successful with women. He was handsome enough, in a quiet, undemonstrative way, but more than that, he was elusive. Women sensed a reserve beneath his quicksilver nature, a reserve that presented an irresistible challenge.

They had no idea how great the challenge really was.

He began to whistle as he went to the bathroom to shower.

CHAPTER
Three

I N THE MORNING, Ashley was the first person
seated in the conference room supplied by the hotel.
She had her folder of notes in front of her and was
sipping coffee when the door opened and the senator
and Meg came in, followed by Damico and several
other advisers. Bringing up the rear was Scott Baker, the
senator's chief of staff.

"Good morning, sweetheart," Fair said to Ashley.
"Sleep well?"

"Fine," Ashley replied, not completely truthfully.

Meg slipped into the chair next to her and whipped
out a pocket tape recorder.

"Gentlemen, Miss Drummond is recording us again,"
Fair said dryly. "I would advise you to use extreme dis-
cretion in your statements."

Meg grinned, and the others smiled tolerantly. Her
compulsive tracking of their every word was a standing
joke, but it contributed to her legendary competence, so
no one really minded.

"I guess I'll begin," Baker said as he sat across from

Ashley. "I have the results of the latest Gallup and Harris polls. We'll go over the numbers and then I'll throw the floor open to discussion."

Baker read off his information, and his listeners contributed their ideas about how to improve Fair's standing in the areas where his following was limited.

"I think we have to schedule a tour of the midwestern states for the late summer," Ashley said firmly. "We haven't been doing well there for a while, and the situation is obviously not improving."

"Another tour so fast on the heels of this one?" Baker said without relish.

"It seems necessary," Ashley replied. "We can do everything else possible, but there's nothing like personal contact, letting the people see and hear Dad in person."

"What do you think, Joe?" Baker asked the senator.

"I think Ashley's right," Fair said.

"The media are always hyping your charisma," Damico added. "The voters can't appreciate that from campaign rhetoric."

Fair nodded. "Okay. Meg and Ashley, you look into it, see what you can arrange."

Meg nodded, and Ashley made a note.

"What's next?" Fair asked.

The meeting proceeded smoothly until Damico announced his concern over several conservative newspapers, also in the Midwest, that were treating the senator rather shabbily.

"Don't we have any contacts in the area, any influence we could use?" Ashley asked when Roger paused in his monologue.

"The editorial control is Republican," Damico replied. "There's not much we can do about that."

"Let's buy some advertising," Meg suggested. "They have to sell us the space if we have the price, no matter who owns the paper."

"What will that prove?" Damico asked. "That we can spend more money? We're getting a bad rap for that already. I say we wait until the tour. That will have the impact we want."

"That will take too long to arrange," Meg replied. "We should move now. The ads will expose the readership to another point of view before Joe gets out there. They're being inundated with slanted information. Let's get our side of the important issues aired even if we have to pay dearly for the privilege."

There was a silence as the assembly considered this idea.

"Do it," the senator said suddenly. "It can't hurt."

"It's going to cost us," Damico said. "That plus the tour will be a chunk of change."

"Find out how much," Fair directed him. "Work up the figures and bring them to the next meeting."

Damico nodded, making a note on the pad in front of him.

It was now Ashley's turn to speak. She waited until her father looked up from his agenda.

"Ash?" he said.

Ashley stood and passed out Xeroxed copies of the fund-raising calendar she had prepared.

"As you can see, Millvale is the key event during the next couple of months," she said when everyone was reading the mimeographed sheet. "At a thousand dollars a plate; it's our best effort so far. We also have commitments for two five-hundred-dollar-a-plate events, but one of those is shaky because I'm not sure we can get the hotel at a low enough rate to make the required profit, and the restaurant manager also wants a guarantee of eight hundred in attendance."

"Eight hundred?" Baker said, making a face.

"I had hoped for a thousand," Damico said.

Meg began punching numbers into her calculator, refiguring the profit from the event.

"I think we can get the bodies together," Ashley went on, "but it will take some dickering to get the hotel down on the price. I'll have it finalized by Wednesday, one way or the other."

"Ashley, this is very impressive," Fair said admiringly, his eyes scanning the sheet before him.

"Thanks."

"You'll be ready to discuss the final figures on this by the next meeting?"

"Yes."

Meg raised her hand. "I hate to interrupt, but if Ashley doesn't leave now she's going to miss the school tour Roger has so thoughtfully arranged."

Roger glanced up from his reading.

"And all the wonderful press coverage he's lined up," Meg added mischievously.

Roger shot Meg a withering look.

"I'm going," Ashley said, rising.

"Why don't you go with Ashley, Meg," the senator said. "I think she could use the company, and we're almost done here."

"Are you sure?" Meg asked.

"Absolutely," Fair replied. "These things are never a lot of fun, and it will help my daughter to have you along. I promise we'll leave your tape recorder running so you won't miss a syllable of our scintillating conversation, all right?"

"Okay," Meg said, and rose from her chair. The two women moved toward the door.

"Lieutenant Martin is waiting for us in the hall," Meg said to Ashley. "I saw him on my way in here."

They slipped out into the hall as the others continued with the meeting.

Martin was leaning against the far wall, smoking. He straightened when he saw them.

"Hello, Lieutenant," Ashley said. "I'll be ready to go in a minute. I just want to pick up our coats inside."

"Miss Drummond is coming with us?"

"Yes, is that all right?"

"Fine," Martin said.

"I presume Sergeant Capo will be going with my father to the VFW hall at eleven?" Ashley asked.

Martin nodded.

Ashley went into her room and left Meg standing with the taciturn policeman.

"So," Meg said after a protracted, uncomfortable silence, "how about those Phillies?"

Martin suppressed a grin, then chuckled.

"Gotcha," Meg said, pleased with herself.

"I guess you did."

"I knew you couldn't be such a hard guy."

"Don't tell anyone else, okay?" Martin said soberly, playing along.

"My lips are sealed," Meg replied solemnly.

Ashley emerged from her room wearing her raincoat and carrying Meg's jacket over her arm. She glanced from one to the other, then back to Meg.

"Here you go," she said, handing Meg her blazer.

"Ladies, the car is waiting for us downstairs," Martin informed them briskly.

They descended to the limo, and Martin got into the front as he had before, while Meg and Ashley rode in the back. The school was only a short distance away, and the principal welcomed them at the door and led them into an auditorium, where the student body was assembled to hear Ashley's address. Flashbulbs popped as she took over the podium after the principal's welcoming introduction. She talked to the kids about the importance of education and their role as the hope of the future, giving the standard "school speech," and then posed for more pictures afterward. She was photographed with the principal, the assistant superintendent, and the president of the student body, an energetic redhead who told her that he hoped her father would "knock 'em dead." Martin and Meg stood on the sidelines, observing the scene, and it wasn't until they were all heading back to the car, surrounded by reporters, that Ashley said in an aside to Meg, "What was that about when I went to get our coats?"

"What was what about?" Meg rejoined innocently.

"You know what I mean. When I got back, you and Martin were both grinning about something."

"Oh, just a joke. Nothing major."

"A joke?"

"Yeah. He's not as dull as he's trying to appear."

"Somehow I guessed that," Ashley replied dryly.

Martin came up behind them, and Ashley didn't pursue it any further.

When they got back to the hotel, Meg went to make some arrangements with the desk clerk, and Ashley was left with Martin.

"Well, thank you, Lieutenant," Ashley began, then staggered suddenly as she was walking, lurching forward erratically.

Martin was at her side instantly, taking her elbow and steadying her against him.

"Are you all right?" he asked worriedly.

"I . . . think so. I just got a little dizzy for a moment."

"Here, sit down over here," he said, leading her to a love seat in the lobby. He sat next to her, leaning forward to watch her face.

"How do you feel now?"

"Better, thank you."

"Do you want a glass of water or something?"

Ashley shook her head. "No, I don't think so."

Martin examined her slight frame and had an inspiration. "Did you eat any breakfast this morning?"

Ashley bit her lip and didn't answer, which was answer enough.

"How about last night?"

Ashley looked at the floor.

"Can you remember the last time you ate anything?" Martin finally asked, rephrasing the question.

Ashley sighed and shrugged.

"I think I know how to solve this problem," Martin said firmly, standing and taking her arm. He marched her directly to the hotel restaurant and confronted the hostess.

"We'd like to be seated, please," he said.

"I'm sorry, breakfast is over and we won't be opening again until twelve-thirty for lunch," the hostess said smoothly.

"This is Senator Joseph Fair's daughter," Martin said briskly, "and I am Lieutenant Martin of the Philadelphia Metropolitan Police." He flashed his badge. "Miss Fair is a guest of this hotel, and I am here on official business. Miss Fair would like to be served, and we don't want to deal with room service's limited selection and the delay involved. I think you could find a way to accommodate her, don't you?"

The hostess gazed into his cobalt eyes for three seconds before capitulating. She unhooked the silken cord that barred their way and said evenly, "Please be seated anywhere you like. I'll bring your menus shortly."

Martin followed Ashley to a table near the window and held the chair for her while she sat. When he was seated across from her she said, "Do you pull that macho-cop act very often?"

"Only when it's necessary."

"And it's necessary now?" she asked.

"To keep you from fainting, yes."

"I wasn't fainting."

"Then what were you doing?"

She thought a moment. "Stumbling?" she suggested.

"Looked like it. You need food."

"Yes, Doctor," Ashley replied meekly.

The hostess returned with menus, and Martin asked her, "What would be fastest?"

"A sandwich, or omelet, I suppose," she said.

He looked at Ashley.

"An omelet," she said.

"With toast," he added. "And some fruit."

"Anything for you?" the woman asked.

"Just coffee."

"I'll give your order to your server. She'll bring your setups in a moment." The hostess left, and Martin said, "You know, you should take better care of yourself. You won't be of any help to your father if you land in the hospital."

"Missing a few meals isn't going to land me in the hospital," Ashley said dismissively.

"How do you know? If you actually do pass out, where do you think they will take you? Disneyland?"

A waitress arrived and deposited placemats with silverware and napkins on the table. When she left, Ashley said, "You're an unlikely looking nurse, Lieutenant Martin."

"Just using common sense," he said gruffly.

"Do you provide this service for all the people you protect?"

"I've never protected anybody before, but most people would have the good judgment to eat once in a while and not try to live on coffee."

"I do eat. Once in a while."

"No appetite?" he asked.

"Not much."

"Why not?"

She shrugged. "I don't know. Busy, nervous. Something."

The waitress came back with the food, and Martin watched, sipping coffee, as Ashley dutifully plowed through the omelet, a slice of toast, and half an apple.

Finally, she held up her hand in surrender and said, "That's it. I'm full. I can't eat another bite. Really."

"You did all right," Martin said.

"Thank you, sir. And thank you, too, for bringing me here. I do feel better."

He nodded. "Good."

"More coffee?" the waitress said at his elbow.

"No, thanks. Just give me the check, please."

The waitress scribbled a total on her pad and ripped off the top sheet, handing it to him.

"You can put that on my father's tab," Ashley told him.

Martin put it on the table with several bills. "It's on me," he said.

Ashley glanced at her watch. "Oh, dear, I'd better get going. My father will be back any minute."

She stood, and Martin followed her out of the restaurant. They rode back up in the elevator, and as she entered the senator's suite she turned and said, "Thank you, Lieutenant. I do appreciate your concern, and I promise to take better care in the future."

Martin nodded, then watched as she disappeared through the door.

By late afternoon, everyone had reassembled in the hotel. They went out in the evening again, to a reception that ran late, and by the time they got back Martin was developing an appreciation for why presidential candidates always looked so tired.

The next day was a break. The senator was closeted with his press aide all day, sending down for room service, and Ashley worked in her room. Martin and Capo sat in Ashley's anteroom, playing cards and watching television, hanging around like mafia soldiers while the don was occupied. Meg Drummond came and went, nodding as she passed the two policemen, finally prompting Capo to say conspiratorially, "I don't think this crew could get dressed in the morning unless that lady told them exactly what to wear."

Martin grinned. "Intimidated, Anthony?" He glanced at the clock. It was eight-thirty P.M.

Capo was outraged. "Who, me? I'm a liberated man. But I'm telling you, she's amazing. There's this computer in the senator's suite, and she's got everything in there, his schedule and appointments and all the information he needs. And she runs that thing like a whiz, pressing buttons, popping discs in and out like they were pieces of toast. She handles the groupies like a Prussian general, too. Nobody gets past her unless she wants them to. It's amazing to watch her in action. She's a roadblock or a gate, depending on what's happening and who wants to pass through."

"Pretty impressive, huh?"

"She impresses the hell out of me," Capo replied, examining his hand. He picked out two cards and placed them on the table.

Martin looked them over and selected one from the deck. As he did, the bedroom door opened and Ashley emerged, reading glasses perched on the end of her nose. She was wearing slacks and carrying a notebook and pencil.

"Gentlemen," she said.

Both cops looked up at her.

"I was just about to call room service for coffee. Would you like some?"

"Thanks, Miss Fair," Capo said.

She walked behind Capo and picked up a book lying on a table by the outer door. On her way back, she peered over Capo's shoulder, pointed with her pencil, and said, "Gin."

She disappeared into her bedroom again.

Capo looked down at his hand, rearranged a few cards, and shrugged.

"Gin," he said, fanning his cards out on the table.

Martin sat back in his chair, laughing helplessly. "I don't believe you," he said.

"Why not?" Capo replied. "It was there all along, I just didn't happen to see it."

"You're hopeless, Capo. I give up."

"Don't give up yet. You owe me ten bucks."

"You actually think you're going to collect on that?"

"All right, all right," Capo said with a wounded air. "But I warn you, I'm keeping track of all this." He took a slip of paper out of his pocket and made a note on it.

"Keep track, Capo. You'll have the college tuition for the kids before you know it."

Capo jammed the note back into his shirt and said, "Mmm, you smell that perfume she leaves behind her? How much you think that stuff costs?"

"You can bet it's beyond your budget, Sergeant," Martin replied dryly. "It would take generations of trust funds to afford that lady."

Capo looked at him for a long moment, then said, "Just what is irritating you, buddy?"

"Nothing."

"Could it be that *you* don't have the trust fund, so *you* can't afford her?"

"What is that supposed to mean?" Martin snapped.

"Figure it out. A smart guy like you shouldn't have much trouble with it."

Martin stacked the cards, not replying.

"So her family has bucks," Capo said, as if Martin had answered. "Is that her fault? You keep acting like she's playing the princess role around here, but I don't see it. I do see her working like a dog and doing everything she can to cooperate with us. I'm sure you've observed the same thing. So I ask myself, what's your problem?"

"I don't have a problem," Martin said gruffly.

"Okay, fine," Capo said, obviously content to drop the subject. He leaned across the table and added in a low tone, "What the hell is she doing in there? She's been at it for hours."

"Legal work."

"Whose? I thought she was on a leave from that job."

Martin shrugged. "Don't ask me. But people from the Justice Department keep calling her."

"What about loverboy?"

"He's back in Washington."

"Trouble in paradise?"

"I don't think so. Apparently he goes back and forth a lot."

"Too bad. That guy makes me want to muss up his hair, which I think is dyed. Did I mention that?"

"You mentioned it," Martin answered, grinning. "You're probably just jealous."

"Not me, Timmy, but I think one of us is," Capo replied seriously.

Martin fixed him with a baleful stare.

"Hey, I'm allowed to offer an opinion on the subject," Capo said defensively. "I'm a . . ."

". . . happily married man," Martin finished for him. "I know, you've told me."

There was a knock at the outer door. "Room service."

Martin got up to answer it, and as he did Meg Drummond stuck her head in the door.

"The senator is about to retire, Sergeant Capo," she said.

"So early?" Capo said.

"Long day tomorrow," Meg replied.

Capo picked up his jacket. "See you in the morning," he said to Martin, and followed Meg into the hall.

The waiter carried the tray in and set it on the cocktail table. Martin signed the slip and gave the boy a tip, then tapped on the connecting door.

"Miss Fair, your coffee's here," he said.

Ashley emerged after a few seconds of silence, lifting her hair off her neck and sighing.

"Wonderful," she said. "I could use a break." She poured for both of them and inquired, "Cream?"

"Black."

She handed Martin his cup and then added cream to hers.

"How are you feeling today?" he asked.

"Fine."

"No dizzy spells?"

"None at all, thank you. The omelet cure must have worked."

She sipped her coffee as she watched him take a deep swallow of his and then put his cup down to light a cigarette. He noticed her scrutiny and said self-consciously, "I hope you don't mind my smoking. I guess I should have asked already."

"I don't mind, Lieutenant. But I'd be careful around Jim. He has a thing about it. Thinks he can get lung cancer from secondhand smoke."

"Yeah, well, maybe he's right," Martin said neutrally, unwilling to get into the subject of Dillon. "Too late for me, anyway. I'd rather smoke than eat."

Ashley chuckled. "That's a terrible thing to say."

"It's the truth."

"Why?"

Martin shrugged. "It's soothing, I suppose. Easy, and steady, and quiet. It's always the same, always rewarding. Few other things in life are that consistent."

"I see."

"It helps me think."

"Do you do a lot of thinking, Lieutenant?" Ashley asked.

He looked at her sharply, to see if she was baiting him, but her gaze was level and serene.

"More of that than anything else," he replied. "Police work is mostly trying to out-think the criminals, regardless of how many car chases you see on TV."

"Then you must be very good at it. I understand you're the youngest lieutenant on the force."

There was no reply to that, and he made none.

"This must be a very boring duty for you," she added.

"It's different," he answered.

Her smile became impish. "It will get more so. To-morrow evening we're going to the opera."

He looked so distressed that she laughed.

"It didn't say that on the itinerary I was given," he objected. "I would have remembered."

"Our plans have changed. We're squeezing this into the schedule. Never been to the opera, Lieutenant?"

He shook his head.

"No worse than a trip to the dentist," she said. "This one's a benefit performance for the ACLU, a big booster of my father's campaign. *La Traviata*."

He lifted his shoulders.

"The story of Camille," she explained.

"Camille?" It sounded vaguely familiar.

"'La Dame aux Camellias.' Violetta. She dies prettily of consumption in the last act."

"Oh, yeah, I remember now. She coughs herself to death, right?" He lifted his cigarette. "Think she was a smoker?"

Ashley giggled. "In the original play, Dumas leads us to believe it was tuberculosis," she sobered. "I'm afraid the occasion requires formal clothes."

"For me?" he asked, aghast.

"For everyone attending. I'm afraid that includes you, Lieutenant. By the way, what is your first name? You weren't baptized 'Lieutenant,' were you?"

"Timothy," he replied. "Tim."

"Well, Tim, we'll have to order something for you. There's a shop not far from here that my father has used. They can send something over tomorrow if you give me your sizes." She went into her room and came back with her yellow legal pad. "Shirt?" she said, pencil poised.

"Fifteen and a half, thirty-five," he replied, feeling silly, as he always did with salespeople in stores.

"Suit?"

"Forty-two long, I guess. I'm not sure."

"That's good enough for a start." She ripped off the top sheet and folded it in half. "I'll give this information to Meg. She can talk to the sergeant about his sizes in the morning. I assume that you do have black shoes?"

"Yes."

"Fine. That ought to do it."

"Where's the performance?" Martin asked.

"At the Met in New York."

"That's a two-hour drive."

Ashley looked embarrassed. "We're taking my uncle's plane. His real-estate business is all over the country. It saves time."

Martin nodded, feeling naive. The company jet. Of course.

"It's really kind of an unobtrusive, ordinary-looking plane," she said gently, reading his mind.

"No Concorde?" Martin said with a sidelong glance.

"No."

Not that you couldn't afford a Concorde if you wanted one, Martin thought.

Ashley studied his pensive face and said, "I sense that all of this is making you a trifle uncomfortable, Lieu . . . Tim."

Martin didn't reply.

"Yes?" she prodded.

"This is an assignment for me. I don't make any judgments," he answered.

"Yes, you do," she said with a slight smile. "And I don't know if I care for being thought of as an 'assignment.' We're just people like everyone else."

"Not like everyone else," he said, since she was pressing him. "You have more money."

"Money can be its own burden," she said.

He snorted. "And why is it always people who have so much of it who say that?"

"Because we know."

He looked extremely skeptical, so she added slowly, "For example, most people don't have enough money to dispose of unwanted children in an acceptable way. The rich do. Boarding schools, summer camps, extensive and prolonged vacations. You never have to see your own child if you don't want to, which is not usually an option available to those without considerable means."

He stared at her, wondering what the hell she was talking about. At the same time he realized that she was deadly serious. The subject was important to her.

She looked up at him and gave a little shake, as if waking from a trance.

"I'm afraid I'm babbling," she said quickly. "And I have too much to do to waste time." She put down her empty cup. "Thanks for the talk, Tim. And the rescue yesterday. I'll see you in the morning."

Martin watched her go back into the bedroom, staring after her with a puzzled expression. Then he sat on the sofa, pouring the rest of the coffee into his cup and lighting a fresh cigarette.

She certainly was different from what he'd expected.

He had to admit, however reluctantly, that Capo was right: she treated him as if she saw a person when she looked at him and not just a blue suit. The rest of them, like Dillon, looked through Martin as if he weren't there, except when they wanted something.

And what was that little recital about disposing of kids? Was she referring to herself, the stepmother packing her off to St. Whosis, that place in Switzerland he'd read about in the background information? And if so, why was she discussing it with *him*, of all people, the cop, the bodyguard, the nobody?

Forget it, he told himself. These people are all off the wall. They have more problems than investments, and they've got a lot of investments.

But he couldn't quite dismiss it, and smoked another cigarette before he went to sleep.

Meg Drummond was on the telephone, having a little trouble with Deacon's Formal Wear.

"Why can't you send the tuxedos over to the hotel by messenger?" she asked wearily.

She listened and then said, "All your delivery trucks are out? We need the clothes for tonight."

She listened again and made a face. "I realize that this is a last-minute order, but the clothes are for people in Senator Fair's party . . ." I should have lied and said they were for Joe, she thought in annoyance as the clerk answered with something else she didn't want to hear.

"I'll send someone over to pick them up, and you can bill us," Megan finally said. Her expression changed as she listened once again, this time in true disbelief. She interrupted the flow of words from the other end to demand, "Since when do you require prepayment? We've dealt with you before and—"

She stopped, looking patiently at the ceiling as the clerk cut her off in reply.

"Well, I don't much care for your new policy," Meg announced irritably. "I'll be over myself in a few minutes to pick up the order. Does your 'new policy' permit the use of credit cards?"

She got her answer and said, "How progressive of you, thank you so much," replacing the phone receiver with a bang. I'm crossing them off my list, she thought, making a mental note. Meg couldn't abide inefficiency in any form; she didn't have time for it.

She walked through the connecting door to Ashley's suite and found the senator's daughter in the bedroom, staring at three gowns displayed on the hotel bed.

"Which one for tonight?" she asked Meg as she spotted her.

"The pearl-gray strapless. You look smashing in it."

Ashley made a face. "I wore that last month to Judith Clinton's. Some of the same people will be there."

"How about the blue?"

"That bib makes me look like Alice in Wonderland," Ashley said in a tired voice.

"You look like Alice in Wonderland anyway, sweets," Meg said, grinning.

"It's not an image I'm trying to cultivate," Ashley said flatly. "And that melon sherbet one makes me look like a tart."

"The color is 'blush,' and it does not," Meg said.

"Damn. I'm going to have to bring a batch of clothes

from Georgetown, or else get more from Carlo," Ashley muttered.

"Why don't you just go out and buy some, like a normal person?" Meg inquired.

Ashley sighed. "Standing around all day getting pinned up like a seamstress's dummy reminds me of Sylvia," she said. "It's so . . . self-indulgent."

"Ashley, you need the clothes," Meg said practically. "You're getting photographed every time you walk out the door."

"Oh, all right. Can we call that woman from Bonwit's, and Jerry from Magnin's? Tell them to send me some rack samples and I'll order by phone, have them fitted here."

"Will do," Meg said, extracting a small spiral notebook from her pocket.

"And remember, full price."

"Right," Meg said. "And what about the designers? Should I call anybody besides Carlo?"

"No, no, they're more trouble than they're worth. Photo credits, guarantee of mention in the gossip columns, blah-blah-blah. At least Carlo doesn't plague me."

"He will," Meg said airily.

"I'll worry about that when the time comes," Ashley said. "Well, what do you think?" she asked again, pointing to the bed.

"The melon one. You look very sexy in it. And it has that matching cape. Perfect."

"It always makes me feel like Jack the Ripper's prime target," Ashley said doubtfully.

"You spent entirely too much time locked up with

those nuns in St. Andrew's," Meg replied, grinning. "There's nothing wrong with looking . . . sensuous."

"For *La Traviata*?"

"For anything. Do you want me to get one of the stylists from the salon downstairs to come up and do your hair?"

"No, thanks. Sylvia is sending Claude over at five o'clock."

"Uh-oh. Did she volunteer him?"

"Yes. I thought as long as she was trying to be nice I'd take her up on it."

"I hope you don't emerge from it looking like Martha Washington," Meg said gloomily.

"I'm sure he could find the time to do you too, if you like," Ashley said mischievously.

"No, thanks," Meg replied, pretending to be horrified. "Who knows what's in that shampoo? And that other stuff he puts on Sylvia's hair twice a week makes her head look like a tequila sunrise. I have a theory that it's affecting her brain. Something certainly is." She glanced at her watch. "Speaking of brains, I'm losing mine. I have to get over to that formal-wear place and pick up the tuxedos for the cops."

"Can't they send the clothes?"

Meg sighed. "No, it's a long story. I'll be back in an hour or so. My car's right downstairs."

"Where are they?" Ashley asked.

"Who?"

"The cops."

"Capo's with your father, and Martin is right outside in the hall. Well, I'm off. See you later."

Ashley waved as Meg left and then shut the bedroom

door behind her. She stripped down to her underwear
and unhooked her bra, dropping it on the carpet. She
tried on the satin dress with its low-cut bodice and spa-
ghetti straps, struggling with the back zipper and then
standing to survey herself in the hotel's pier glass. The
hem of the dress dragged over her feet, and she hoisted
the skirt to her calves as she went to the closet and got
the matching shoes, stepping into them and whirling to
see the effect.

There. That was better. It had been a long time since
she'd put the gown on, primarily because Jim had dis-
liked it the first time she wore it. She took the cape, of
the same material as the dress and lined with ivory silk
charmeuse, down from its hook. She settled it over her
shoulders, sweeping her hair out of the way. The cloak
swirled to her ankles as she fastened it at the throat with
its large mother-of-pearl button.

She had to admit that the result was quite dramatic.
Oh, why not? Maybe Meg was right. Who knew how
long she'd be able to get away with outfits like this one?
She'd be heading for shirtwaists and twin sets soon
enough.

She went to the wall safe and got her mother's dia-
mond pendant earrings, ordered from Van Cleef and
Arpels by grandmother Fair as a wedding present for her
son's wife. Ashley tried them on and examined her reflection critically. They were fabulous, of course, but
too gaudy a combination with the elaborate dress; she
looked like a Christmas tree. She put them back and
tried on a set of Majorcan pearls, a single strand neck-
lace with 8mm stud earrings. That was it. Understated,
elegant. Perfect.

Satisfied, Ashley took everything off and put it away, then slipped on the Chinese print robe she had brought back from Hong Kong. She lay down on the bed, wishing she had time for a nap but aware that she had promised to call Harry at two with her thoughts on the file he'd sent her. Which was now sitting on the bedside table, staring at her accusingly.

She picked it up reluctantly, lifting the cover, and a yellow slip of paper fell out of it and fluttered to the bed. It was her note from the previous night, listing Martin's sizes. 15 and a half, 34, she read. Jim was 15, 33. Martin's neck was bigger, his arms longer. Martin was taller, too, tall and strong. She recalled the strength of his arms around her during their brief dance. He'd made her feel like a drift of swan's down.

Then she crumpled the paper and tossed it to the floor, disgusted with herself. What on earth was wrong with her? She couldn't concentrate at all lately; the slightest thing distracted her.

She propped a pillow behind her head and set the file in her lap, taking her pencil in hand.

Meg exited from the side door of the hotel and then walked around to the parking lot. She was standing next to her car, fishing in her bag for the keys, when she realized that one of the tires was flat. The rim was sitting flush on the ground, the rubber squashed around it like a fallen soufflé.

Great. This was just what she needed. She considered going back upstairs and getting the keys to the limo, but she would have to take care of this sooner or later. There was a can of tire inflater in the glove compartment, if she could just get the thing blown up she could drive to a garage and have it changed.

She unlocked the car and retrieved the can of sealer, which had a set of incomprehensible instructions printed on its side. She was directed to pull the pin and unscrew the valve caps, then insert the nozzle and wait until the tire inflated to thirty pounds of pressure. How was she supposed to know when thirty pounds of pressure was reached? She was standing with the can in her hand, stymied, when she felt a presence at her elbow.

"May I help?" a man said pleasantly.

She glanced up inquiringly. He was an olive-skinned blond in his thirties with hazel eyes and an engaging smile. He was wearing a dark business suit and carrying a burgundy leather briefcase.

All of her mother's warnings about conversing with strangers came flooding into her mind. "No, thanks, I don't think that will be necessary," she replied. "I have this can of stuff here . . ."

Ransom had heard this before and was ready for it. He went down on one knee, surveying the tire and shaking his head. "I don't think that will hold for any length of time. You'd be much safer if you just let me change it for you. Do you have a spare in the trunk?"

"Well, yes, but . . ." Meg rambled, stalling.

He was already removing his jacket, revealing a crisp white shirt and a lean torso. "Look," he said, holding up his hand, "you're right to be cautious, but I'm perfectly safe, I assure you. I'll just change the tire and go. My car is right over there. I'll get my jack and toolbox and be right back, okay?"

Meg watched him walk away, noting his rangy build,

unsure about taking his help. He unlocked the trunk of a gray Mercedes and removed several bulky items, returning promptly to deposit them on the ground next to her.

"You'll ruin your suit," she protested weakly as he knelt and began to remove what had to be the valve caps from her tire.

"Nah," he replied. "I've got this down to a science. You'll be on the road in ten minutes, I promise."

He was as good as his word. She stood by and watched as he quickly and neatly exchanged the good tire for the bad one, finishing the procedure by tossing the flat into her trunk, slamming the lid, then dusting his palms on his thighs.

"I don't know how to thank you," she said inadequately as he shouldered back into his jacket.

"No need," he said, grinning. He had very white teeth, the incisors slightly uneven. "I have a Sir Walter Raleigh complex."

Meg smiled back at last. "Well, Walter, it's nice to meet you. I'm Meg Drummond."

Ransom removed a silver case from his inside pocket and extracted an embossed card. "Peter Ransom," he said, giving it to her and then shaking her hand.

"So you often rescue ladies in distress?" Meg asked.

"As often as possible. Are you sure you'll be all right now? You don't want me to follow you?"

"No, thank you," Meg said quickly. "I'll be fine. But I really do appreciate your help."

He made a self-deprecating gesture. "Glad to be of service. I'll be on my way now, if you don't mind." He winked. "But get your tires checked in the future."

, Meg laughed. "I will." She watched him return to his car, get in, and drive away.

What a nice man, she thought as she got into her own compact and turned the key in the ignition. Well-spoken and obviously prosperous. To think he would take time out from what must be a busy schedule to help her that way.

People weren't as callous as everyone said.

Ransom drove for several blocks and then pulled over to the side of the road, elated. It had gone supremely well. She'd reacted exactly as anticipated: she was intelligent but basically innocent, the type of person who believed in other people, as befitted the top aide to a notorious do-gooder like Senator Fair.

And she was a lot prettier than her pictures.

This was going to be a piece of cake.

Capo stuck his head through the hall door and grinned when he saw Martin.

"Looking for company, sailor?" he said, winking and gesturing to the tuxedo Martin was wearing.

"Don't laugh at *me,* Tony. You look just as ridiculous," Martin replied, tugging at his cummerbund.

"I feel like I'm getting married again," Capo said.

"I wore a suit when I got married. The last time I put on one of these straitjackets was for Maryann's senior prom. And that was twenty years ago," Martin said.

"They got us the same outfit," Capo noted. "We look like the Bobbsey Twins."

"The Bobbsey Twins are a boy and a girl," Martin said.

"A couple of fools, then," Capo said.

"I'll go along with that," Martin agreed. He stared at his reflection in the mirror and adjusted his bow tie, then fingered the studs in his shirt. To his everlasting gratitude they had ordered a simple black tux with a plain, off-white shirt. The only glamorous touch was the satin stripe on each of the pants legs. Still, he felt strange. It was a good thing Rourke wasn't around to see this. He'd laugh himself sick.

Meg Drummond breezed past Capo and pronounced, "Gentlemen, you look very handsome. Sergeant Capo, you're a vision."

"A vision of what?" Martin mumbled. "Armageddon?"

"I heard that," Capo said to him in a low tone. To Meg he said, "You look pretty nice yourself."

"Thank you, Sergeant," she said, smiling. She was wearing a soft-violet Grecian-style dress that flattered her dark coloring and left one smooth shoulder bare. "The senator is finished dressing, so I imagine we'll be leaving soon."

The bedroom door opened and Ashley emerged. Her hair was piled on top of her head, curling tendrils escaping at her neckline and temples. She was wearing the satin dress, luminous pearls gleaming around her slender throat and at her ears. The cape was folded over her arm.

A moment of silence greeted her arrival. Capo turned aside and rolled his eyes at Martin, tapping his heart with his closed fist. Martin kept his face expressionless, meeting Ashley's blue gaze briefly and then looking away.

"Dad ready?" Ashley said to Meg.

Meg nodded.

"Sylvia is meeting us at the airport, right?"

"Right," Meg confirmed.

The senator came through the connecting doors, leaving behind in the bedroom the four or five political advisers that surrounded him almost constantly, like a hovering cloud. He was wearing a gray tuxedo with a ruffled shirt and a scarlet cummerbund. His thick silvering hair was carefully styled, and his perennially tanned skin glowed with a patina of health.

"Well, well," he said jovially, "aren't our boys in blue smashing this evening? And my dear, you are looking especially lovely." He leaned over to kiss Ashley's brow.

"Thank you," she said politely.

Martin watched the interchange closely.

"Where's Jim?" the senator asked, looking around the room. "Is he taking a direct flight to New York?"

"He can't make it," Ashley replied shortly. "He called a couple of hours ago."

"Oh, what a shame," Fair said. "Well, I guess we'd better get on the road, then. Will is having the plane fueled, and it'll be waiting for us at the airport."

That was their cue to leave, and they filed out, the senator conferring in a low tone with Meg, the two policemen bringing up the rear with his daughter. There were two cars waiting for them at the curb. When Fair and Meg got into the back seat of one, still talking, Capo jumped in next to the driver.

That left Ashley and Martin standing with the doorman.

"Would you sit with me?" Ashley said to Martin. "I always feel uncomfortable being chauffeured around alone in that vast back seat, like the old lady in *Driving Miss Daisy*."

He opened the door, and she moved past him, sliding over to allow him to get in next to her. The driver, who had his instructions, pulled away as soon as the door closed.

The lights of the city streamed past them in a blur as they headed to the airport. After a silent interval, Ashley said to him, "Tell me some more about your work. You got me interested the other night."

Martin turned his head, feeling a stab of sympathy for her. And reluctant admiration. She'd been stood up at the last minute by her boyfriend. Now, on her way to this shindig alone, she was gallantly trying to make conversation with a semistranger whose only connection with her was the badge he carried in his wallet.

"I work homicide," he replied. "Investigating murders."

"It seems inappropriate to ask if you enjoy that," Ashley said slowly, "but do you?"

"I enjoy solving the puzzle, putting together the clues, the evidence. I like bringing justice to somebody who really deserves to get it."

"Do you find many of the . . . perpetrators? Isn't that the word?"

"That's the word. We find enough of them. More than the newspapers would lead you to believe. Reporters love to go on about all the 'unsolved murders,' but we do all right."

"In my profession, it's fashionable to take a dim view

of policemen," she said with a note of amusement in her voice.

"Yeah, I know. We put them in the jails and you get them out," he replied.

"It's not quite as simple as that. Surely you agree that in a democracy even a person accused of a crime should have certain rights."

"I agree in principle. But if you saw, firsthand, some of the slimeballs those laws put back on the streets, you might change your mind."

"I have seen them," she said quietly. "During my last year of law school I interned at a federal prison and wrote appeals for incarcerated felons."

"They must have had a great time with you," Martin couldn't stop himself from saying.

"There were some problems in the beginning, but once they got used to thinking of me as their lawyer, things settled down."

"Did you have a guard in the room with you when you met with the prisoners?"

"At all times."

"I'm relieved to hear it. It's nice to know that the penal administration is still somewhat in touch with reality."

"I gather that you feel women don't belong in certain branches of the law?"

"I didn't say that. Most people, of either sex, don't belong inside prisons. Cons will do anything, use anybody, to get out. Lawyers, teachers, social workers, anybody going in to a prison on a daily basis is inviting a hostage situation."

"How would you suggest convicts talk to their law-yers, visit with their families?"

"There's a wonderful invention called the telephone. You just pick up the receiver and dial, and you can talk to anybody you want."

"Are you suggesting that prisoners never be permitted personal visitation by *anyone* during the course of their terms?" She sounded as if she couldn't believe it.

"Why not? They're in prison, for God's sake, not at summer camp. Weekend furloughs, work release, tutor-ial programs—next thing you know they'll be importing hairdressers and masseurs to make sure the poor con-victs are comfortable."

"Lieutenant, I'm glad you're not in Congress making the laws," she said dryly. "You're very tough."

He noticed his demotion from "Tim" to "Lieutenant" and wondered if it had anything to do with the content of his remarks. "After seventeen years on the force, I have to be," he said. He looked over at her, a dim out-line in the darkened car.

She didn't comment.

"Tell me something," he said. "When you were work-ing with the cons, didn't you ever meet one of them that you wanted to wall up someplace with a bunch of bricks, like that guy in the Edgar Allan Poe story?"

To his surprise, she suddenly burst out laughing. "What are you talking about?"

"I'm serious. I mean somebody so bad, such a low-life, that you never wanted him to see daylight again. Somebody you wanted to make sure would never get out to hurt anyone else."

There was a long silence, and then she said in a small

voice, "I used to feel that way about the child moles-
ters."

"There, you see?"

"But I wasn't proud of feeling that way. I believe that
our constitution provides the same protections for every
person, regardless of what that person has done."

"That's what you believe, what you want to believe,"
Martin said. "But that's not what you feel."

Ashley shook her head as if to clear it. "How did we
get into this? I was trying to make polite chitchat, and
the next thing I know I'm defending the concept of con-
stitutional democracy."

He laughed. "And to me."

"Why not you?" Ashley replied, turning her head to
look at him.

There was a silence while they examined one another.

"I don't think of myself as an especially articulate
spokesman for any point of view," he finally said
quietly.

"You should. You boxed me into a corner very nicely.
I don't like being forced to confront the differences between the way I want things to be and the way they
actually are."

"No idealist does."

"Is that what I am?"

"You talk like one."

She sighed and turned to look out at the passing landscape. "I guess I do. I *know* I do. I wish I could stop."

He fought back a smile. "Why would you want to
stop?"

"Because I know it makes me sound like a college
freshman who's just discovered the *Federalist Papers*."

He bit his lower lip, hard, and said in a strangled voice, "Not a freshman, no."

"At least a sophomore, right? A sophomore enrolled in 'History 203—The Foundations of the American Justice System.'"

They were laughing together when the driver entered the airport, skirting the commercial terminals and heading for the small private airfield at the rear. There a plane was waiting, its lights on, its pilot standing next to the portable steps. He was wearing a leather flight jacket and smoking a cigarette.

Bomber jacket, Martin thought with irritation as they got out of the cars and walked toward the plane. The guy was actually wearing a bomber jacket, like John Wayne in one of those World War II movies. Were they going to bomb New York?

You're just annoyed because your little ride with her ladyship is over, he said to himself. You were really enjoying her company back there, weren't you? Well, don't get too used to it. If golden boy Dillon had shown up as planned, you would have been talking to the dashboard in the front seat.

They got aboard the plane, a Cessna twelve-seater, and Ashley fell into conversation with Meg and her father. Martin sat right behind the pilot with Capo and amused himself during the half-hour flight by watching the little green Day-Glo plane bobbing up and down on the instrument panel. When they landed and homed in on the runway, a beeper sounded, the noise becoming more insistent until it merged into a single tone as they locked into the approach signal. They landed as smoothly as an Olympic diver cuts the water.

There were two cars waiting for them when they got off the plane. Martin was amazed at how effortless travel was for these people; no merciless traffic, no frenzied terminals, no flagging cabs that sped past in the rain. Money could accomplish anything.

The drive in from the airport took longer than the plane flight, but they arrived at the Metropolitan Opera House in plenty of time. The fountain on the esplanade sprayed them with mist as they passed, and Martin's eyes, accustomed to the night outside, were dazzled by the brilliantly lit, ornate lobby. The senator garnered a round of applause as he entered, and they were shown to a box, where Sylvia Fair was already seated.

Martin looked around before the house lights went down. The place was huge, and glittering, not least because of the jewelry worn by the female patrons of the arts. The low hum of conversation fell to a hush as the lights dimmed and the curtain rose.

He couldn't make much of the story, which seemed to involve doomed love and Violetta dying, as advertised, in the end. The singing, which sounded suspiciously like screaming to him, gave him a headache. At the interval he bolted seltzer water with two aspirin, smoking until the sounding of the bell-like gong called them back for more culture.

Ashley had been seated next to him throughout, and as they finally got up to leave, she whispered, "I don't think you enjoyed the performance very much."

He looked at her, couldn't lie, and shook his head. "I don't understand that kind of music. I like the Temptations."

"Smokey Robinson?"

"Yeah."

"So do I."

He turned as the senator merged with the crowd and shook hands, edging toward the staircase. "Where's he going?" Martin asked, glancing around for Capo.

"There's a reception at the Dining Car just down the block," Ashley replied.

"We have to walk out on the street?" Martin demanded. Why hadn't anyone told him this? And why was that damned senator always running away from him?

"Sergeant Capo is with him," Ashley said gently. "I know my father is difficult to keep track of, but you can relax."

They joined the crush of people pouring through the lobby and out into the west-side spring night. A steady stream of humanity flowed away from Lincoln Center and toward the restaurant, and they followed along in its wake.

They were greeted at the door by a blue-haired matron, who kissed Ashley and viewed Martin with undisguised interest. Ashley introduced him as "Timothy Martin," and the woman's eyes followed them as they walked inside.

"They don't have to know you're a cop," Ashley explained.

"Who's sponsoring this again?" Martin asked suspiciously.

"American Civil Liberties Union," she replied.

He decided to keep a low profile.

The restaurant was one of those theme clubs so popular with the quickly sated, well-heeled crowd who patronized it. It was decorated and furnished like a thirties railroad dining car, complete with oakwood paneling, fringed lamps, and red plush carpeting. The walls were hung with prints of movie posters from the period, and stars like Jean Harlow, James Cagney, Spencer Tracy, and Joan Blondell were displayed for the diners, dressed in the exaggerated fashions of the Depression, frozen in their youth for all time.

The guests sampled the buffet as the senator and his wife made the rounds. Ashley followed him, circling the place once and then returning to stand next to Martin. She took a glass of wine from a passing server and sipped it sparingly.

"I feel like I'm falling down on the job," she observed.

"Can't take any more flesh pressing?" Martin asked.

She shook her head.

"Want something to eat?"

She looked as though she didn't know one way or the other.

"Isn't that caviar?" he inquired.

She smiled. "Yes."

"I've always wanted to try that." He scooped some of the grayish black eggs onto a cracker and popped it into his mouth. His eyes widened with alarm.

Ashley smiled.

"Gah," he said, swallowing. "Tastes like soap. Heavily salted, mushy soap."

"It's an acquired taste."

"No, no. *Beer* is an acquired taste. That stuff is worse than the earache medicine I used to take when I was a kid."

"It costs a fortune, too."

He shook his head in wonderment. "I'd love to ditch this place and get a hamburger," he said.

"I'd love to go with you," she replied wistfully.

"Would you really like to get out of here?"

"You bet."

"Then why don't you just go?"

She gazed at him, then shook her head, her expression fatalistic. "That isn't done, Lieutenant. People in my position can't follow their whims like that." She selected a smoked oyster and then put it back again. "I'm supposed to be here, and here I'll stay. I may not be charming the faithful at the moment, but at least I'm showing my face." She made a quick sandwich and took two bites before dumping it in the trash. No wonder she stayed so slim.

Martin surveyed the room, and after a while he began to notice that people were eyeing him steadily.

"Is it my paranoid police personality," he finally said to Ashley, "or are these people staring at me?"

"Your status is somewhat unclear," she replied.

"What?"

"Jim isn't here, and they think you're my date."

He could feel his face growing warm. "Oh."

She walked away, leaving him to look after her, his head banging like the percussion section in a marimba band.

He took two more aspirin, wishing for a double Jack Daniel's but settling for a club soda. When he looked up, there was a stylish brunette with a martini in her hand standing next to him, giving him a slow once-over.

"You're here with Ashley?" she said. She had lustrous

black hair, flawless olive skin, and a predatory expression.

"Uh . . . yeah."

"What do you think of her?"

"I beg your pardon?"

"Is she any good in the sack?"

Martin almost dropped his glass.

"I've always wondered," she went on, unmindful of his reaction, "if all that sweetness is an act. And I like your shoulders. So if you get tired of sucking on that particular honeycomb . . ."

"Excuse me," he said in a strong voice, and fled. He almost crashed into Capo, who was standing against the far wall, looking bored.

"Quite a group," Martin said, downing half his drink in one gulp.

Capo shrugged. "My ears are still ringing from all that yelling. I wish I was home in bed."

"We'll be out of here in an hour, once the senator says a few gracious words."

"Let's hope it's a few."

Ashley returned, and a moment later the voluptuous brunette appeared at her elbow.

"Hello, Carmen," Ashley said evenly, with an obvious lack of enthusiasm.

"Who's your friend?" Carmen asked.

Ashley performed the introductions. "Timothy Martin, Carmen Hughes."

"Did you like the Verdi?" Carmen asked Martin. "I thought I've heard him better done."

Martin said nothing.

"Of course, I really prefer his *Rigoletto*," Carmen ventured. "Don't you?"

"I don't know," Martin said. "I've never heard it."

"But my all-time favorite is *Aida*. There's nothing to compare to that exotic setting, the aria in Act One, the triumphal march in Act Two. What do you think, Timothy?"

"Carmen," Ashley tried to interrupt, her eyes on Martin's face.

"I'm talking to him," Carmen snapped.

Martin finished his drink and set his glass down smartly. "Look, miss," he said to Carmen. "I went to college nights, on the GI bill, and held down a full-time job while I majored in police science. I didn't have a lot of time for the opera." He turned his back on all of them and walked to the door, pushing through it and gulping lungfuls of the fresh night air. He stayed outside for a blessed minute, and when he turned to go back, Ashley was behind him.

"Tim, don't let Carmen get to you," she said quietly.

He didn't answer.

"I'm sure she wasn't trying to make you feel . . ."

"Yes, she was."

"All right, she was. But she was just getting back at you for giving her the brush-off earlier."

He looked at her.

"Yes, I saw it. And she's not used to that, believe me. Her sultry come-on, or her daddy's money, can usually get her just about any man she wants."

"I didn't handle her very well," he admitted.

"You handled her just fine, the only way you could. Subtlety doesn't work with Carmen."

"What was she talking about, anyway? Who's Verdi?"

"The composer."

"You told me Dumas wrote the thing."

"He did. Verdi wrote the opera based on the Dumas play."

"Oh." He shrugged. "I guess Carmen will have to look beyond me for the type of company she obviously prefers."

"Unfortunately for me, I'm part of the company she prefers." Ashley sighed.

Martin studied her for a long moment and then said, "What are you doing here, with this group? Do you really feel that you belong with them?"

It was the wrong thing to say. Her face became blank, expressionless, and she replied in a cool tone, "Please don't judge all of us by Carmen Hughes."

She left him standing on the sidewalk. He jammed his hands into his pockets, rocked back on his heels, and closed his eyes. Damn it. Why hadn't he kept his mouth shut? A couple of conversations with her when she had nothing better to do did not make them best buddies.

And he'd been right about one thing. She could definitely put on the mistress of the manor act when she chose.

Then he remembered why he was there, and went back inside to watch the Fairs.

Ashley was now "working the room," possibly to avoid any further interaction with Martin. She kept it up until her father spoke, and the party broke up shortly afterward.

The senator and Mrs. Fair were staying overnight in

the city, so Capo left with them, and Meg rode back to the airport with Ashley and Martin. The two women sat together, and Martin was relegated to the front seat, where he spent the travel time brooding about his unprofessional behavior. He said nothing during the subsequent plane ride and trip back to the hotel, but when Meg left and Ashley was heading into the bedroom, he called, "Miss Fair?"

She turned and looked at him.

"I want to apologize for what I said earlier, at the restaurant. I spoke out of turn."

Ashley shook her head, interrupting him. She had taken her hair down during the plane ride, and it now cascaded over her bare shoulders, making her look very young.

"It was my fault," she said. "I shouldn't have reacted the way I did. I'm afraid that Carmen is a sore point with me."

He waited.

"We were at school together in Europe," she explained. "Her grandfather was the Costa Rican ambassador during my dad's first term in the Senate. He opposed some international-trade legislation that would have favored Ambassador Mantegna's country, and, as kids will, we carried the rivalry over into our own lives."

"I see."

"I'm afraid that Carmen has never outgrown it," Ashley added ruefully.

Martin listened, thinking that the color of her dress flattered her pale complexion.

"I should have told everyone why you were there,"

she added softly. "You became a target because she thought you were my date." She brushed her hair back off her forehead, smiling wanly. "At least that was one reason. I don't mean to discount the impact of your considerable personal charms."

Martin watched her, wondering why she was being so candid. He knew enough about her already to realize that she hid a lot beneath the family's glowing persona.

"Why didn't you tell them why I was there?" he asked quietly.

She sighed, looking away from him. "I'm not sure. They've seen me with Jim for so long. I guess I wanted them to think that some other man would be interested in me."

"Of course they know other men would be interested in you," he said gently, wondering how she could doubt it.

"Someone like you?" she added, and he realized with concern that she was very close to tears.

"Ashley, what's the matter?" he said, unconsciously calling her by her familiar name for the first time. "What's wrong?"

She shook her head rapidly, closing her eyes. "Nothing. I'm just tired. Forgive me."

Martin watched her trying to recover her composure, his gaze fixed on her face.

"Good night, Lieutenant," she said softly. "I'll see you in the morning." She stepped through the door and closed it behind her.

Tim, he said to her silently. You're supposed to be calling me Tim, remember?

Ashley walked to her bed and sat on it, listening to

him undressing in the next room, trying not to picture him without his shirt. Without his pants. She stood and tore off her gown savagely, dropping it in a heap on the floor.

Damn Jim, anyway. He knew how she hated to go to these things alone, and so he backs out two hours before she has to get on the stupid plane, leaving her vulnerable to . . .

To what? Martin hadn't done anything, except look so heart-stoppingly gorgeous in that rented tux that Carmen had homed in on him like a circling vulture, ready to sink her scarlet claws into his hard, masculine flesh.

What an irresistible combination for her, Ashley thought bitterly. All that wavy black hair, those aquamarine eyes, and my date to boot. I'm surprised she didn't trip over her Charles Jourdan sandals in her mad rush to get to him.

And then when he froze her out—what had she said to him to make him look so rattled? He didn't rattle easily—she'd asked a few questions and quickly determined the right approach to embarrass him. God, she was vile. Ashley wished she had her in the room right now so she could slap her. Martin was worth ten of Carmen's effete, opera-aficionado pals. And on some level she sensed that, which had helped to bring on this evening's revolting display.

Martin had sidestepped her perfectly, of course, but Ashley still felt bad about it. Bad that it had happened to him, bad that it was one of her father's invited guests who had treated him so shabbily. It appeared that he'd dismissed it without a second thought, but she couldn't.

She heard a thump from next door and tried to imagine what he was doing out there. Probably smoking three cigarettes at once, wondering what kind of lunatics he was mixed up with and wishing he were back in homicide solving a nice, simple murder.

She took off her jewelry and went to the safe to put it away.

CHAPTER
Four

RANSOM WAITED a week before he called Meg. Waiting was not as difficult for him as it was for most people, and he fully expected to reap the rewards of his patience in the end. He passed the time reading up on the Philadelphia area and expanding his knowledge of the job he was supposed to have, so that he could discuss it intelligently.

The phone rang at a little after nine in the morning in the Fair hotel suite and was answered by the senator's press aide. Damico listened, said, "Hang on," and handed the receiver to Meg.

"Who is it?" she asked him, putting down the speech she was proofreading and reaching to take the phone, covering the mouthpiece with her hand.

Damico shrugged.

"Thanks, Roger," she said dryly. The man treated reporters as though they were an invading army and played Torquemada with delivery boys, but he was too busy to ask who was calling her.

"Hello?" she said.

"Margaret, this is Peter Ransom."

The name drew a blank. She was silent long enough to convince Ransom that he should clarify, and he added, "Walter Raleigh."

She laughed. "Oh, yes, of course. My savior. How are you?"

"Fine, and you?"

"Good. I'm sorry I didn't remember your name. We're very busy here and . . ." She paused. "How did you find me?"

"Well, I met you in the hotel parking lot, so I asked the clerk at the registration desk. He told me you were Senator Fair's assistant."

"I see. How did you get this number?"

There was a soft chuckle from the other end of the line. "You're a careful lady."

"I try to be."

"That's always wise. So, let's see, what did I do? Oh, yeah. There were no rooms registered to the senator when I asked, but I knew his group must be staying there. It was a process of elimination. I finally recognized the name of one of the campaign aids. Kirchner, right?"

"Yes. He signed for the rooms. It helps to deflect unwanted communications."

"I hope this isn't one of them."

Meg relaxed. "Of course not. But you went to some trouble to get in touch with me."

"I wanted to see you again." His tone was low, friendly without being too intimate.

Meg hesitated. She really didn't know this man, but she had to admit that what she recalled about him inter-

ested her. And his persistence in finding her was flatter-
ing.

"Just lunch," he said, correctly interpreting her hesi-
tation. "You can bring your own car and meet me
there."

"Today?" Meg asked, mentally running through her
schedule.

"I know it's last-minute, but I really would like to see
you. I know you must be very busy, and it may be tough
for us to get together if we wait too long."

Meg thought just a moment longer. She did want to
see him again, and if they didn't hit it off she could
always leave. It was only lunch, after all.

"All right," she said. "How about one o'clock?"

"Fine. Fiore's downtown? Do you know where it is?"

"Yes, I've been there. But I have to be back by three
to leave for Bucks County."

"No problem. I'll see you there. Good-bye." He hung
up quickly, before she could change her mind.

Meg moved to replace the receiver, and then dropped
it into her lap. She grabbed her purse and rummaged
through it, locating her wallet and extracting Ransom's
business card from the billfold where she'd stuck it. The
card gave a center-city address and a local number. She
picked up the receiver and pressed the button for the
tone, dialing the exchange listed on the card.

"Premier Leasing," a woman's voice answered on the
second ring.

"Peter Ransom, please," Meg said.

"I'm sorry, Mr. Ransom is out of the office today.
May I take a message for him?"

"No, that's all right, thank you," Meg said, and hung

up the phone. Well, he apparently worked where he said he did. Beyond that, she would have to see.

She'd meet him for lunch.

She picked up her pencil and went back to proofreading the speech.

Ransom selected a brick-red tie to go with the navy pin-striped suit and set the clothes out on his bed. He'd already scuffed and then polished the shoes, sent the new suits to the cleaners and the shirts to the laundry. Everything was ready.

He went into the living room and sat on the couch, propping his feet on the coffee table and lighting a cigarette.

He would have to be on his guard and be careful not to rush her. She was more wary than she had seemed the first time he met her. But he wasn't worried. His willingness to take things slow contributed in large part to his success.

An abandoned, illegitimate child, Ransom had been raised in the oppressive atmosphere of state orphanages, where delayed gratification was a way of life. If you cleaned the common room every day for a week, you'd get a slice of cake for dinner on Saturday night. If you kept your slate clean of demerits for three months, you'd go on the group trip to the movies on Sunday afternoon. He endured, without love or indeed any genuine interest shown him, because he was a loner who cultivated self-reliance as a means of survival.

When he was sixteen, he ran away from the home and lied about his age to join the army. He found the service environment of rigid rules and blind obedience to orders familiar and even comfortable, enabling him to adjust quickly and prosper. He watched kids several years older than he, away from their families for the first time, cry themselves to sleep in their bunks. He observed their weakness and realized that it showcased his own strength. He had never forgotten the lesson, and from that period ceased to think of himself as less than those who'd had the benefit of homes and parents. He was only different, and in some ways, superior.

Ransom lay back against the sofa and closed his eyes, remembering his first tour of duty in Vietnam. He was a big kid with a mature demeanor, and nobody had guessed how young he was. Especially when he held his own with the most seasoned of the veterans "in country," never flinching, never turning away from the worst of it. He'd volunteered for more Asian tours when he could have been stationed Stateside and was decorated several times, learning warfare as a profession with the ease of a natural predator. His superiors had recognized his ability and sent him to Special Forces School, and that experience marked his final transformation into the trained, expert killing machine who'd been hired to dispatch Senator Fair.

Ransom glanced at the wall clock and decided he had time for a second cigarette. He smoked it slowly, indulging himself in an unusually reflective mood. To him, the past was dust and he rarely examined it; his real life had begun when he found his current calling.

With the end of the war, he, like other veterans, had returned to an unappreciative nation and a series of unsatisfactory jobs. He was ripe for the picking when his former Green Beret colonel recruited him and several others like him for mercenary work at home. Ransom quickly became an elite contract killer, a top performer in his chosen field, much in demand for the difficult assignments that required his special touch. And enough of those came his way to make him a rich man in a short period of time.

He relied on the colonel, his "contact," to set up deals with clients willing to pay handsomely for his specialized skill, and so he lived the life of a nomad, traveling and assuming a new identity to complete each job. He was wanted by the FBI and Interpol as several different people, since the police hadn't realized yet that the same man was the culprit in many varied cases. But it was only a matter of time before they did; they weren't as smart as he was, but they weren't idiots, either. He'd been thinking lately of dropping out for a while, taking an extended vacation when this deal was done. He could go back to work any time he wanted. People with a pecuniary interest in murder were always in the market for what he had to sell.

Ransom stood and crushed out his cigarette, going to the bedroom to change. As he dressed for his date with Meg, he reviewed what he would say to her, how he would direct the conversation. It never occurred to him that he might not be in control of the situation. He always was. He enjoyed success not only because of his brilliant planning and excellent marksmanship, but because his life was devoid of emotional involvement. He regarded people as the means to an end—his next completed contract. And the goal of his work was simple: the accumulation of wealth.

Money represented neither luxuries nor pleasures,

since he indulged himself in few of either, but rather the security of knowing he would never be at the mercy of public institutions again. To that end he lived simply and invested well, going from project to project like a judicious performer choosing vehicles for advancement, acquiring a reputation for accuracy and positive outcome.

He didn't expect that this case would jeopardize it.

Meg did not feel like battling the city traffic in her own car, and she disdained the senator's limo, instead taking a cab to the restaurant. She didn't want to be ostentatious, and the town car was hard to miss. In addition, the drivers talked. She preferred to keep this to herself for a while, until she decided if it really was worth pursuing

She had dressed with care, selecting a two-piece dove-gray outfit, a sleeveless dress, and matching cardigan jacket that flattered her dark coloring. She always made the most of her looks, choosing clothes in dark blue and navy, shades of lavender and gray, sometimes cherry red, anything that enhanced what nature had given her. And she had a superb figure, which she kept in trim with a closely supervised diet and the constant activity involved with working for the senator. So she was ready for the great love of her life. He was tardy, she had to admit, but he might yet appear. At the moment, however, she was more concerned about getting back in time to keep her schedule for the rest of the day, and she checked her memory against the leather-bound calendar in her purse. Everything seemed to be in order, and she relaxed, sitting back against the seat for the crosstown ride.

Ransom was waiting inside the lobby of the restaurant, stationed at the bow window watching for Meg's arrival. He had called ahead for a reservation and bribed the maître d' for a good table, secluded and away from the kitchen noise. The dining room was crowded but subdued, the sort of place where conversation never rose above a low murmur. He had chosen it for that reason; he would be able to talk to her and draw her out, make the first meeting count for as much as possible. He felt tense and a little nervous, as he always did before setting a plan in motion, but he was glad he was getting his plan underway.

He stepped forward as Meg walked through the door. She looked around briefly, caught his eye, and smiled.

She looked nice, he thought as he closed the distance between them. She had been wearing jeans and a sweater when they met, but now she was more dressed up, with a knee-length skirt and high heels that flattered her legs. She had good legs, he noticed, a good figure in fact, not willowy and slight like the Fair girl's but full-bodied and curvaceous.

This might turn out to be quite pleasurable.

"I wasn't sure I would recognize you," she greeted him as he took her hand and shook it.

"I was certain I would know you," he replied.

They were shown to their table, and Ransom said as they sat, "You look lovely."

"Thank you," she replied neutrally.

Too much, he thought quickly. No more flattery; she doesn't like it and she'll see through it. Remember how bright she is.

"I'm glad you decided to come," he added.

She looked at him and nodded. "So am I."

There, that was better. "I imagine you don't meet many men the way you met me."

She grinned. "It's something to keep in mind if I ever get lonely. I can always have another flat tire. It beats putting ads in the personals columns."

"I can't believe you'd ever have to do that." Careful, not too obsequious.

"Maybe not. But I did have a number of blind dates in college."

"Really?"

"Really. I had this very popular roommate who was convinced I was burying my youthful potential under a bunch of political science textbooks. I had a work scholarship and a tough curriculum, so I didn't have a wealth of time to pursue a social life. She was always fixing me up with somebody, usually a friend of her current boyfriend. She had a lot of boyfriends, so I had quite a few arranged dates."

"Did any of them work out?"

"Some of them, for a while. They weren't all as bad as the guy in the gorilla suit."

Ransom beckoned the waiter closer, leaning forward to say to Meg, "The guy in the gorilla suit?"

"It was a Halloween party, and . . . well, it's a long story."

"Something from the bar?" Ransom asked as the waiter appeared at his elbow.

Meg shook her head. "I have to work this afternoon. Just club soda with a slice of lime, please."

"I'll have the same," Ransom said to the waiter.

The man left, and Ransom said to Meg, "Tell me about the Halloween party."

"Are you sure you want to hear it?" God, she thought, why had she brought up such an adolescent subject? She must be jumpier than she'd realized.

He nodded, smiling.

"Well," she said, refolding her linen napkin in her lap, "it was October of my sophomore year, and Karen, that's my roommate, was going to a Halloween party sponsored by her boyfriend Tom's fraternity. I was just going to stay in the dorm that weekend and catch up on some work, but she wouldn't hear of it. Tom had a friend, of course, a nice guy, she said, kind of shy but really a wonderful person underneath it all. You know the routine."

Ransom smiled again. He didn't, he'd never had a blind date in his life and very few enlightened ones, but he pretended to go along with her.

"And so I dressed up as Fay Wray. You know, that lady in the King Kong movie? The ape is carrying her around when the planes are dive-bombing him on the Empire State Building."

Ransom nodded. He had seen the film in the army.

"So my date shows up in the gorilla suit, which I expected. But he's huge, I mean really big, a linebacker on the football team, six foot four and two hundred and fifty pounds. And he can't talk to me because the head of the suit muffles everything he says, so in order to carry on a conversation he has to take the head off and carry it under his arm like that coach driver in 'The Legend of Sleepy Hollow.'"

"I see." He was, indeed, beginning to get the picture.

"So there we were, at the dance, and he's lumbering around in this suit, can't hear, can't talk, can hardly see, and is crashing into everything, including me. And I'm trying to communicate with hand gestures and standing next to this human obelisk and wishing I was back in my room reading the last three chapters of *Lyndon Baines Johnson: The Exercise of Power,* which was my assignment for the weekend." Please don't let him be bored with this, Meg thought, wishing she didn't have to finish the story.

"And?" he said.

"That wasn't the worst of it."

"What was the worst of it?"

"He apparently fancied himself as something of a clown, and every once in a while he would grab me and haul me into the air, literally over his head, and beat his breast with his free hand, making what he imagined to be gorilla noises."

"Oh."

"He dislocated my wrist."

Ransom said nothing, listening in disbelief.

"So we wound up the festivities in the emergency room of the local hospital, having my wrist put in a cast." She took a sip of the drink the waiter had just deposited in front of her. "And that was my last blind date."

"I'm not surprised."

"Karen stopped suggesting them after that."

"I'm amazed you left her alive to say anything at all."

"Oh, it wasn't her fault. She was trying to be helpful. She really thought I was missing out on something."

"But you didn't."

Meg shrugged. "I guess I figured if something was meant to happen, it would."

"A fatalist."

"Maybe."

"So am I. There's only so much you can control in life. The rest is just chance."

"Like flat tires."

"Like that." He fiddled with the salt shaker and asked, "So how did you wind up in your present job? I would think you'd be awfully young for such a responsible position."

"Senator Fair likes to project a youthful image."

"I'm sure that's not the only reason."

"I'm good at what I do," she said in a matter-of-fact tone. "I've been fascinated by politics all my life. I volunteered to work on the senator's state campaigns when I was in college and joined his staff when I graduated. I moved up from there."

"You make it sound easy."

She shook her head. "It wasn't. But it was what I wanted to do. I've had to make sacrifices, of course, but you always have to sacrifice to get what you want, no matter what it is."

"No regrets, then?"

"None."

"Do you believe in the senator that much?"

"I believe in what he stands for, his goals. I couldn't work for him if I didn't."

The waiter returned and they ordered, spinach salad and quiche for Meg, prosciutto with melon and flounder française for Ransom. When the server had taken the menus and gone, Meg said, "Enough about me. Tell me about you. What do you do at Premier Leasing?"

"I lease office space for business concerns. Larger outfits have their own real-estate people, but smaller businesses don't have the time or the money to employ a full-time representative. They contact me with their requests and I find the right kind of site for expansion, a warehouse, a factory, whatever they need. I take a percentage of the purchase price or the lease as my fee." He had actually done just that years ago, so he could speak of it convincingly.

"I see. Is that interesting work?"

"No."

Meg burst out laughing. "At least you're honest."

He shrugged. "It pays the bills until I can get enough money together to start my own agency."

"That's your plan?"

He nodded. "There's a big future in commercial real estate in this area. Many companies in New York and Washington are finding the cost of doing business in the home area too high and are looking to move, not too far, to keep expenses down. Philadelphia is very appealing in that respect; it has a metropolitan environment, but real estate is cheaper than in comparable cities."

"You seem to know all about it."

"I've been studying the market for a while."

The waiter brought their appetizers, and Ransom cut his ham into several slices as Meg dug into her salad.

"How did you get into real estate?" she asked.

Careful. "I was a business major in college, and a friend's father had a local agency. He just handled residential listings, but it got me started. My friend and I used to work there during the summers, and when I graduated from school I got my license."

"Where did you go to school?"

"UCLA," he said promptly. He had actually taken a few courses there, and had a fake diploma from the place, courtesy of a former lover who worked for a lithographer, but if she checked with the registrar's office he would be in trouble. The trick was to make sure she never got suspicious enough to check.

"Did you like California?"

"I liked it well enough. The climate is great, but boring after a while. Sunshine every day. It got to the point where I was praying for a monsoon." He had lived there when he was discharged from the army at a base near Los Angeles, simply because he didn't have the money to travel anywhere else.

"I've heard that about the climate. Of course, the earthquakes do provide a change."

"We weren't having any earthquakes when I was there. I missed the change of seasons, so I came back east."

"Do you have any family?"

"All dead," he said shortly, in a tone that intimated that he did not want to discuss it. He assumed Meg's good manners would prevent her from pursuing the subject, and he was right.

"My parents still live in the house where I was raised, in Doylestown," she said. "That's north of here, quite rural. My father has a grain-feed business."

"Any brothers or sisters?" One of them might show up and interfere with his plan.

"I have a younger brother in medical school in Iowa."

Good. Medical students tended to be very busy, and Iowa was far away.

"Why did he go there?" Ransom asked.

"That's the only place he got into school. It's difficult to get admitted. You have to go where they'll take you."

"Your parents must be very proud of both of you." How well he had assimilated the nuances of polite conversation. He always knew the proper thing to say.

"Yes, they are," she replied.

"Do they come to see you often?"

"Almost never. My father has to be surgically removed from his office, and my mother doesn't like to travel. If I want to see them, I have to go there."

"You must be different from your mother. Your work involves a lot of travel, doesn't it?"

Meg nodded. "Especially now. We're set to cover the whole state in the next six weeks or so." She giggled as the waiter removed her salad plate. "They're even giving us a police escort for the trip."

Ransom's fork paused in the act of carrying the last bit of melon to his mouth. "Police?" he said.

"Yup. The commissioner assigned them to us himself. Two Philadelphia cops, a sergeant and a lieutenant."

Damn. "A lieutenant. I'm surprised they would send someone with that high a rank. Rather a waste, isn't it, for such a routine duty?"

"I think the cops feel the same way, but they're pretty much doing what they're told. Ashley feels better having them around, though. She wasn't happy about it in the beginning, but I can see that she's changing her mind."

"The senator's daughter?"

"Yes."

"I've seen her pictures in the papers. Very photogenic."

"You could say that. She's gorgeous."

"I haven't read anything about the police bodyguards."

A furrow appeared between Meg's dark brows. "Would they mention that in the newspapers?"

"Perhaps not," Ransom replied hastily, aware that he should change the subject. "Have you been keeping tabs on the senator's potential opponent? How is the other side doing?"

Meg shook her head. "Too early to tell for sure. We're following the polls, but as we get closer to summer they will become much more important. Right now they're not as accurate as we'd like; there's too much time for things to change."

"Your man is assumed to be the underdog."

"Like Harry Truman after the war?" Meg asked, grinning. "Like John Kennedy in 1960?"

"I can see that you won't give up until the swearing-in ceremony."

"Not even then. There's always the future, the next term. Four years isn't very long when you consider a lifetime or a century."

The waiter brought the main course, and Ransom watched Meg remove the bacon bits from her quiche with a single tine of her fork. She looked up and caught him studying her.

"I don't like bacon," she explained sheepishly.

"Would you prefer something else?" he asked, glancing around for the waiter.

"Oh, no. This is fine. I've mutilated it sufficiently."

He smiled. "Your name is Margaret, but you prefer Meg?"

She nodded.

"Why? Margaret is such a charming name."

"It means 'a pearl.' Difficult to live up to, don't you think? Especially for someone with my coloring."

"There are black pearls, just the shade of your hair. They're far more rare and valuable than the white ones."

She looked up at him, and he could see her examining him for sincerity. He marshaled all his resources to project it.

She looked down again. "'Margaret' always makes me feel like I'm back in fourth grade." She lowered her voice to a male register. "'Margaret, how do you explain this failing grade in conduct?'" she said, imitating her father.

"You got poor grades in elementary school?" he asked in surprise.

"Not in academic subjects. In behavior, deportment."

"I can't believe you misbehaved."

"I didn't misbehave, really, but the school had a demerits system. You lost points if you broke the rules. I didn't cut class or sass the teachers, but I was always reading novels during arithmetic and doing homework when I finished the test early, that sort of thing. Each incident added up, and the total usually caught up with me at report time."

"Sounds like the place I was in," Ransom said dryly.

"Where was that?"

"A boarding school," he said lightly, surprised at himself for making the admission. Why had he told her that?

"So you understand what I mean," she said.

"Yes, I do, Meg."

She smiled. Then she glanced at her watch and said, "Oh, dear. I'm afraid I have to get going, I really lost track of the time."

"Can't you have some dessert, coffee?"

"Maybe just coffee, but then I have to run."

"All right."

The waiter cleared the plates, and while they waited for the coffee Ransom said, "I'd like to take you to dinner soon."

She hesitated.

"No gorilla suits, I promise," he said.

She smiled. "Okay. I'll give you the number in New Hope where we'll be staying. You can call me there."

He held her gaze. "Meg, I like you. I like you a lot. Please don't make me leave here without a firm commitment."

"I'm very busy with the campaign," she said weakly.

"Saturday night?" he asked.

"I'm sorry, I have a political dinner. There are functions to attend most weekends."

"Thursday, then. Is anything happening Thursday night?"

"No."

"We'll make it an early evening. Where will you be staying?"

"The Chanticleer Hotel in New Hope."

"I'll pick you up in the lobby at eight. Chez Ondine is

only a short distance away, if I remember correctly. Would that be all right?"

"Yes."

"I'll have you back by ten-thirty."

"Okay," she agreed. The waiter poured the coffee, and as she sipped it she checked her watch again.

"My car is out in the parking lot," Ransom said, watching her. "I'll drive you back."

"I wouldn't think of it, that's all the way across town in the midday traffic," Meg replied firmly. "I'll go by cab, the way I came."

He saw that she would brook no argument, and so he signaled the maître d', who was standing at the entrance to the dining room. When the man appeared at his side, Ransom took a folded bill from his wallet and said, "Please call the lady a cab. She'll need it in ten minutes."

"Very good, sir," the maître d' said, and went to the desk to use the telephone.

"Thank you," Meg said to Ransom.

They drank their coffee and made small talk until the maître d' returned and said, "The lady's cab is here."

Ransom rose and pulled out Meg's chair, then walked her to the door. They emerged into the afternoon sunshine and turned to each other to say good-bye.

The taxi was waiting at the curb.

"Eight o'clock on Thursday," Ransom reminded her.

"Eight o'clock."

"Until then."

Meg nodded and climbed into the cab. Ransom stood on the sidewalk and watched it disappear around the corner, then he turned back into the restaurant and went directly to the bar.

"Jameson's straight up, no ice," he said to the bartender. The barman nodded and went for the bottle while Ransom sat on the leather stool and studied his reflection in the Victorian mirror.

By all rational standards it had gone very well. She had seemed to enjoy his company and he'd made another date with her. If their relationship continued in this vein, he would be able to accomplish his mission with no problem. Yet he was vaguely uneasy. Why?

It was Meg, he realized. He really never *liked* anyone; respect was the closest he could come to affection. But she was attractive and pleasant, witty and bright. Worthy of respect. Why couldn't she have been the dull, driven career woman he'd expected, a thing, a patsy it would have been easy to use and discard? Instead she was a person, a personality, and he didn't like that.

His drink came, and he bolted it, asked for another. Something was off center, he mused, something was wrong with him. He was thinking about vacations, giving away unnecessary information to a mark, considering the feelings of a woman whose trust he was plotting to abuse. How many other people had he violated in the past without even losing his concentration? He must be slipping, getting old.

Oh, what the hell, he thought. It was probably just starting-gate tension. He had never hit anyone as prominent as Fair before, finding his clientele primarily among businessmen who wanted to eliminate rivals and husbands who wanted to eliminate their wives. He felt different this time because the situation *was* different.

His target was a U.S. senator, and that was bound to generate some jitters. Nothing to worry about, certainly.

But when the second drink came he bolted that too.

The next day, Meg glanced up from her computer terminal to find Capo standing three feet away from her, smoking languidly.

"Sergeant Capo," she said, "I would appreciate it if you would take that cigarette into the other room. I'm wearing my contact lenses, and the haze bothers my eyes."

Capo crushed out the cigarette and came closer, which wasn't exactly the reaction she'd anticipated.

"You don't always wear them, huh?" he said.

"No, but for prolonged close work they're helpful."

"You can't see without them?"

"Not well. I need to wear them or my glasses," she answered, continuing to type.

"I've got great eyes myself," Capo volunteered. "Twenty-twenty, twenty-fifteen, something like that. I can read billboards, signs on the road, anything."

"How fortunate for you," Meg observed, not looking up.

"What are you working on?" he asked, peering over her shoulder.

"I'm revising the senator's schedule," she replied.

"He's a pretty busy guy."

Meg's fingers ceased their activity. "Sergeant Capo, are you waiting for something?"

"Not really. The senator's taking a nap. I guess I'm waiting for him to wake up." He grinned, displaying teeth as perfect as his eyesight.

"Where's Lieutenant Martin?"

"He's with Miss Fair at the VA hospital, remember?"

So, no hope of distracting him with his buddy, she thought. Capo seemed nonchalant, but he missed nothing, and she wanted a break from his penetrating gaze for a little while.

"The flowers just came?" he asked, gesturing to the large basket of gladiolas on her desk.

"Yes."

"Who are they from?"

Meg's thumb hit the space bar, and the computer jumped a line. "A friend," she said stiffly.

"Boyfriend?" Capo asked, picking up the enclosure envelope.

"A man, Sergeant. Does that serve to make it any clearer?" Meg replied archly.

"Don't get huffy," he said equably. "I'm just doing my job." He examined the card, which featured a caricature of a gorilla on its cover. He opened it and read the legend aloud: "'I'm just ape over you.'"

"It's an inside joke, Sergeant," Meg said. "I wouldn't expect you to understand."

"I understand your friend's got classy handwriting," he said dryly, replacing the card.

"That's the florist's handwriting," Meg answered, annoyed. "The order was placed over the phone."

"How do you know?"

"It came through the Teleflora service. The tag is on the basket. Sergeant, is all of this leading somewhere? I resent the invasion of my privacy, and I don't see what this has to do with Senator Fair."

"I'm just checking on what comes in and goes out. I

don't think that's unreasonable. Bombs and other dangerous devices can be concealed in almost anything."

"Feel free to search the gladiolas for fuses, Sergeant," Meg said sarcastically, and went back to her typing.

"Miss Drummond?" Capo intoned with infuriating calm.

She looked up with exaggerated patience.

"I've already told you that you can call me Tony," he confided, and winked.

He ambled back into the hall as Meg rolled her eyes and then returned her attention to her work.

Ashley had returned from the hospital and was in her bedroom reading when her father knocked on her door.

"Honey, are you busy?" Fair said.

"No, Dad, come on in."

Fair entered his daughter's hotel room and sat gingerly on the edge of her bed. He was wearing one of his outrageously expensive but interchangeable dark suits, and his thick hair was neatly combed. His namesake and Ashley's half brother, Joe, looked just like him, right down to the high-bridged nose and widow's peak.

"I just thought I'd take a moment to come in and chat," Fair said. "We're both so busy that we rarely get a chance to talk in private."

Ashley waited. Her father never wasted time; this visit had a purpose.

"I don't think I ever thanked you properly for giving up your job to work on my campaign," Fair said.

"I didn't give it up, Dad, I just took a leave of absence."

"Nevertheless, you made a big change in your life for me, and I want you to know I appreciate it."

Ashley smiled.

Fair sighed, and she could see that he was choosing his words carefully.

"I'm aware," he began, "that you and Sylvia have not been the best of friends."

"We just have different interests, Dad, that's all," Ashley said quickly. Too quickly.

Fair shook his head. "No. You felt excluded when she had the children. I never should have sent you away to school."

"Dad, it doesn't matter now," Ashley said uncomfortably.

"Yes, it does. You said that was what you wanted, and I just went along because it seemed best at the time. But I did see, later, that I'd made a mistake."

"Dad, don't do this. It serves no purpose."

"It was your mother, you see," Fair said, as if she hadn't spoken. "Sylvia could never forget that I loved her first; she saw your mother's shadow everywhere. And you looked just like her. Still do."

Ashley was silent.

"I had hoped, at first, that since you were close in age to Sylvia you might find things in common and get along. But there was too much resentment, I guess, on both sides, and I just took the easy way out. I was always busy, always preoccupied, and your going away to school seemed to solve so many problems."

"It did."

"But not for you, eh?" Fair said.

"Dad, it was so long ago. We all survived it."

"Did you survive it?"

"Of course."

"When you volunteered to work with me on the campaign, I thought, She understands now, she wants to be a part of my life. I felt that it would be a healing time for both of us."

"It has been," Ashley said gently. "That's why I wanted to do it."

"So you forgive me?"

"There's nothing to forgive. I've thought about it, and in your place I don't know that I would have done any differently. Sylvia was your wife, you wanted her to be happy, and it wasn't as though you were sending me to a concentration camp. I got a wonderful education, and by the time I got out of school Sylvia felt more secure in her position. We've been able to bury a lot of those old bones."

"Is that really true?" Fair asked.

Ashley was astonished to see that there were tears in his eyes. She got up and embraced him.

"Dad, it's true. I just couldn't carry a child's resentment into adulthood. There were too many mature feelings crowding it out."

"Ashley, I love you," her father said, hugging her close. "You're my first child, and no one will ever take your place in my heart."

Ashley was silent, her throat closing with emotion.

Fair held her off to look at her. "When you were born, your mother and I didn't know how to contain our joy. You were such a beautiful baby, and she had such high hopes for you." He closed his eyes. "I can't bear the thought that I let her down where you're concerned."

"You didn't." Ashley stepped back and smiled at him. "You didn't, Dad. I've done what I wanted with my life."

"But you always seem so lonely."

Ashley had no reply.

"You're not in love with Jim Dillon, are you?"

Ashley didn't answer, refusing to meet his eyes.

Fair stood. "Well, that's your business. I won't pry. But I'm glad we had this talk, and if there's ever anything you need, you won't hesitate to come to me, will you?"

"I won't."

He kissed the top of her head, then wiped his eyes. He walked to the door, glanced back at her once, smiled, and then closed the door behind him.

Well, Ashley thought, who would have thought he had it in him? She knew how hard it had been for him to come to her, and she admired him for it.

She smiled to herself, picked up her book again, and stared at the pages until the tears started to flow.

Several nights later, Martin was looking out the window of Ashley's New Hope hotel suite, studying the marquee lights reflected in the wet pavement below. The barge canal across the street was dappled with raindrops, and the wind from the river behind him whipped the trees inside out and back again. It was very late, but he was wide awake. They were moving west in a couple of days, to a Carbon County steel town known to be a Democratic stronghold.

It didn't matter to Martin where they were; the routine was always the same.

He rubbed his eyes and tried to resist the temptation to have another cigarette. He lost the battle and lit up, standing, the restlessness he felt prodding him into motion. He was physically tired, but mentally too alert to sleep. The fatigue was nothing new. They were all tired from the demanding schedule, but the ceaseless activity wasn't the hardest part of Martin's job. The candidate was extremely difficult to protect. He considered himself a man of the people, and liked to mingle, shaking hands and engaging in close contact, disregarding the instructions of his bodyguards. Martin felt as though he was playing football again, chasing a broken-field runner who eluded his grasp. Just that evening Ashley had persuaded her father to listen to Capo's recommendation that he stick to the dais when Fair wanted to parade through the crowd, gladhanding the masses. Even so, the experience had been taxing for the two cops. Capo was asleep in the adjoining suite, done in after accompanying the Fairs to another of the seemingly endless receptions, and Martin was left with a half-empty pack of Camels and raging insomnia.

He was remembering Dillon kissing Ashley good-bye in the hallway earlier that night, and it was keeping him awake.

After the night at the opera—it *was* like a Marx Brothers movie, Martin thought sourly—Dillon had returned with a vengeance, as if to make up for his peccadillo on that occasion. He escorted Ashley, both of them dressed to kill, to some affair almost every evening. As she passed ahead of him on Dillon's arm, smelling deli-

ciously of that tantalizing perfume, Martin wanted to
take her aside and tell her that she didn't have to play
the role anymore, that the world wouldn't fall apart if
she just gave it all up and did what she wanted. But of
course he said nothing, merely trailed them through
each public event like a shadow, watching the somber-
ness of Ashley's expression in repose change to animation when she found herself observed.

Martin was drawn to her, sensing a loneliness beneath
her perfect exterior, a loneliness that matched his beat
for beat. He daily confirmed his original opinion that
she wasn't in love with Dillon; he knew that from the
way her gray eyes passed over Dillon's face to settle on
his own. He caught her watching him at odd times, but
when he would meet her eyes her gaze would shift away
from him, and he wondered if he was imagining things.

But he wasn't imagining the way she would thank
Dillon for the gifts he sent with a mild, passionless appreciation, or how she took his phone calls with friendly
regard but a noticeable lack of delight.

I'd make her respond, Martin thought fiercely, exhaling a stream of smoke. She wouldn't be so cool, so
distant with me. Then he realized what he was thinking
and stubbed his cigarette out with a vengeance.

No more of that, he instructed himself. Distraction,
that was the answer. He switched on the portable television the management had thoughtfully provided and
tried to watch the late movie. It was one of those black-
and-white set pieces from the early sixties with cheap
production values and a moody jazz score. It proved
incomprehensible and he turned the set off again, going
back to the window and sitting on the edge of an easy

chair. He drew aside the hotel curtain to look down at the rainy, windswept street.

In a little more than a month it would be over, and he'd never see her again.

The thought should have brought comfort, but what he felt was more like despair.

Inside her bedroom, Ashley could hear him moving about restlessly. They were both awake, both looking for something to do. The impulse to go out and see him was overwhelming, but she was trying to talk herself out of it.

Could she really risk a personal relationship with this man? She was drawn to him so powerfully that reason was sublimated, but she knew that he was as different from her as frost from fire. She felt that she was at a turning point, and that if she did what she was thinking of doing, a line would be crossed that night, forever.

She thought a moment longer and then stood, tying the sash of her robe.

Martin lit another cigarette with resignation. He was dragging on it, his eyes narrowed against the curling smoke, when he felt that he was not alone.

"I'm sorry to disturb, you, Tim," Ashley said, standing by the door. "I couldn't sleep."

"That's all right," he replied. "I just didn't hear you come in."

"Can't sleep either?"

She was wearing a pink batiste full-length dressing down, sprigged all over with tiny flowers and belted at her narrow waist.

He shook his head.

"Too many parties," Ashley said sagely. "You get

pumped up for them and then afterward you can't come down. Believe me, I know."

"I guess that's what it is," he answered, hardly aware of what he was saying. She was backlit by the standing lamp behind her, and he could see the outline of her legs through the thin material covering them.

"I've just been wishing that I could take a walk," she said.

"At two in the morning?"

"I'm hungry. I want a pastrami sandwich."

He smiled. "Ever heard of room service?"

"Room service stops at midnight. Plus it doesn't offer deli items." She smiled conspiratorially. "One of the local people at the reception told me that the Lambertville Diner across the river in Jersey has the best pastrami sandwiches in the area. And it's open all night."

He watched her warily, wondering where this was leading.

"I can never eat at these political things," she said.

"Yes, I know. I've had some experience with your habits in that area, remember?"

"But I'm starving now."

"That's a good sign."

"Do you want to join me for a snack?"

"You're not thinking of walking over there now?" Martin said. "It's the middle of the night."

"Why not? I'm not under house arrest here, am I?"

"Of course not, but . . ."

"Then why can't I go?"

"It's raining."

"I like rain, especially at night. It would be all right,

wouldn't it? I wouldn't be breaking the rules or anything?"

"I suppose it would be all right," Martin conceded reluctantly. "If I went with you," he added.

"Then let's go. Just give me a minute to change."

She disappeared into her room, and Martin spent the time until her return wondering if it was really happening. When she came back she was wearing jeans and a sweater with a hooded mackintosh that made her look about sixteen. He bent to pick up his jacket, adjusting his shoulder holster as he did so.

She eyed it soberly, but said nothing.

"Ready?" he said.

"Ready," she replied.

Martin fell into step beside her, feeling as if he were on his first date. He'd had his share of women in the years since his divorce, including the few he would always remember, but he had never known a lady like this. She made him feel awkward, outclassed. And large. Very large.

They descended in the elevator, accompanied by Muzak, and emerged into the lobby, which was almost deserted.

The desk clerk looked up from his glossy magazine, appearing a little nonplussed to see Ashley Fair dressed like a high-school cheerleader and taking off into a rainstorm with her father's bodyguard. But he forgot it instantly, going back to the latest romantic escapades of his favorite TV star.

Ashley pulled her hood up and they stepped through the door. Martin glanced out at the rain, which had let up somewhat and was now only a drifting mist. He glanced back at her, saying, "Maybe I should get one of the cars."

"Oh, no, I'd like to walk. Unless you mind getting a little wet."

He turned up the collar of his trenchcoat and said truthfully, "I don't mind at all."

They set off for the bridge that connected Pennsylvania and New Jersey. It was built to accommodate vehicle traffic down the middle with footpaths on either side. Occasionally a car whooshed past them, creating a plume of spray from the sitting puddles. The streetlights were dim and pearled with moisture, the night air fresh and invigorating, washed clean by the storm.

"It's nice, isn't it?" Meg asked, looking up at him.

He nodded. Surprisingly, it was.

They didn't say much as they walked across the bridge, but the silence was companionable. The moon appeared intermittently, sometimes obscured by the dissipating rain clouds, and the whole landscape had that eerie stillness associated with the early hours of the morning.

On the other side of the bridge Martin saw the flashing neon sign of the diner on the facing street. It hung over a ramshackle clapboard building that leaned drunkenly toward the sidewalk and seemed to be supported by the more respectable structures on either side.

"Is that it?" he asked, pointing.

"Has to be. The lady I spoke to said you couldn't miss it. You can't miss that."

"Are you sure you want to go there?" he asked, squinting into the distance.

"Why not?"

He glanced down at her. "It looks like a dive."

Ashley laughed lightly. "You should see some of the places I've been, campaigning for my father."

He sighed doubtfully.

"You'll protect me, won't you?" she asked playfully, shooting him a sidelong glance.

"If I remember correctly, that's why I'm here," he replied, shaking his head.

"Oh, good," she said, like a little kid, and ran ahead of him, turning to urge him onward.

When they arrived, Martin's worst fears were confirmed. The interior of the diner kept unsavory pace with the exterior, and the scattered customers, nursing cups of coffee or shoveling in the blue plate special, looked like extras from *On the Waterfront*.

"I'll probably get canned for bringing you here," Martin muttered to Ashley as they entered and he got an even more detailed look at their surroundings.

"It's the middle of the night. No one will ever have to know," Ashley replied.

"I think they'll find out if you become the next local crime statistic," he muttered.

"You would never let that happen, Lieutenant," Ashley observed confidently. She looked around expectantly. "I wonder where the hostess is."

"Don't strain your eyes," Martin said to her. "In places like this, you're lucky there's a roof, much less a hostess."

"Do you spend a lot of time in places like this?" Ashley asked.

"Too much," he responded.

A harried waitress in a faded pink uniform emerged

from the kitchen carrying a tray and said to them, "Just sit anywhere you like, folks." She barged past them and deposited two cheeseburgers in front of a huge man in a red flannel shirt. He was reading the racing form.

"I can smell the pastrami," Ashley whispered.

"I think that's my career reducing itself to ashes," Martin countered darkly.

"Let's sit here," Ashley said, ignoring him. She selected a booth and slid onto one of the seats. Its vinyl cover was ripped and marked with ink, the table next to it cracked and stained with wear.

Martin slid in across from her and said, "I can't believe I let you talk me into this."

"Something tells me that doesn't happen to you very often," Ashley replied archly.

"It's been happening to me a lot more lately," he said dryly, and she laughed.

The menus were covered with plastic and propped in a stainless-steel stand on the table. Martin removed them and handed one to Ashley. He studied the bill of fare, which was about what he'd expected.

The same waitress approached them and said to Ashley, "What'll it be, hon?"

"I'll have a pastrami sandwich, please," Ashley said, in the tone she must have used to order dinner at the senator's country club.

The waitress looked at Martin expectantly.

"The same," he said, replacing the menus. "And a cup of coffee."

"I'll have coffee too," Ashley added.

The waitress scribbled and said, "Be right up." She

padded off down the aisle, rubber-soled shoes squeaking.

"Well, if the meat is poisoned, at least we'll die together," Martin said philosophically.

"Did you notice the group over there in the corner?" Ashley asked sotto voce.

Martin glanced in the direction she was indicating and saw three young girls in their late teens, dressed in leather jackets. They were heavily made up and had elaborate, post-punk hairdos. The giggled loudly when they saw that he was looking at them.

"Fugitives from the first act of *Macbeth*," he said. "Isn't it a little early for Halloween?"

"They're watching us," Ashley told him, amused. "Or rather, they're watching you."

"Why aren't they home in bed?" he said sourly.

"Why aren't we?" Ashley countered. Then she realized fully what she had said and blushed furiously, her pale skin coloring to the roots of her hair.

The waitress returned with the coffee, and Martin got busy drinking it, pretending he didn't realize that Ashley was embarrassed. When she had recovered sufficiently, she took a sip of her drink and said, "I hope my father wasn't too much trouble for you tonight. Sometimes he loses sight of why you're with us."

"Thanks for helping me with him," Martin replied. "He always feels that Capo and I are overdoing the precautions."

"I worry about him." Ashley sighed. "He thinks that nothing can touch him."

"That's why he thinks he can be President," Martin observed. "It's part of the package."

"That's true," Ashley said. "But I still wish he would be more careful."

"You love him very much, don't you?" Martin said quietly.

"Yes, I do. In spite of the fact that until the last few years I hardly saw him."

Martin listened, surprised by her candor.

"My mother died when I was very little, and when my father remarried and had his new family, I was kind of the odd man out, if you know what I mean."

"I know your stepmother sent you away to school," Martin said.

Ashley shrugged. "I resented it at the time, but I realize now it was better for all of us. It wouldn't have been fun for me to stay around and spoil things for everybody, including myself."

"But I notice you keep your distance from your stepmother."

"Oh, she's all right. Now that I'm an adult myself, I can appreciate how threatened she was by the constant reminder of the first marriage, especially since I look just like my mother. My father was just talking to me about that recently, and I realized what an impossible position he was in with both Sylvia and me when I was younger."

"So you've resolved your feelings for him?"

Ashley set her cup down decisively. "I think so. My father is a good man, some would say a great man, but he has his faults, like everyone else. In personal matters he finds it difficult to confront things, but he has been making the effort, despite how tough it is for him. But he loves me, he loves my stepmother, and he desperately wants the relationship he has with each of us."

"Sylvia's not exactly a help with the campaign, is she?" Martin asked carefully.

"You noticed that," Ashley said flatly.

"Yes."

"Every candidate has some liability. I guess she's ours."

The waitress brought their sandwiches. Ashley bit into hers and said, "I am vindicated."

"Really?" Martin took a bite of his, swallowed, and said, "Son of a gun, you're right. It's terrific."

"Don't ever challenge my restaurant recommendations again," she said smugly.

"Never. But I must say your taste for deli food surprises me."

"Why? I'm not quite as highbrow as you seem to think. In fact, we share a common heritage. 'Fair' is a translation of the Gaelic 'Finn,' you know."

"I wouldn't call that 'common.' You're lace curtain, and I'm afraid I'm shanty all the way."

"The lace goes back only a couple of generations," Ashley said, putting down her sandwich and wiping her lips with a paper napkin. "When my great-grandfather Finn first came to this country, he was a land speculator. He was locked up several times for cheating people on phony deals and narrowly avoided being prosecuted for bigamy."

"Bigamy?" Martin said, looking at her.

"Seems he had one wife in the old country and one here. He neglected to sever his connection from the first one over the water before he took the second one in Philadelphia."

"Funny how that stuff never made it into your father's official campaign biography," Martin said dryly.

"We've polished up the image since then. Great-grandaddy Finn flourished almost a hundred years ago, and the less savory details of his career were conveniently forgotten while the money he pirated remained. The family, rechristened 'Fair' to remove the taint of the old sod, married well, into the right families, invested in legitimate businesses, cleaned up the act. And look how far we've come today," she concluded, saluting him with her cup.

"But you remember your origins. And you're telling me. Why?"

"It's a matter of public record," Ashley replied, shrugging. "The history is there for anyone who cares to look. We downplay it, but we can't obliterate it. We even have a branch of the original Finns, descended from the first wife, floating around the eastern seaboard someplace. They emigrated after the old man and got into the printing business."

"Did your father buy them off?" Martin asked, fascinated.

"No, he gave them a job," Ashley replied, laughing. "They do all the campaign fliers and leaflets."

"That was smart," Martin said admiringly.

"Joe Fair didn't get where he is by letting the undesirables rear their ugly heads and make trouble," Ashley said dryly.

"Politics," Martin said, shaking his head.

"Some people would be just as mystified by police

work," she replied. "Is it the only thing you thought you'd be good at?"

"Well, I used to know all the Temptations' routines, but there's not much call for that nowadays."

She laughed. She played with her empty cup for a moment before saying, "Anthony told me that you're divorced."

"Anthony?"

"Sergeant Capo."

"How did that subject come up?" he asked, thinking that "Anthony" had a big mouth.

"I asked him," she said ingenuously. "How long were you married?"

"Two years," he said shortly.

"What happened? If you don't mind telling me," she added hastily, youthful training overcoming her curiosity.

"I don't mind. She left me."

Ashley was silent, finding that hard to believe.

"She left me for a music teacher," he added.

Ashley managed not to laugh, but her smile was impish. "That must have been quite a change from you," she said in a restrained voice.

"That's what she wanted. A change from me."

"Why?"

"I didn't pay enough attention to her, I guess. She was very pretty, very popular in school, used to getting what she wanted."

"You make her sound spoiled," Ashley interjected.

"I don't know if she was spoiled, exactly; she told me she was lonely. I couldn't get home much, what with working and going to school, and this teacher had regular hours. You know teachers: evenings, weekends, and summers off, lots of free time. Maryann wasn't good at being alone; she liked company."

"A difficult schedule would never make a decision like that for me," Ashley said softly.

"You know how she met him?" Martin said.

Ashley shook her head.

"She had studied the piano in school, and I suggested she take it up again to fill her evenings when I was at college. Guess who was giving the lessons?" He laughed mirthlessly.

"That must have been awful for you," Ashley said sympathetically.

He sat back and took out his cigarettes, shaking the last one loose from the pack. "It was fourteen years ago. She has three kids now. I understand she's very happy. I was just her first real romance, a mistake." He put the cigarette in his mouth and lit it, talking around it. "She used to tell me I loved the police department more than her."

"Did you?" Ashley murmured.

He inhaled deeply and then exhaled through his nose. "I didn't love anything or anybody more than her."

Ashley looked away, her heart pounding. She wondered with sudden, stabbing insight what it would be like for him to say that about her.

"More coffee?" The waitress had reappeared, brandishing the glass coffeepot and yawning.

Martin glanced at Ashley, who shook her head.

"No, thanks, just the check," Martin said.

"Right." The woman yanked the checkpad out of her

pocket, scribbled on it quickly, and ripped off the top sheet cleanly, palming it neatly onto the table.

Martin picked it up and rose to his feet in the same motion.

"I'm going to get cigarettes," he said to Ashley.

The waitress waited until he had left for the machine by the entrance and then said to Ashley, "I was you, honey, I wouldn't let that one get away."

"I beg your pardon?" Ashley said, astonished.

The waitress shrugged. "I figure by the way you were talking that you're just starting out. But let me tell ya, guys like him aren't exactly thick on the ground these days."

"Guys like him?" Ashley repeated numbly, wondering why the waitress felt she needed such advice.

"The ones who treat a woman like china, open doors, show some manners. They're hard to come by. Even those twinkies know it." She jammed her thumb in the direction of the three bikettes, who were still staring in their direction.

Ashley looked around helplessly, praying that Martin wouldn't come back in time to overhear this surreal conversation.

"Don't worry, hon, he really seems to like you," the waitress concluded. "Good luck. G'night, now." She walked away, leaving Ashley benumbed in her wake.

Martin returned to put a tip on the table. He glanced at Ashley's face and said, "Are you okay?"

"Sure. Fine."

"We'd better get going."

She stood briskly, disguising a strong desire to extend their outing as long as she could.

They headed for the door, where Martin paid the bill. As he turned away from the register, one of the three teenagers waved at him.

Ashley was amazed to see him blow the table a kiss.

The girls shrieked with delight, collapsing in fits of hysterical laughter.

"Do you acquire a following wherever you go?" she asked him as they left.

"The ones I want to follow me never do," he replied briefly.

Outside, the rain had stopped. They stood on the sidewalk and contemplated the gleaming pavements of the deserted streets.

"I hate to go back," she admitted quietly.

"I can't keep you out all night," Martin said. "You have to be up very early."

Ashley nodded silently and followed him when he turned toward the road. The return trip seemed to go much too quickly, and she found herself back in the suite's sitting room in no time, looking up at him as he closed the door to the hall.

"Thank you, Tim," she said, giving him her hand. "That was a much-needed break. I get so caught up in this rat race with my father, having to be the senator's daughter every minute of every day, that I forget what it feels like to relax."

"Any time," he said quietly, holding her fingers in his.

"Good night."

"Good night," he responded, releasing her.

She went into her bedroom and closed the door.

Martin sat on the sofa and looked at the floor. He felt

like going to sleep about as much as he felt like joining a monastery. He was so keyed up he was fully capable of kicking in her door and . . .

He yanked his new pack of cigarettes out of his pocket and lit one, resigned to waiting out the night.

On the other side of the connecting wall, Ashley undressed in the dark. She was fighting a compelling desire to go back out to him.

You had to do that, she told herself savagely. You had to invite him to go out, spend time alone with him, make it even harder on yourself in the long run.

She pulled a nightgown over her head and climbed into bed, staring at the ceiling.

She was still staring at it when she heard the dawn birds begin to sing.

CHAPTER
Five

ASHLEY DIALED campaign headquarters in Harrisburg by rote, without even looking at the numbers. She called the place so often she felt as if she could do it in her sleep.

"Joseph Fair for President," one of the staffers answered.

"Carol, is that you?" Ashley asked.

"Oh, hi, Miss Fair."

"Hi, Carol. Listen, something has just come up, and we're going to need another thousand campaign buttons by the end of the week."

There was an audible groan from the other end of the line.

"I knew that would not be good news," Ashley said sympathetically, "but it can't be helped."

"That 'Occasion Outfitters' who produce them is a real pain in the neck. I know the price was right, but they take forever to do anything. I'll try, but I can't promise anything."

"I know they're a problem; we won't use them in the future. But for the moment we need them."

"Okay, I'll do my best," Carol said resignedly.

"I'm sure you can handle it, Carol." Ashley knew that Carol was a grumbler, but a hard worker who produced results. Ashley glanced down at her notes. "Carol, is Tom Clancy there by any chance?"

"He's at the copy desk. Do you want me to get him?"

"Please."

Ashley waited until Clancy picked up the phone.

"Ashley?" he said.

"Hi, Tom. I was talking to Roger this morning and told him I was going to call you."

Tom waited. He was Damico's press liaison and knew he was about to receive instructions.

"Tom, they're still running that picture of my father from the senatorial race. You know, the one taken the morning after the election when his tie was askew and he had five-o'clock shadow?"

"I know," Clancy responded wearily, "I saw it in the *Evening Post* yesterday."

"I thought we pulled that from all the press files."

"We did, but somebody must still have a copy of it. You know we can't prevent them from using it if they have it."

Ashley knew only too well. "Isn't there anything we can do?"

"I know Bob Hagerty at the *Post*," Clancy said after a moment. "I could call him and ask him to do me a personal favor. He owes me one."

"Good."

"I don't know if he'll do it, Ash. They're awfully touchy over there, especially about that First Amendment stuff."

"It's worth the attempt, at least. Ask him to destroy the negative, okay, Tom?"

"I will."

"Thanks a lot. Good-bye."

Ashley was hanging up the phone when Meg entered and announced, "Strategy meeting in five."

Ashley glanced down at the long list of calls she had yet to make in consternation.

"Can't you give that job to somebody else?" Meg asked, following her glance.

Ashley shook her head.

"I know," Meg said. "Nobody gets the troops to perform like you do."

Ashley let that pass without comment.

"Did you get to Clancy about that picture?" Meg asked.

Ashley nodded. "Tops on my agenda."

"Your dad looks like he's coming off a five-day drunk in it."

"Clancy's going to try to get rid of it."

"That thing keeps popping up like the proverbial bad penny. I'd like to kill the photographer who took it."

"Todd Gaines of the *Sun*."

"You know?"

Ashley tapped her temple with a forefinger. "He's on my hit list."

"Ah-ha. Okay."

Ashley stood. "I guess this will have to wait until

later," she said, folding her telephone notes and putting the paper into her pocket.

They went into the hall and headed for the conference room.

Meg was stepping into her shoes that Thursday night when Ashley knocked at her hotel-room door.

"Come in," she called.

Ashley entered and saw the navy silk tailored dress, the sapphire earrings, and said, "Big date?"

"I don't know. We'll see," Meg replied.

"Is this the same guy who sent you the flowers?"

Meg nodded.

"He must be really taken with you."

"So far, anyway."

"Don't be such a pessimist." Ashley sat on Meg's bed, crossing her legs at the ankle. "What does he do?"

"He leases commercial real estate. He's working on getting his own agency."

"Sounds prosperous. How did you meet him?"

Meg grinned at her. "Have you been taking lessons from my mother on the sly?"

"Sorry," Ashley said sheepishly. "I didn't mean to grill you. But you don't usually show this much interest in your social life, and I'm curious about him."

"I met him when he fixed the flat on my car."

"Ah-ha. The chivalrous type. I'm a sucker for them myself."

"It's too soon to mail the wedding invitations, Ash."

"Spoilsport. When do I get to meet him?"

"All in good time. I want to make sure I'm sold on him first, all right?"

"You're sold on him. I haven't seen that dress since the famous Carter Hastings affair. And that was a long time ago."

Meg groaned. "Did you have to bring him up?"

"You were besotted with him at the time."

"Please don't remind me of my past stupidity."

"Nobody could have guessed he was using you to get to my father. He was much cleverer than most of them. We were all fooled."

"I hope he went back to Arizona and drowned in that kidney-shaped swimming pool he was so proud of. What a jerk."

"I gather this new guy . . . What's his name?"

"Peter Ransom."

"Peter is different?"

"Different from Carter, yes. For example, he listened to my gorilla-suit story with a fairly straight face and did not suggest my commitment at the end of it."

"Margaret Drummond, you didn't tell him about that on your first date!" Ashley said, aghast.

"Why not? I figure if they can't pass the acid test they're not worth it. Throw 'em into the shark tank right away and see if they can swim to safety."

Ashley narrowed her eyes.

"All right," Meg admitted, seeing her expression, "I didn't exactly mean to tell him. The story sort of slipped out because I was nervous, but he handled it very well."

"What does he look like?"

"He's attractive. Not a showstopper, but certainly worth a second glance. And there's something about him . . ."

"What?"

"I don't know, an intensity or something. You feel it when you're with him."

"Oh, boy."

"Don't get carried away," Meg said airily. "I'm going to take my time and be sensible."

Ashley coughed delicately.

"Ye of little faith," Meg muttered under her breath. She squinted at the clock. "What time is it?"

"You'd better clean your contacts, Meg. You can't see much if you can't see that clock at six feet away. It's five minutes to eight."

"Uh-oh. I've got to hurry." She picked up her bag and began tossing in keys and other odd items.

Ashley sighed. "And I've lots of work to do. I guess I'll see you in the morning." She ambled out of the room, and Meg cast a parting glance at herself in the mirror, pausing to moisten her contacts with lens cleaner and then dropping the bottle into her purse.

She was as ready as she'd ever be, and as she walked into the hall she stopped to lock her door behind her.

The two cops were lounging outside the senator's suite, smoking and talking. They nodded to her as she passed. Fair was in a meeting with his advisers, and she was glad to have been excused.

Ransom was waiting for her in the lobby. This time he was wearing a slate-gray suit with a gray-and-black-striped tie. He smiled when he saw her and walked over to her, taking both of her hands in his.

"It's so good to see you," he said warmly.

"Hi, Peter," Meg greeted him.

"My car is waiting outside with the valet," he told her, leading her toward the front door.

The car was the same 300D he'd had when she met him. They drove to the restaurant, a French provincial chateau only a few miles away, and were shown to a table immediately. A screen of standing plants separated them from the rest of the patrons and created a tiny alcove where they could dine in complete privacy.

"This is wonderful," Meg said to him as they sat facing one another across a square glass table covered with a snowy linen cloth. The waiter lit the fat beeswax candle, which was surrounded by a ring of miniature carnations and set inside a crystal hurricane lamp. The flame burst into life, illuminating their faces with a flickering glow.

"Would you like a drink?" Ransom asked her.

"If you're having something," Meg replied.

Ransom consulted the wine list and ordered an expensive Taittinger brut champagne. The sommelier brought the bottle, wrapped in a cloth and set in a bucket of ice. Ransom tasted it when half a glass was poured out for his consideration.

"That's fine," he said, and the server filled his glass, then Meg's, and replaced the bottle in its icy bed.

"Some people like this at room temperature, but I prefer it cold," he said to Meg.

"It's very nice," she said appreciatively, sipping slowly from her glass.

"I've been looking forward to this very much," Ransom said.

Meg smiled and said nothing.

"So tell me what's new with the campaign," he prodded her, sitting back and observing her.

"Things are quiet at the moment, but that won't last," she replied sagely.

"How do you know?"

"After a while, you learn to recognize the lull before the storm. There will be a crisis soon. I can feel it."

"How are you getting along with your police escort?"

"Oh, they're all right. They're trying to keep a low profile, but it's difficult, because they're both pretty big." She grinned.

"I didn't see them at the hotel."

"They were upstairs with the senator. They stick pretty close to him all the time."

"So do you, no?"

"Not physically, but I have to keep track of what he's doing."

"What do you use, notebooks, tape recorders, videos?"

"Computer. I'm hooked into a main frame at the office, and I have a desktop model for travel."

"A very modern approach. My secretary uses an IBM, but I understand they're quite complicated. Is that right?"

She nodded, taking another sip of her wine.

"What kind do you take with you when you move around?"

"Apple II. It's the easiest to use."

"That's convenient."

She nodded. "I keep it in my room."

Ransom exhaled silently, guarding his expression. "I think we'd better look these over," he said, indicating their elaborate, tassled menus, still closed on the table.

"That waiter over there keeps looking at me expectantly."

Meg opened hers and examined the two sheets of foolscap fastened to the cover with a cotter pin. The dishes offered were handwritten and obviously changed every day.

"What's good?" Meg asked, her appetite fleeing before the onslaught of the visual stimulus.

"I've had the seafood Provençale, and I can recommend it."

"Fine," Meg said, closing her menu.

"And how about the pâté de foie gras first?" he asked. She nodded. She didn't care.

Ransom gave their order to the waiter and then refilled Meg's glass, saying, "I guess you haven't been here before, have you?"

She shook her head. "A campaign is more about tuna sandwiches in hotel rooms than dinners in a place like this."

"Then I'm glad I was able to provide you with a change of scene from all that."

"I must admit it's very restful to get away from it for an evening," Meg said to him. "As soon as I left the hotel, I felt as if a weight had been lifted from my shoulders."

"Is all the hype getting to you?"

"The frenetic pace is. I didn't have such a key position during the last election, and so I've never experienced the fever from this perspective. Sometimes I don't know how the senator keeps on going. He just gets up every day and plunges back into the game."

"He doesn't miss many of his scheduled engagements, then?"

"No. He keeps on plugging even when he's sick."

"I guess he doesn't want to disappoint anybody."

"He rarely does."

The waiter brought the appetizer and Ransom prepared it for Meg, spreading the pâté on thin slices of baguette and adding purple onion and finely chopped egg. Her reaction was enthusiastic, and he kept her wineglass filled during the first course and the main dish as well, encouraging her to feel at ease.

By the end of the meal she wasn't drunk, but she was relaxed.

"So what's your itinerary for the next few weeks?" Ransom asked as the waiter cleared the plates and swept the table free of crumbs.

"Everywhere," she replied. "Crisscrossing the state."

"How do you keep track of where you're going?"

"It isn't easy. I have a separate disk just for the schedule of appearances."

"So I'll have to trail you all over like a camp follower?" he said, smiling.

"If you want to see me."

"I want to see you," Ransom replied quietly, holding her gaze.

The waiter placed a glass dish of almond chocolate mousse in front of each of them. He brought a chased-silver pot of coffee and filled two thin china cups, setting a pitcher of cream and a bowl of sugar in the center of the table.

"Tomorrow it's back to room service," Meg said glumly, sipping her coffee.

"Another campaign sacrifice? I would think that the cuisine at some of the affairs you attend might be quite good."

"Who gets to eat at those things? I run around the whole time and wind up having egg salad on rye back in my room."

"Yet you wouldn't trade your job for anyone's."

"That's right."

"You're a complicated woman."

"More than you know," she replied mysteriously.

By the time Ransom had paid the check and called for the car, Meg was feeling the effects of wine, food, and a full day. She was openly yawning as Ransom drove back to the hotel, and hadn't the energy to protest when he said he would walk her to the elevator.

He pushed the button and watched the light go on as the car descended to the first floor.

"Here we are," he said as the doors slid open in front of them.

Meg turned to him. "Thank you. I had a lovely time."

He lifted her chin with his forefinger and bent to kiss her lightly on the mouth. "Good night, Meg. I enjoyed myself too. I'll call you in the morning."

"Good night, Peter." She stepped through the doors, and they shut behind her. She was exhausted. The prospect of getting undressed for bed was overwhelming, at the moment ranking right up there with cleaning the refrigerator and emptying the vacuum bag. She decided to compromise and sleep in her underwear. That monumental decision made, she leaned against the wall of the elevator with her eyes closed until it stopped at her floor.

Ransom walked back through the lobby, his mind racing.

The next day, Capo sauntered into the lounge of the senator's suite where Martin was reading a newspaper, and said cheerfully, "Guess what? We've got the weekend off."

Martin looked up at him questioningly.

"The senator's canceled his appointments for the next couple of days to spend the time 'closeted with his advisers,' according to the press release."

"What does that mean?"

"Oh, I don't know, there's some kind of media crisis. I heard them talking. The Republicans dug up a bunch of new dirt and word leaked that they're planning a negative ad campaign. Fair's press people need this time to figure out how to counteract it, and they don't want the senator exposed to reporters until they can decide what to do. So he's holing up here, and we're not needed."

"What about his daughter?"

"Are you ready for this? She's slipping away for a romantic weekend with Dillon aboard the family yacht, no less. Our presence will not be required there either, so we're sprung until Sunday night, when they're having the charity auction at Penn's Landing."

While Martin should have been pleased at the prospect of the free time, the knowledge of how Ashley would be spending it dulled his reaction.

"When did they tell you this?" he asked.

"While you were downstairs. Good news, huh?"

Martin nodded thoughtfully.

"You could look a little happier about it," Capo said.

"The fund-raiser tonight is canceled too?"

"Yup. Everything. I already called Lorraine, and she says to come to dinner at eight o'clock. She'll make the pot roast you like, and get that cheesecake too."

"Sounds great. Thanks," Martin replied absently.

"What's the matter with you?" Capo asked him. "We're out of here, old buddy, we're on the lam until Sunday night. I'll tell you something. The senator may be the last, best hope this country has, like the TV spot says, but I'm not sorry that I won't be looking at his face for a couple of days, and I'm sure he feels the same about me."

Martin said nothing.

"But of course, the girl's easier on the eyes," Capo said, watching his friend's face.

"The yacht's already in?" Martin asked thoughtfully, ignoring the comment.

"Docked last night. Dillon and the girl are driving back to Philly this afternoon." He frowned. "What do you care?"

"I just wondered."

"Well, stop wondering. Until we get back, she's not your responsibility, so forget her."

"When can we leave?"

"As soon as she does. She's packing for the weekend in the other room right now."

Martin got up and headed for the connecting door.

"Where are you going?" Capo demanded.

Martin didn't answer, just kept walking, and Capo stood looking after him with a concerned expression on his face.

Ashley glanced up from loading her overnight bag

and saw Martin standing in the doorway of her bedroom.

"Hi," she said.

He nodded.

"I guess you heard about the change of plans."

"Yeah."

"I'm sure you're looking forward to the time off."

He didn't respond to that, but asked instead, "How come the auction is still on? Why didn't you cancel that too?"

"The plans were too elaborate. The furniture and art works have already been shipped to the docks and stored in a warehouse there. Plus I think Roger Damico is pretty certain they'll have something worked out by then."

"Are you concerned about the ad campaign? Capo told me what's going on."

She sighed and pushed back a pale lock of hair. "These things always come up in politics. You have to be ready to deal with them at a moment's notice. And we are. I wanted to stay and help Roger, but my father is insisting I take some time off. And to tell you the truth, I didn't give him a big argument. I'm beat."

"Does the problem have anything to do with that other family you told me about, the printing Finns?"

She smiled. "No, it's a little worse than that, although having them surface right now would not exactly be helpful." She closed the hasps on her case and straightened up. "When my father was in law school, he was accused of cheating on the moot-court competition. He was later exonerated and the whole thing was dropped. But the other side has gotten wind of it. They're trying to make it look bad, like Dad really did cheat and my grandfather bought everybody off to keep it quiet, shove it under the rug."

"How could they make it look like that?" Martin asked.

"My grandfather endowed a chair in international law at the school the same year."

"What does that mean?"

"He gave the school the money to hire an expert in the field, pay his salary, buy the required books, et cetera."

"I see. It seems like he came across with the goods to keep his kid in the school."

"Right."

Martin leaned back against the doorjamb and folded his arms. "What's a moot-court competition?"

"It's the trial by fire at the end of the first year of law school. You're given a fictionalized case and you have to do the research, prepare the arguments, write the briefs, and represent your client before a panel of teachers, with one of them playing the role of the judge. It's important to do well, because it's the closest you come as a student to participating in the real thing."

"Who accused your father of cheating?"

"I don't know all the details, but apparently my dad was representing the defendant in the case and the student representing the plaintiff left his notes unattended in the library. My father was seen in the vicinity and was suspected of reading the notes and getting a jump on the opposition's argument."

"But wasn't that the other kid's fault for leaving his stuff around to be seen?"

"That was stupid, maybe, but not a violation of the honor code. Stealing his ideas would have been. But all the reference materials to be used in the case were gathered in that one area of the library, so my father had a valid reason for being there, and that's why the whole thing eventually became so cloudy."

"It sounds like a big deal over nothing to me."

"That's because you've never been to law school. The competition for grades is merciless. Some people will do anything to beat out another student by just a couple of points."

"A great system," Martin said dryly.

"It doesn't exactly foster camaraderie," Ashley admitted.

"Can your father's opponent really make an issue out of something like that in the campaign? It happened, what, thirty years ago?"

"Would you want a cheat for your president?" Ashley countered. "All sorts of things go on behind closed doors, before elections and after, that the public doesn't know about; deals are made, trade-offs sanctioned, payoffs given to the right people. But the image is everything. If a candidate won the Congressional Medal of Honor but also beats his wife, the voters will elect him on the medal, because they'll know about that. His domestic situation will remain a secret, unless somebody from the other side finds out about it and uses it."

Martin was silent. He knew she was right.

She moved to lift her case off the bed, and he stepped up behind her, taking it and saying, "I'll carry this down for you."

He followed her out into the sitting room, where she

said to Capo, "Good-bye, Anthony. Have a nice week-end."

"Bye," Capo murmured, watching the two of them walk past him. Cozy duo, he couldn't help noticing. He sighed heavily, shaking his head. Bound to be trouble there, he thought.

They went down in the elevator, and Martin said to her, "So you'll be glad to get away from this for a couple of days."

She looked at him, studying his expression, and replied quietly, "A change is usually welcome."

They emerged from the elevator and saw Dillon moving toward them across the lobby. He stopped in front of Ashley, kissed her, and said brusquely to Martin, "I'll take that."

Martin surrendered the case, feeling as if he was giving up the woman herself.

"Ready?" Dillon said to Ashley.

She nodded.

"Let's go," Dillon said.

Ashley took a step, looked over her shoulder at Martin, and said, "Good-bye, Tim. I'll see you Sunday night."

Martin watched them go, his expression bleak, and then went back upstairs to the suite.

Ashley stared out the window of Dillon's 528i, barely listening to his monologue on a case he was trying in district court.

Why did she feel that she had left with the wrong man?

"And so I filed for a continuance," Dillon was saying,

"but Judge Masters was in a bear of a mood. She wanted to know why I needed more time when we'd spent three weeks in discovery and the case was taking far too long already. . . ." He looked over at her and realized that she was not listening.

"Ashley?"

She started and turned to him. "What?"

"You're in another world, darling. What's the matter?"

She shrugged.

"Are you concerned about that law school thing with your father? Don't worry, they'll unearth some old professor and get him to say that your dad was the most sterling example of honesty ever to pass through the hallowed halls of . . . where'd he go?"

"Penn."

"Right. It'll blow over, you'll see."

She nodded. That was not the source of her distraction.

"It'll be good just to settle in on the boat and relax. Did your father request that the crew stay aboard?"

"Yes."

Dillon smiled, pleased.

Ashley looked away from him, annoyed. God forbid he should have to fix his own scotch, she thought. She felt that he enjoyed the amenities of wealth a little too much.

"We could take a cruise around the basin this evening, if you like. The weather should be right for it."

"Okay."

"Dinner on the water. How does that sound?"

"That might be nice," she replied, feeling guilty. He

was acting the way he always acted. It wasn't his fault that behavior she'd once tolerated, accepted, she now found irritating.

"I've missed you, Ash. I can't wait for us to be alone together tonight."

Ashley studied the passing trees, biting her lip. He would want to make love, and she didn't know if she could go through with it. If she refused him, he would want an explanation, and there would be a discussion about it.

Maybe she should just go to bed with him and get it over with; he wouldn't know her heart wasn't in it.

She put her head back against the seat and closed her eyes.

Her problem was that sleeping with Dillon now would feel like a betrayal.

Lorraine Capo opened her front door in Northeast Philadelphia and caroled, "Timmy, come on in."

The house was a semidetached ranch with a stone front that shared one exterior wall with its twin next door. The floor plan was railroad style, with the living room, dining room, and kitchen in a line front to back, the bedrooms off to one side.

Martin entered, shedding his jacket. Lorraine beamed at him, black hair shining, fresh skin glowing.

She patted his cheek and said to her husband, "Look how gorgeous. Tony, why can't we find this man a wife?"

"It's not for lack of trying on your part, Lori," Martin said dryly.

Capo said nothing, thinking his own thoughts on that particular subject.

"Smells good," Martin observed, commenting on the dinner still in the oven.

"You always say the same thing," Lorraine told him. "What do you live on back at that apartment of yours, dog food?"

"Just about. Anything that comes in a can. Where are the kids?"

"The baby's sleeping, hopefully down for the night," Capo replied. "And Michael is . . ."

The four-year-old boy burst in from the back of the house, running past his mother to Martin and grabbing him about the knees. Martin responded by picking him up and hauling him above his head while the child screeched with delight.

"I guess we know where Mike is," Lorraine said acerbically. She went back into the kitchen to check on the roast.

"Want a beer?" Capo said.

Martin nodded.

"You promised that next time you came you would show me how to switch the tracks on my train set," Mike complained.

Martin looked over at Capo, who rolled his eyes.

"Go on," Capo said. "I'll get the beer and bring it in to you."

Martin and the boy departed for the child's bedroom, and Capo went into the kitchen, where his wife was removing the sputtering roast pan from the oven.

"Where'd they go?" she asked her husband.

"They're in Mikie's bedroom with the trains," he replied. He opened the refrigerator door and pulled out two cans of beer, popping the top on one of them for himself.

"This will be ready in just a minute," she said, taking the padded glove off her hand and opening a drawer to remove a carving knife. "What do you think about Dottie Calandria for Tim?" she asked.

"Who's Dottie Calandria?" Capo said, taking a healthy swallow of his beer.

"You know, Betty Rizzo's sister. You met her at the christening for Betty's little girl, Rhonda."

"Is Dottie the one with the mustache?" Capo inquired.

His wife stared at him in exasperation. "She does not have a mustache," she said firmly. "She has dark hair, that's all, and . . ."

"She looks like Tom Selleck. She must shave twice a day."

"Anthony Capo, you should be ashamed of yourself. That's a cruel thing to say."

"I'm not fixing my friend up with her, and that's final. Tim would never go for it anyway. How many times have you tried to get him to go along with one of your ideas? Has he ever listened, even once?"

"There's always a first time," Lorraine said stubbornly.

"Not for Dottie Calandria," Capo replied flatly.

"All right, all right. But he's lonely. Just looking at him you can see that."

"Tim can find his own women."

"But that's the problem. He's not looking. Not seriously, anyway. Those dates he has are always one-night stands, a couple of weeks at the most. He bolts as soon as the woman really starts getting involved with him."

Don't be too sure of that, Capo thought gloomily, sipping his drink.

"Not that I blame him after Maryann," Lorraine said, "but that was a long time ago. Is he going to spend the rest of his life nursing his wounds about that?"

"Lori, I don't know," Capo said wearily. "But I wish you would find something else to do. Why don't you work on the peace campaign, or the energy crisis, and leave Tim alone? Everybody in the world doesn't have to be married."

Lorraine scooped butter from a stick and mixed it in with a pot of vegetables sitting on the stove. "Fine," she said crisply, replacing the lid on the pot. "I'm going to freshen up. You set the table while I'm gone." She breezed past him, going into their bedroom.

Martin stuck his head into the kitchen. "Hey, where's my beer?"

Capo handed him the second can and said, "Did you get Mikie set up in there?"

"Yeah, he's planning a collision between the B & O and the Langhorne-Reading Railroads." Martin took a belt of his drink and asked, "Are we supposed to be doing something in here?"

"Setting the table, I think," Capo replied, nodding to the adjoining dining room.

"Let's do it."

They put out the plates and silverware, discussing the Phillies game while they did so. Martin's back was to Lorraine when she entered the room with her son.

In an instant he seemed to be surrounded by a scent

he knew all too well. In the irrational, instinctive second before he realized that Ashley could not possibly be there, he believed she was, and he whirled suddenly, heart pounding, his expression dazed.

"Tim, my goodness," Lorraine said, staring at him. "What is it?"

"Your perfume," he mumbled. "I thought . . ." He stopped, his gaze moving guiltily to Capo.

His friend understood in an instant. "I gave it to Lori for her birthday," he explained quietly. "I could afford only a teaspoon of the stuff. It costs two hundred and fifty bucks an ounce."

"What's this about my perfume?" Lorraine asked, bewildered.

"You've got it bad, man," Capo said to Martin in a soft voice.

Martin refused to meet his eyes.

"There's something going on here I don't understand," Lorraine said loudly.

"The perfume I gave you is the same brand Ashley Fair uses," Capo explained to her. "I liked it, so I asked her what it was and where to get it."

"I see," Lorraine said slowly. "I wondered why you suddenly developed such good taste. It's the nicest scent you've given me in eight years, Tony. I love it."

"Tim likes it too, don't you, Timmo?" Capo said softly.

Martin didn't reply, and Lorraine looked from one to the other before intervening to say briskly, "Well, come on, let's eat before everything is ruined. Michael, come with me and help me bring in the food."

Her son followed her out, and the men maintained a

silence until they were all gathered around the dinner table. Michael said grace and then Lorraine kept up the conversation as they passed the dishes and ate. Martin did not seem to have much appetite and contributed little to the chatter, which consisted mainly of Michael's doings at nursery school and Lorraine's inquiries about the senator and his entourage. Capo answered her questions, sometimes asking confirmation from Martin, who agreed with a nod or a grunt when it was indicated. They had cleared the table and Lorraine was getting the coffee when Capo said to Martin, "Tim, I think we'd better talk about it."

"About what?"

"About the rise in unemployment in the rural Southwest. What do you think?"

Lorraine returned with dessert, and no more was said until they had finished the meal and she'd gone with Michael to supervise his change into pajamas.

"Tim, don't you think you're losing your grip on reality?" Capo began again.

Martin regarded him dispassionately.

"This girl's father is a U.S. senator running for president. She's almost engaged to her lawyer boyfriend, and his daddy has almost as much money as her daddy. Where do you fit into all of that?"

Martin said nothing.

"She couldn't be seriously interested in you," Capo told him gently.

"I never said that she was." It was Martin's first comment on the subject.

"Then what are we talking about?"

"I don't know, Tony. Why don't you tell me?" Martin replied dryly. "You seem to be heading this discussion."

"You don't think she feels the same way."

Martin sighed. "I haven't discussed it with her."

"But you admit that you're hung up on her."

Martin stared at the tablecloth morosely. "I guess so, Tony. Since you're obviously on top of the whole situation, there isn't any point in denying it."

"Then it's the thunderbolt," Capo said with conviction.

Martin glared at him. He had heard about the thunderbolt before, unfortunately.

"Don't look at me that way, Tim. You know it's true. I just didn't recognize it, 'cause you're so good at hiding your feelings. When you were looking at Dillon like you wanted to kill him, I thought it was because the guy's a wimp. Sometimes I feel like killing him myself, and I'm not in love with his girl. But it's the thunderbolt, no doubt about it."

Martin eyed him balefully. Capo was assuming his Sicilian *pezzonovante* personality, the retired man of the world sitting in the hills above Palermo, sipping strega and reflecting on the vagaries of life.

"Tony, if you start that crap with me tonight, I'm going to belt you," Martin said wearily.

"Okay, okay. But you have to admit it's crazy, Tim. All these years, all the women you've been with, and *this* is the one you choose?"

"It's not a matter of choosing. You should know that."

"Are you sure she doesn't know?"

Martin shrugged. "She's a nice person. We talk. She thinks we're friends. Funny thing is, I guess we are."

"What are you going to do?"

"Nothing. There's nothing to do. I'll finish out the assignment and then I'll never see her again."

"That's rough," Capo murmured.

"I assume that I'll get over it. 'Men have died and worms have eaten them, but not for love.'"

"Where did you hear that?"

"My father used to say it."

"Your father was a cop."

"My father was a cop with a library card."

"You think too much, Tim."

"I guess that's true."

Lorraine came in with her pajama-clad son, and they had more coffee. After the dishes were put away and Michael put to bed, Martin rose to get his coat.

"Can't you stay a little longer?" Lorraine asked as he was shrugging into his jacket.

"No, thanks, Lori. I haven't been home since we started this gig, and I've got a lot to do."

"Well, take care," she said, kissing him on the cheek.

"I will."

The second the door closed behind him, she turned to her husband and said, "Something is wrong with him."

"Tell me about it," Capo muttered.

"What's going on?"

"I think," Capo said, "he's in love."

"With who?" Lorraine said, thunderstruck.

"With Ashley Fair." Capo rose and went into the kitchen to get another beer, leaving his wife to stare after him in amazement.

* * *

Martin drove the short distance to his apartment in Trevose in a thoughtful mood.

Curiously enough, his conversation with Capo had made him feel better. It was good to finally admit what he'd been concealing and deal with it honestly.

He parked his car and walked up the path to his door, unlocking it and switching on the overhead light automatically. His place was a typical bachelor pad, nothing extraordinary, light on decor and heavy on the items important to him: stereo speakers, stacks of tapes and records, books on police procedure, history, and athletics. He went into the bedroom in the dark, stretched out on the king-sized bed—a luxury he considered a necessity because of his height—still wearing his jacket, and folded his arms behind his head.

He hadn't felt this way in twenty years. No, that wasn't true. He had *never* felt like this before. He'd been proud of Maryann, proud of their status as a couple, because she was pretty and popular and a girl the other guys admired. They seemed to belong together: she was captain of the color guard and he was a running back on the football team. They looked good in pictures, he so tall and dark, she with the same height and coloring, like matched bookends. He had let it all happen, cruising along without effort through the pins and the prom and the rings. He had liked Maryann, loved her dearly in a way that he now realized was boyish and as much a part of his youth as the high jump he could no longer scale. But the consuming passion he felt for Ashley, the jealous possessiveness that made him want to knock Dillon down every time the lawyer looked at her, the need to protect her from everything and everybody and have her with him at all times, was new.

Capo was right. It was the thunderbolt, the exquisitely apt Sicilian expression for the stroke of Cupid's arrow, the instant and irrevocable wound of love.

Martin sat up and tore off his jacket, dropping it, with the sleeves inside out, onto the floor. He lay back down and rolled over on his side, hoping for sleep.

Ashley crept up the steps from the cabin belowdecks and leaned over the railing of the *Fair Play,* letting the cool night breeze wash over her face. The water lapped gently against the hull as she pulled the collar of her robe closer about her neck and tightened the belt, snuggling into its warmth.

Dillon was asleep. She had pleaded illness and pretended to rest in the guest cabin until he drifted off himself.

It was only a matter of time, she thought now. She couldn't hold him off forever, and the prospect of engaging in more debates on the subject made her want to jump overboard.

What was the right thing to do? She was truly fond of Jim and didn't want to hurt his feelings, but surely it was wrong to let him continue planning for something that she was increasingly convinced would never be.

There was a sound from belowdecks, and she closed her eyes.

"Ashley?" Dillon called.

"Up here."

He clambered up the steps, wearing only a faded pair

of running shorts. She noted with detachment his finely tuned body, his charmingly touseled hair.

"What are you doing out here by yourself?" he asked.

"Just getting a breath of air."

"I thought you were sleeping."

"I thought *you* were."

"I must have heard you walking past my cabin and it woke me up." He came up behind her and put his arms around her waist. "Feeling better?"

"Um-hm."

"Want to go below and sleep with me this time?" he whispered, kissing her neck.

Ashley stiffened, and he released her.

"Ash, what is it? You've been acting weird all day, since I picked you up this morning."

"I'm just tired, Jim. I've been keeping a pretty hectic schedule. You can understand that."

"Do you think you should take some time off from the campaign, drop out for a while and rest?"

"Oh, no, it's not that bad. I'll get over it. I just think I should go back to bed. Alone."

"All right," he said, sighing. "Let's do it." They went below, and Dillon went back into the master cabin, while Ashley slipped into the guest-room bunk.

In seconds the boat was silent again, leaving Ashley to her troubled thoughts.

On Sunday night, the *Fair Play* was lit up like the Lincoln Memorial when Martin and Capo approached it. A huge striped circuslike tent was set up on the dock where it was moored, and workers were proceeding in and out of the tent with pieces of furniture wrapped in padding and canvases wrapped in brown paper and cushioned with Styrofoam.

"Gee, do you think I'll get to feed the elephants?" Capo said to Martin as they paused in the opening created by the lifted flaps. Inside, rows of folding chairs faced a makeshift stage with a podium and a canvas backdrop.

"You think these people would just rent an auditorium," Capo said disgustedly. "What are we doing down here on the docks?"

"You're not a bored millionaire," Martin replied. "They're always trying to outdo each other in originality. This is original."

"I'll grant you that. Ringling Brothers wouldn't have had this thing; it's too small, and the stripes are blue instead of red."

"A circus purist, Tony?"

Capo shot him a look and said, "We'd better get on the boat. They must be about ready."

They were met at the end of the dock by a uniformed crewman who checked their badges and then revealed himself to be a member of the harbor police.

"Welcome aboard," he said, stepping aside.

"Welcome aboard?" Capo muttered to Martin. "What is this, McHale's Navy?"

The yacht was fitted with amber teakwood and gleaming brass. Ashley and her father were waiting in the main salon, which had an oversized gray and black rug with a geometrical border design spread on the floor and frosted-glass art deco lamps on the walls. Martin realized that the room had undoubtedly been done by a high-priced decorator, but to him the place had a cold, stylized feel, not Ashley at all.

But it did look like the senator's wife.

Ashley was wearing a strapless blue cocktail dress with a fitted bodice and bell-shaped skirt. Martin had not seen it before; it made her look sophisticated, older than she was. Even though she was beautiful, he realized that seeing her this way disturbed him. It made her seem part of the world her relatives inhabited, and more remote from him.

Ashley turned, and her face lit up when she saw him. She left her father and came to the two cops, saying, "Tim."

He looked down at her, not smiling, but his gaze was intimate all the same.

"Hi," he said.

"How was your time off?" she asked, never taking her eyes from his face.

"Dull," he replied.

"Not relaxing?"

"I guess dull qualifies for relaxing," he answered. "Did you clear up the problem with your father's record?"

She smiled cynically. "Yes. My father's staff found something just as bad on the opposition side, and we traded dirt. So the final word is nobody's saying anything in either camp."

"Remember me?" Capo asked dryly at Martin's side.

Ashley laughed. "And the irrepressible Sergeant Capo. How was your family?"

"Still there."

"I'm sure they were very glad to see you."

"Seemed like it," he said, and grinned.

"Ashley," her father called from across the room, "somebody is here to see you."

She turned, and they all saw a slim, dark, elegantly handsome man in a well-cut suit smiling at her.

"Carlo," she said, and went to take his hands. She kissed him on the cheek.

"Carlo?" Capo said in a low tone to Martin. "Are you telling me she has *another* boyfriend? The competition's getting stiffer, Timmo."

"Shut up," Martin muttered savagely.

Ashley chattered away to her friend, and they were soon joined by Meg and the senator's wife. Drinks were served by a uniformed maid, and the two policemen faded into the background. It was some time before Ashley walked past with Carlo, and then stopped abruptly, taking him by the hand to the corner where Martin stood.

"Tim, I'd like you to meet Giancarlo Deslourdes, my favorite designer. He saw you from across the room and requested an introduction. He whipped up the dress I'm wearing just for me."

Martin shook hands with the couturier, who assessed him with worldy dark eyes.

"Darling, he's prettier than the dress," Carlo drawled to Ashley.

Martin stiffened.

"Oh, look, he's getting nervous," Carlo said. "Ash, I'm so grateful; you've made my night. Now I'm going over to the tent, where I will try to recover from this sensational experience. I'll see you there. And let me know what you think of the scent."

"I will," she said.

He winked at Martin. "Take care, handsome."

He left, and Martin fixed Ashley with a narrow, gimlet stare. "Thanks a lot."

She giggled wickedly. "He wanted to meet you."

"Why didn't you ask me if I wanted to meet him?"

"Oh, he's all right. An opportunist in the business sense, but generally harmless."

"Not to twelve-year-old boys, I'll bet."

She shook her head. "You're such a cop. Every minute, all the time. I don't judge anyone else's personal life. Besides, Carlo confines his pursuits to those beyond the age of consent."

"That's what they all say," Martin observed darkly. "Until you find them with a stable full of kidnapped fourth-graders posing for porno films."

Her mouth tightened. "Mr. Straight Arrow," she said flatly.

"You got it. And what was the 'scent' he was talking about?"

"He created a new perfume for me." She held up her wrist for him to sniff the sample.

He bent his head. "I like your old one better," he said quietly, straightening, his senses reeling from the almost-contact with her skin.

She held his gaze. "Thank you."

"How do you create a perfume?" he asked dryly to dispel the mood; there were too many observers. "In the same way God created the heaven and the earth in seven days?"

"That isn't very funny. It's quite an honor to have exclusive use of it during the trial period."

"What's it called?"

"'Tristesse.'"

Martin's expression changed, and he looked down at her seriously. "Sadness?" he said, translating. "He named a perfume for you and he called it 'sadness'?"

"I don't think he named it for me," she said uncomfortably, aware of what he was thinking. "That was the name he had in mind before he asked me to wear it. He says it best expresses the scent's haunting, evocative quality. And 'tristesse' doesn't mean sadness, exactly."

"I took high-school French," Martin said flatly. "That's just what it means."

She shook her head. "It's more a sense of loneliness, a longing for fulfillment." She stopped suddenly, realizing that she was making things worse.

He was watching her closely.

"Excuse me," she blurted. "I just saw Jim." She fled, leaving Martin to stare after her in consternation.

The salon was filling fast, and at eight o'clock a crew member stepped into the room and struck a triangular chime to indicate that it was time to adjourn to the tent. The group filed out, moving along the dock to the scene of the auction.

Quite a bit of the audience was already in place, and there was light applause when the senator entered with his entourage. When they were seated, the auctioneer ascended the stage and took his place at the podium. There was a rustling of programs as people consulted the listing of antiques and art works to be sold, all donated by friends of the senator. The proceeds would be split between the Save the Children Foundation, one of his favorite charities, and his campaign fund, with the former taking the lion's share.

Martin moved up close to the stage, behind the woman preparing to take phone bids at a small side table. Ashley was only a few feet away, sitting with Dillon on the aisle.

The auctioneer made the standard introductions, and then cleared his throat to say, "Our first item up for bid is a Wyeth from the Helga series, which you all know caused a sensation in the art world when it was discovered. This was donated by the artist himself, and it goes without mention that . . ."

Martin tuned out, glancing around at the crowd, who all seemed absorbed in what the auctioneer was saying.

Capo sidled up next to him and said, "Some show, huh?"

Martin nodded. They watched the audience react to the auctioneer's prodding, lifting discreet fingers or signaling with their programs to indicate a bid.

"A subdued group," Capo observed. "The auctions my wife goes to, you can't hear the bids for the screaming. Of course, they're usually auctioning off stuff like ceramic flamingos for the front lawn, so I guess it's understandable."

Capo seemed to find the auction interesting for a while, but as it became repetitive, proceeding through the art to the furniture, his restlessness increased.

"What's a Queen Anne lowboy?" Capo asked Martin as the item was announced.

"That," Martin replied, indicating the waist-high chest with gracefully curved legs that appeared on the stage.

"Would you pay that for it?" Capo asked as the auctioneer set the opening bid.

"I wouldn't pay that for the house it sat in," Martin answered dryly.

Capo shook his head. "I'm going to take a walk around the perimeter," he announced. "I'll be back in a few minutes."

Martin nodded.

The show went on, through the Louis Quinze chairs and the Regency toilette tables, the rustic American Colonial pines and maples, catalogued by period and country of origin, until Martin's attention was drifting in a fog of boredom. He was standing with his back against the tent wall, his gaze straight ahead and his arms folded, when a loud report sounded in the room, like the sharp crack of a gunshot.

Ashley leaped to her feet, and Martin was at her side in an instant, his gun drawn, forgetting that his primary responsibility was the senator. She turned to him, and his arm came around her waist.

"Are you all right?" he said to her.

She nodded shakily, and her head rested on his shoulder for a second before he released her, reassured.

Dillon watched the scene with a fixed, grim expression.

Capo materialized next to the senator, who was also unharmed. The two cops then ran to the front of the tent, trying to determine what was going on as the crowd panicked around them.

"You handle them. I'm going backstage," Martin barked to Capo.

The sergeant leaped to the podium, grabbing the mike

from the stunned auctioneer, and said into it, "Calm down, folks. Everybody's all right, nobody's hurt. We're investigating the disturbance, and we would appreciate your cooperation. Please return to your seats and remain there until we can determine the source of the problem."

Martin threw back the canvas flaps that concealed the backstage area and almost stumbled over the pile of paintings at his feet. Someone had lined them up next to one another, and when one fell they all did, like dominoes, causing the last one to hit the floor with a bang and create the noise they'd heard. Tremendously relieved, he exhaled heavily, then went out front to take the mike from Capo.

"It's all right, folks. There was an accident backstage that accounts for the noise," he announced. "There's nothing wrong. Let's all settle down and get on with the show."

They obeyed him, but the rest of the evening had an air of anticlimax, and the auctioneer wrapped things up in a hurry. Ashley avoided Martin's eyes as she went back to the yacht with Dillon, and he followed with Capo, taking up their watch at the entrance to the boat. The family was staying aboard for the night, and then the campaign was moving on to Carbondale and the coal district in the morning.

"So, a little excitement at last," Capo said to Martin as they lounged against the railing up top, smoking.

"I'm glad it turned out to be a false alarm," Martin replied.

"I saw what happened with the girl."

"It was nothing."

"It didn't look like nothing. Maybe there's hope for you."

Martin was silent, and Capo changed the subject. "Where are we bunking tonight?" he asked.

"There's a guest cabin below," Martin answered.

"With Ashley and loverboy right down the hall?" Capo inquired. "That will be a little tough on you, won't it?"

"He won't stay aboard the yacht when her father is here," Martin replied shortly.

Capo received that in silence, then said, "You've made quite a study of her behavior."

"I haven't had much else to do," Martin replied.

"I've been around too, and I can't predict her every move. But then, I'm not obsessed with her, and you are."

"Be quiet, will you?" Martin murmured, nodding toward the harbor policeman, who was still lingering on the dock.

Capo subsided, and they both fell to smoking silently, lost in their own thoughts. Neither had any idea of the conversation about to take place belowdecks, in Ashley's cabin.

James Dillon, of Dillon and Hunley, was not happy. He was pacing, waiting for Ashley to come out of the adjoining lavatory. He was thinking about that moment of intimacy between Ashley and the cop when the artwork fell. It was frozen in his mind like a tableau. Martin had rushed to her side as if she were the most important thing in the world to him and her safety mattered above all else. And she had turned into his arms as if to a haven, all pretense of polite distance gone.

What the hell was going on? As far as he knew, Ashley had done little more than exchange pleasantries with the guy, but there was no mistaking the tone of that encounter. Dillon had the gut instinct of a seasoned but unsuccessful campaigner, and he sensed that the tall, pale-eyed cop was touching Ashley where he never had, and never could.

Ashley entered the room wearing her Chinese robe and carrying her dress over her arm.

"Jim, are you still here?" she greeted him. "I thought you'd gone home." She hung up her dress and began to brush her hair.

"Ashley, I want to talk to you."

"Jim, can't it wait? I'm tired, and I'd like to get to bed."

"It can't wait."

"All right, I'm listening." She was examining her hair length in the mirror.

"Look at me."

She turned and faced him, surprised at his imperious tone. "What is it?" she asked.

"I want to know what's going on between you and that cop."

"Which cop?"

"Don't play dumb, Ashley, it's out of character. How many cops do you have hanging around all the time?"

"You mean Lieutenant Martin or Sergeant Capo, I take it."

"Martin, the quiet one. What are you up to with him?"

Her expression changed. "Up to?"

"I saw you with him when the paintings fell backstage."

Her gaze shifted away from his. "So?"

"That's all you have to say about it? 'So'?"

"What do you want me to say?"

"I want you to tell me about the relationship you have obviously been developing with him behind my back. When that noise sounded, he went for you like a greyhound at the gate. I thought he was supposed to be protecting your *father*."

"The policemen are for both of us," she replied coolly. "You know that."

"He seemed to be solely interested in you."

"He was just doing his job, Jim."

"He's been doing a lot more than his job. You've been spending time alone with him, haven't you?"

"Jim, I don't want to be interrogated about this right now," she said. "I would like to get some sleep, and I suggest you go home and do the same."

"I deserve an explanation, Ashley," he said quietly.

Ashley hesitated. Perhaps he did.

"The night you canceled to go to the opera, he rode in the car with me," she said wearily, "and I . . . talked to him. And once we went out for a sandwich. That's all. Basically."

"You went out for a sandwich? When? I don't remember that."

"It was late. You had gone home. I was hungry and I couldn't sleep and . . ."

"Couldn't sleep? You're having midnight snacks with this guy?"

"Don't make it sound so . . ."

"Intimate? Apparently it was. I can see what's happening, Ash. Despite what seems to be your low opinion of my perceptual capacity, I can see it all very well."

"Jim, don't you think you're making a pretty big deal out of one incident?"

"It's not one incident; I've been subliminally aware of it all along. I see you talking to him, the way he is around you. I just didn't think it merited comment until now. But I should make it clear that I don't want you getting close to this man."

His commanding attitude irritated her. "Jim, you can't tell me how to choose my friends."

"Friends! He wants more than friendship from you."

"I'm going to ignore that," she said frostily.

"All right, all right," Dillon said, sensing that he had gone too far. "Let's assume he wants to be 'friends.' What do you have in common with him? For God's sake, Ashley, he does shift work for a Philadelphia precinct! He hangs out with his flatfoot buddies and drinks beer and watches the Super Bowl on the station-house TV."

"All criminal pursuits, certainly," she murmured sarcastically.

"You know what I mean."

"And you don't know him!" she flared back defiantly. "Maybe I'm not the snob you are, Jim, did you ever consider that? Maybe I find beer and football and working two jobs to get through college a refreshing change from overindulged dilettantes and homosexual designers. Did that ever occur to you?"

Her defense of Martin infuriated him. "Oh, I see.

You'll be giving your money away to charity next and going to live with him in some crummy apartment?"

"I am not going to continue this ridiculous conversation," she said haughtily. "Good night."

"Don't pull that princess act on me. I'm not as easily impressed with it as he is. I've seen it before, remember?"

Ashley said nothing, trying to hold her temper in check.

"This is the real reason you wouldn't sleep with me the other night," he said accusingly. "You weren't tired, or sick, or any other damn thing. You've got the hots for that cop!"

Ashley dug her nails into her palms. What could she say?

"I want you to get rid of him," Dillon said definitively. "Call the Philadelphia police and tell them to assign someone else."

"I will not!" Ashley replied, shocked.

"Yes, you will."

"I am not going to jeopardize that man's career by asking for a replacement," she said in an outraged tone.

"Career! Will you listen to yourself? He's a cop, for God's sake. Wake up. Are you planning to attend the Policemen's Ball with him, you in a Giancarlo and he in a bargain-basement suit? Accessorized with his shield, of course."

"I will not dignify that with a reply." She whirled, turning her back on him.

"Maybe you'd like to go to that first night next week by yourself?" he said childishly over her shoulder.

"I can handle it," Ashley answered coolly.

"And don't call me at the last minute, either. I'll be busy." Dillon stormed out of the cabin, up the stairs, and almost into the two policemen on deck. He shot Martin one murderous glance and then hurried off the boat, vanishing into the night.

"Uh-oh. Looks like a tiff with Lady Ashley. He must have noticed you making time with his girlfriend tonight."

Martin made no reply, looking in the direction of Dillon's disappearance.

"I'm not knocking it, of course. If I weren't . . ."

". . . happily married," Martin supplied for him.

"Right. I might be making a play for the dainty, diligent Miss Drummond."

Martin started to laugh. "Are you kidding? She scares me to death. If Fair is elected, the woman will be running the country. Besides, haven't you seen all the flowers and gifts she's been getting? Somebody's hot on the trail, boy." He grinned. "Somebody braver than you or me."

"Speak for yourself. Did you see her in that red dress the other night? Not half bad." He leaned in closer. "I think she's getting to like me," he confided. "As a friend, of course," he added quickly.

"How did you come to that startling conclusion?" Martin asked, amused, shaking his head.

"I can just sense these things."

"Tony, you're deranged. You try your macho routine with her and she'll land you a karate chop that'll send you into next week. You'll wind up out cold on the floor with her sitting on you."

"She takes karate lessons?" Capo said, horrified.

"I heard her talking about it."

"Geez."

"Bear it in mind."

Their voices drifted out over the water as Ashley, still shaking from the loathsome scene with Dillon, fell exhausted into bed.

The next morning, Ransom strolled into a store called Computers Unlimited and asked for an Apple II.

"We have a demonstration model right over here," the salesman said, indicating an ivory box with a printer attached on one side and a disk drive on the other.

"How do you use it?" Ransom asked.

The man stared at him. "You've never used one?"

"I've never used any computer."

The salesman looked dismayed.

"Look," Ransom said to revive his flagging interest, "I have to buy a whole fleet of personal computers to outfit my business, but I want to try one model first and see how I like it. This one was recommended by a friend, and I thought you could demonstrate it for me, give me some pointers to get me started."

"Certainly, sir," the clerk said, his attitude becoming more cooperative as he envisioned a large commission. "Just sit here in front of the console, and I'll be right with you."

The frustrated but patient salesman wound up demonstrating the computer's use, on and off between serving other customers, for about two hours. By then, Ransom was confident of his ability to run the machine, and bought it, promising to return for "the rest" when he was more efficient with his initial purchase.

He took the box back to his apartment and stayed up half the night playing with it, learning what it could and could not do, especially studying its ability to copy information from other disks. He read the manual from cover to cover, and finally went to bed about three A.M., his eyes aching with the strain of reading the display terminal.

When the time came to use the knowledge he had gained, he would be ready.

CHAPTER
Six

FOR THE next three weeks, Ransom pursued Meg with the apparent single-minded determination of a man in love. Lunches and dinners segued to country drives and concerts and long walks as he gained her confidence and her trust. She was falling for him, as they all did, and falling right into his plans.

One evening, as he was driving to pick her up in a town called Lowalla, he pulled over to the shoulder of the road and flicked on his dashboard light. He consulted his map again and made sure of the route, but then, as the traffic flowed past him on the left, instead of pulling back into it, he remained sitting motionless in the driver's seat. He rested his folded arms on the leather-clad steering wheel, lost in thought.

Things were not going exactly as he had anticipated. Technically, everything was right; Meg was shaping up nicely, he had learned the computer in short order, and it was just a matter of time before he got to it and found out what he needed to know. There was only a brief period left in the senator's tour, but he felt confident of his ability to accomplish his mission; the plan was building to a climax, as it always did, and that was fine.

For the first time in his memory, *he* was the problem.

It was bothering him that he was using her, and that was new. Her smiles and laughter, arch looks, and witty comments filled his mind when he was trying to concentrate and kept him awake at night. He wanted her, of course, but such desire was a constant with him; this tenderness was not.

And he was afraid there was no other word for what he felt.

Unless it was love.

He shook his head, as if emerging from a dream. No, that couldn't be true. He had never loved anything or anybody but himself. He was almost proud of that fact, the way the monk is proud of his chastity and the hermit proud of his self-imposed isolation. Ransom was not touched by the weaknesses other people contended with, and that was his chief asset. If he had been denied things that most of them had, like family and home and a loving childhood, then he had gained something in return: an unashamed self-interest as a trade-off, justified by the fact that nobody else on earth was interested in him.

Was that changing now? The thought terrified him in a way that no physical force did, and part of him wanted to run from Meg and get as far away from her as he could.

But of course, that was impossible. He was stuck in this situation until he ended it with the senator's death. He had never abandoned a contract in the middle of the chase, and he was not going to do it now. His reputation for reliability would be ruined, his future in jeopardy. All because a dark-eyed woman smiled at him in a certain way? No. It was not going to happen.

He sat up straight and glanced over his shoulder, then checked his mirrors. If he stayed here any longer, he might attract the attention of a cop, and that was the last thing he wanted.

He put his directional signal on and pulled back into the stream of moving cars.

Meg found Ashley sprawled on the bed in her room, reading a *Federal Reporter*.

"Fascinating?" Meg asked.

"You have no idea," Ashley replied dryly, putting the book facedown on the coverlet.

"The Millvale fund-raiser is set for eight next Thursday evening," Meg announced. "Your stepmother is meeting your dad at the dinner. The others are coming later."

"If I never hear that word 'fund-raiser' again when all this is over, it will be entirely too soon. Can't we start referring to them some other way?"

"Cattle call?" Meg suggested, and Ashley giggled.

"Will Jim be going with you?" Meg inquired delicately.

"I doubt it," Ashley replied crisply.

"I gather the fight was pretty bad."

Ashley nodded bleakly.

"I noticed that he's been making himself scarce since the night of the auction."

"Very astute. We had an argument down in my cabin, and I'm afraid I didn't handle it very well. I really detest scenes, and he wouldn't let me alone, making accusations and demanding I answer them when I was so tired I could hardly see."

"What kind of accusations?"

"About . . . another man."

Meg studied her friend, wondering how much she should say.

"Why don't you just tell Jim how you feel?" she finally asked gently. "It will hurt him less in the long run to hear the truth now."

"How do I feel?" Ashley inquired dryly.

"You don't love Jim Dillon. I think you once wanted to, because he fit in and you had similar backgrounds and all of those things that people who aren't in love believe are so important. But that reasoning no longer applies. The comparison is making that obvious."

"Comparison?" Ashley inquired, her eyes sliding away from Meg's. But she knew.

Meg sighed. "Do you want me to play dumb, or do you want me to tell you the truth?"

Ashley winced. "The truth, Doc."

"I saw a play once in which a character says, 'The only thing more obvious than two people looking longingly at one another is two people trying not to.'"

"Oh," Ashley said in a small voice. She cleared her throat. "How long have you known?"

"A while."

"And you said nothing to me?"

"What is there to say? You've got a situation on your hands."

"Thank you so much."

"How does Martin feel?" Meg asked.

Ashley threw up her hands. "Who knows? He doesn't say much to begin with. He's here in an official capacity, and up until quite recently he's been watching me trotting out nearly every night with my 'boyfriend.' What is he supposed to feel? It doesn't exactly make for the romance of the century."

"He's going to realize that Jim hasn't been around lately."

"I'm sure he has, but he's been far too reticent to ask me about it."

"Gentlemanly, you mean."

"You have to admit that it's a pretty awkward situation."

Meg was silent.

"Well?" Ashley said, staring at her.

Meg threw up her hands. "Don't look at me!"

"Why not? You seem to be doing quite well in the very department we're discussing. I haven't wanted to push this, but am I ever going to meet the mystery man who's been turning your hotel rooms into a floating greenhouse? We never get to see each other anymore. Every free minute that you have, you're off someplace with him."

"You'll meet him soon," Meg said, coloring faintly.

"Isn't he coming to Millvale?"

Meg shook her head. "He has a business trip. He won't be back until a few days afterward."

"Oh, too bad. I'm looking forward to meeting him."

"You will. I'm going out with him later tonight, but you'll be gone already."

"That's okay. We'll get together when we can arrange it. Where are you going tonight?"

"To the movies. There's a retro house a few blocks from here, and it's showing *Notorious*. I saw the marquee when we drove into town. I've never seen the film on a wide screen, only on TV."

"That's a real three-hanky weeper. Better bring a box of Kleenex; your contacts will wash right out of your eyes when Cary Grant saves Ingrid in the end. And what's this with the movies? He was taking you to so many expensive night spots, you were running out of clothes to wear. What happened?"

"I've been encouraging him to tone it down a little. I really prefer simpler pastimes, you know that."

"If he thought a big night out was a pizza in a bowling alley, you'd be complaining." Ashley grinned.

"I don't think so," Meg said, smiling back. "I'd enjoy his company anywhere."

"Ah-ha, like that, is it?" Ashley sat up and swung her legs over the side of the bed.

"It is."

"Did you see Lieutenant Martin outside?" Ashley asked.

"Yup. Your father is taking a nap, so he and Capo are in suspended animation."

"What's he doing?"

"Reading the *Times*. Sports section, I think."

Ashley received that news in perturbed silence.

"Then again, he may have a woman stashed in one of the rooms down the hall. I didn't check."

"That is not funny, Margaret."

"Why don't you go out and talk to him?"

"I'm not going to hang out in the corridor, chatting like a schoolgirl with a pass from study hall."

"You're right. It's a much better idea to sit in here and stew," Meg said innocently.

"I'm not stewing, I'm reading." Ashley picked up her book and waved it in the air.

"I'm convinced," Meg replied. She turned to go and added over her shoulder, "Ladies Auxiliary luncheon at one tomorrow. Don't forget your white gloves and pillbox hat."

Ashley fell flat on the bed and put her hands over her ears.

"I knew that would cheer you up," Meg said in parting.

Ashley watched her go, then picked up her book again, determined to work.

Meg stepped into the hall and confronted the two policemen, who were still reading the newspaper. Martin looked up briefly, then continued to read, while Capo caught her eye and said, "Stepping out tonight again, Meg?"

"If that's all right with you, Anthony," she said briskly, putting her hands behind her back and regarding him with a piquant, schoolmarmish gaze.

"Same guy?" he inquired.

"Yes, the same guy." She held up one hand in warning. "I know. You're about to tell me I shouldn't be going steady at my tender age. I promise I won't get pinned until at least my sophomore year."

"I don't know, Meggie," Capo said, shaking his head. "Next thing you know you'll be married. Kids, diapers, Little League, a van, and a collie, the whole shot. Then what will the senator do?"

"If it's all right with you, I'll worry about that when the time comes," Meg replied dryly.

"How come we never see this guy?" Capo asked.

"I imagine because he's a Kremlin spy," Meg replied.

"Stranger things have happened," Capo said airily.

Martin, accustomed to the banter between these two, was ignoring the exchange.

"Stow your police paranoia for once, won't you?" Meg said as she moved on down the hall. "He's a real-estate agent. I call his office all the time."

"Somebody has to sub for your father when he's not around," Capo called to her retreating back.

She made a face at him over her shoulder and then disappeared into her room.

Capo sat staring after her thoughtfully for a while, then said, "Hey, Tim."

Martin looked over at him.

"You notice how we never see the boyfriend?"

"What? Which boyfriend? We've got a few of them running around here."

"Meg Drummond's. We never see him."

"You want to get something going with him, Tony?" Martin asked, folding his paper.

"You know what I mean. He always picks her up in the lobby, drops her off at the elevator wherever we're staying. She's been going out with him for a while, and we've never even seen him."

"So what? Maybe she doesn't want to march him past us like he's a prize bull on display. I can't blame her."

"But didn't he show up about the same time we did? Isn't that a coincidence?"

Martin shrugged. "I really don't know how long she's been going out with him."

"I still think it's funny," Capo muttered.

"You're just jealous. You can't have her, but you don't want anybody else to have her either."

"He sells real estate," Capo grumbled, shaking out his paper.

"Who?"

"The boyfriend."

"Lots of money in that," Martin observed.

"My uncle Louie sells real estate. He has all these plaques hanging in his office totaling up how many millions he's sold each year."

"Oh, yeah?"

"You don't think she's dating Uncle Louie, do you?"

"I don't think so, Tony."

"It sure would be news to Aunt Angelina." Capo scanned the headlines and then added, "The guy is probably balding, with a paunch, wears glasses, a real loser."

"Probably," Martin agreed, humoring him.

"I'm going to try to get a look at him," Capo concluded.

"You do that."

Both men resumed reading.

Meg was ready early that evening, and sat in her room thinking about the night ahead. She was wearing a cherry-red knit sweater and skirt. Ransom seemed to favor red; he always complimented her when she wore it.

Meg had much to think about concerning her relationship with him. She knew she was falling in love, but his response over the past few weeks puzzled her. While he called her as much as ever and wanted to see her almost daily, he seemed to be withdrawing in some subtle, indefinable way. In the beginning, he had been very amorous, kissing and touching her at every opportunity. Now, though his involvement with her had definitely increased, he was almost remote, restricting contact as if he were afraid it would take him too far. And he had not tried to get her into bed, which she found bewildering. He was a physical man, and unless she was grossly misinterpreting his signals, which she doubted, he found her desirable. So what was going on? She didn't know.

She did know that she dreaded losing him, that he had become as much a part of her life as her job or her family. But she had no idea how to pin him down on something she found so elusive herself. So she resolved to wait and do nothing, see where things would go on their own.

She stood abruptly and switched off the lights in her room, preparing to leave.

Several hours later, Ransom and Meg emerged from the movie house. Meg was still blotting her eyes with a tissue, and he was strolling along with a preoccupied air, his hands in his pockets.

"What did you think of the movie?" Meg asked as they headed down the block in the direction of the hotel.

He shrugged. "I don't go much for that cornball stuff."

"Why corny? I thought it was wonderful."

"I just don't believe that people could fall in love like

that and then go through what they did, surmount all those obstacles to be together. It's unrealistic."

"Why?"

"Life isn't like that. If something doesn't work out, you move on to something else."

Meg was silent for a long moment. "Is that how you really feel?"

"I've never known anything different."

"So if it isn't easy and simple, you drop it?"

He stopped walking and looked down at her. "We're talking about a movie here, Meg."

"Are we?"

"What do you mean?"

"Is that your philosophy of life? In Cary Grant's position, you would have written Ingrid Bergman off?"

"I knew we should have gone to see *Death Wish Ten: The Annihilation*," he said darkly.

"Answer the question."

"The story was sentimental, that's all I'm saying."

"That's what makes it a classic."

"I guess so," he conceded.

"Though I confess I've always had some sympathy for the Claude Rains character, which is certainly not the idea," Meg said acerbically.

"Why?"

"Well, he does love Ingrid, and she is deceiving him. His love for her, and his refusal to believe that odious mother of his that Ingrid is plotting against him, eventually cause his downfall."

"Do you think Ingrid is justified in deceiving him?" Ransom asked carefully.

"Obviously the screenwriter wants you to think that.

Rains is a criminal and Ingrid is drafted into service to get him. But it's not so easy for me to see it that way. I can put myself in his position and imagine being so in love with someone that I would be unable to see the flaws or listen to any criticism of the person that I loved."

"Can you?" he murmured.

"Yes."

"And you would overlook anything to be with him? Anything at all?" Ransom inquired.

"I don't know. It hasn't happened to me. But I suspect that's how I would feel."

He received that in silence.

"I guess that makes me a hopeless romantic, huh?" she asked.

"Probably," he said.

"An endangered species?" Meg said playfully.

"Almost extinct," he agreed. "It's a tough life for that breed in the eighties."

He glanced at his watch. It was eleven o'clock. If he kept her out past midnight, the other members of the senator's entourage would most likely be in bed.

"I'm hungry. Let's get something to eat in here," he suggested, stopping by the door of a sandwich shop.

"'Café Splendide'?" Meg said, reading the name stenciled on the front window.

"Something tells me it might have a hard time living up to that billing," Ransom suggested.

They walked through the door into a clean, well-lit restaurant with scattered tables topped by paper covers under glass. The patrons appeared to be middle class and decidedly upstanding.

"Doesn't look too bad," Ransom qualified his earlier statement as they sat down. "Where are we, again?"

"Lowalla."

"The Café Splendide in Lowalla, Pennsylvania. Doesn't that sound like an off-Broadway play?"

"Look, they can probably cook a hamburger as well as anybody else, right?"

"Let's hope so."

They ordered hamburgers and coffee and sat waiting while Ransom tried to stretch out the time until their return to the hotel.

"You're very quiet," Meg commented, watching his face. "Is there a big deal pending or something?"

He nodded, seizing on the excuse. "A shopping mall."

"That sounds pretty big."

"I've spent a lot of time setting it up, and if it falls through I'm out the time and the money." Why was lying to her becoming so awfully difficult?

"That's the nature of the business, isn't it?" Meg asked.

"Yeah."

"Are you sure that's all? It isn't anything I've done?"

"What could you have done?" he asked, as if the possibility of her doing something to upset him were ludicrous.

"I don't know. Lately you just seem sort of . . . distant."

So she had picked up on his confusion. But he'd come too far to let her slip away from him now, he had to hold on until he had finished what he'd set out to do.

"Do I?" he said, favoring her with his most charming

smile. "I'm sorry. I guess I have been sort of preoccupied. I'll try to do better."

"You don't have to try with me, Peter. You should know that."

The food came, but Ransom was so busy ruminating on how to get into her room that night that he paid it scant attention.

"I thought you said you were hungry," Meg reminded him.

He nodded and picked up his burger, taking a huge bite. He made short work of it, hardly tasting it, and was draining his cup dutifully when she said shyly, not looking at him, "Would you like to come back to my room tonight?"

He froze momentarily, his heart banging in his chest. Was it really going to be that easy?

"Are you sure about this, Meg?" he asked quietly, not wanting to seem too eager.

She nodded. She looked a little nervous, but her gaze was steady.

Ransom paid the bill. It was five to twelve. They walked back to the hotel at a leisurely pace, holding hands, both thinking about what was ahead of them.

The lobby was almost deserted, and they were the only people in the hall as they approached Meg's room.

"Everybody else in bed?" Ransom asked.

"Guess so."

"What about the cops?"

"They sleep in the sitting rooms with the senator and Ashley." She unlocked her door, and they entered. The room was shaped like an L, with a small nook where she had placed her computer on the hotel's cherry secretary. The stem of the L contained a bed and twin night-stands, with an occasional chair and a standing lamp.

Everything was very neat.

"Would you like a drink?" she asked, switching on a shaded lamp on the dresser. It was the only illumination in the darkened room.

He shook his head. Alcohol might make him drowsy later, and he had to be sharp.

"I'm going to have some sparkling water," she said.

He realized that she was giving herself something to do, and watched her as she went to the small refrigerator provided by the hotel and took out a bottle of mineral water. She looked nice, he thought; she was not a stunner on first impression, but her quiet, understated looks grew on you. At least, they did on him. He liked her in red. He had noticed that not many women were able to wear the color successfully, but she could.

She sipped at her drink, then put it down.

"I need a few moments in the bathroom," she said.

He nodded.

As soon as she had closed the door behind her, he took a packet of powder from his pocket and ripped off the top. Listening carefully for her return, he dumped the contents of the tiny bag into her glass and watched the crystals swirl around in the liquid and then disappear. When the powder was dissolved, he picked up the glass, satisfied.

That would cause her to sleep through any noise he might make later on.

When she came out again, he handed her the glass, and in her nervousness she drained it and set it on the bedside table. She turned to face him.

"It's been a long time for me," she said softly. "I'm not sure how to do this."

"Then let me do it," he said, stepping closer. He touched her shoulder and she turned into his arms.

"Just hold me," she whispered. "Just hold me for a while."

Ransom frowned against her hair, though he did as she said. He was good at lovemaking, in the same methodical way he was good at everything else, but he didn't like cuddling. It made him feel lost, inadequate, and control was always his goal. He was a technician, nothing more.

But as he stood with Meg nestled against his shoulder, something changed. He began to feel more comfortable, off stage, as if it were okay to be himself, if he could still remember who that was. She sighed and pulled him closer, and he smoothed her hair gently. She always smelled the same way, clean, like soap or shampoo. It reminded him of shower day at the orphanage, or laundry day when they changed the bed linens, two almost-pleasant memories he had of that place. In fact, she reminded him of everything good that had ever happened to him. When she turned her face up for his kiss, he took his time, savoring the experience, so that he could remember it later when she was no longer a part of his life.

He pulled the sweater over her head and dropped it on the floor. Her body was richer than he would have imagined. Clothing leaned her, disguising ripeness. He removed her bra, cupping her breasts in his hands as he did so, and then the rest of her clothes, setting her on the bed.

Meg watched him undress in the semidarkness. He unzipped his jacket, took it off, and pulled his polo shirt over his head. She held her breath as he unbuckled his pants, and put up her arms to encircle his neck when he knelt on the bed to join her.

She gasped with the shock of his naked skin against hers. He wished for more light, to see her better, to remember, but became lost in her immediately, the feel of her warm flesh under his hands, her yielding body beneath his. She followed where he led instinctively, her less varied experience giving way to his mastery of the art. But as he made love to her, he felt his skills gradually desert him, and felt fifteen again, raw and untutored and flooded with tenderness.

The first time for any couple is always the excitement of the unknown, and of learning each other. But for Ransom there was this new dimension; he forgot about pressing the right buttons and simply loved Meg, pausing to kiss her and hold her close when she clung to him, prolonging the act for his own satisfaction as much as hers. His time with her became a unique experience during which the ghosts of his former lovers receded and were silenced.

And when it was over, with Meg asleep next to him, he was wide awake.

If he had been able to see his own expression, he would have known that he was frightened.

He did know that he didn't want to leave the bed. Usually, once he was finished with a woman he was out of bed and into the shower before his heartbeat had returned to normal, but this time he wanted to linger. Meg felt so sweet and warm beside him, and he could still hear her little sounds of pleasure, the way she'd said his name in his ear at the height of her passion.

Or what she thought was his name.

Ransom forced himself to get up and pull on his pants. The computer sat like an obelisk on the desk. He hesitated, then approached it resolutely.

He had a job to do, and he was going to do it.

The machine sounded a tone when it went on, and he glanced at Meg, but she didn't stir. The master disk sat in its slot, and he pushed it in, opening up with that. Then he glanced at the stack of floppies in a clear plastic box next to the console.

The box was locked.

He stared at it, his bare chest heaving, as if he could force it to yield up its secrets with the intensity of his gaze.

Of course it was locked. Cleaning people and hotel staff came into the room every day. Meg would want to safeguard her notes.

The information he needed was on the disks, the computer of no use to him without them.

He thought for a long moment, fighting panic. If he couldn't get to the disks, all bets were off. He would have to formulate a new plan, and he simply didn't have the time.

Think, he instructed himself. Where would she keep the key? She had a ring in her purse on which she kept her car keys, but he had never examined it closely.

He got up and went to her purse, which she had dropped on the chair next to the door. He took it into the bathroom and shut the door, examining the bag's contents by the light over the sink.

The ring held several keys, only one of which was small enough to fit the lock on the box. Holding his breath, he crept back to the desk and tried it.

The lock yielded, and the lid of the box sprang up smartly.

He released his breath in an audible sigh. He set the key ring aside and put the purse back on the chair, then returned to the computer.

He riffled through the disks quickly, reading the labels. He located one marked "Building Plans" with the dates of several fund-raisers and dinners following the words. He booted it up quickly, and saw diagrams and schematics as he scanned from page to page. He set the machine to copy the document onto one of the blank disks he'd brought with him, and then flipped through the rest of Meg's disks as it did so. He found two others that looked promising and copied them also.

The machine hummed along; the keyboard was virtually silent and the rest of the process relatively quiet. He couldn't be sure he was getting what he needed, but if he didn't this time, he would just have to try again. And soon.

He ran into trouble when he was shutting down. In his haste to log off, he entered an incorrect command and the machine beeped loudly to alert him of it, flashing a remedial instruction.

Meg rolled over, mumbling, as Ransom shot to his feet, standing to block the glowing computer screen.

"Wassa madder?" Meg said, her words slurred from sleep and the dope he had given her.

"Nothing," Ransom replied soothingly. "Go back to sleep."

"Heard something?" she muttered, peering drunkenly through the darkness at him.

She had been wearing her glasses that night, and now they were lying on the bedside table. He knew that without them she wouldn't be able to see across the room, even if it were fully lit and she had her wits about her, which she certainly didn't.

"That was me, in the bathroom. I'm sorry." He waited, still afraid she would recognize the sound she'd heard, a sound she heard routinely every day. But he knew she couldn't remain conscious for long; the drug would pull her back under soon.

"Come back to bed," she finally said sleepily, her head lolling on the pillow.

"In a minute. I'll be right there," he replied, relieved that she was clearly succumbing to the dope.

Ransom waited tensely until she subsided and he could hear that she was breathing deeply again. He went back to the machine and shut it down carefully, sweating profusely.

That had been close. Meg was in love with him, but she was the furthest thing from stupid. It would have been difficult to explain to her why he'd felt an irresistible urge to play with her computer in the middle of the night.

He pocketed the copies he'd made and relocked the box of disks, slipping the key ring back into her purse. Then he took off his pants, pulled back the sheet, and climbed into the bed.

Meg turned to him instantly, and he held her in his arms until the bedside clock read six.

He got up, and she opened her eyes. She was apparently a light sleeper.

"Got to go," he said, bending to kiss her forehead as he buttoned his shirt.

"Can't you stay for breakfast?" she asked, sitting up, a lock of dark hair falling over one eye like a comma.

"I've got an early meeting on the mall project," he lied quickly, reaching for the rest of his clothes. "I'll call you tonight. You'll still be here, right?"

She nodded, falling back groggily. What was the matter with her head? It felt as if it was filled with cotton.

"Eight o'clock," he said.

He was through the door before she could comment.

The only person he saw on his way out was the desk clerk.

Ransom had never felt worse in his life.

Martin was up at six-thirty, drinking room-service coffee and hoping that Ashley would emerge from her room before too long. She had nothing to attend until the luncheon at one, but sometimes she stayed inside working for hours on end. He had resolved that today he would ask her what was going on with Dillon.

It was still none of his business, but if he had to wonder about it any longer, he would surely go mad.

Dillon had vanished after the auction, when he and Capo had seen him leaving in a huff, and Martin wondered if the lawyer's disappearance had anything to do with him. The phone calls had stopped, the gifts no longer arrived, and Ashley attended everything alone.

All in all, from Martin's point of view it was a very interesting development.

He had showered and shaved in the separate room Meg always reserved for that purpose, but now he was back in Ashley's suite, waiting. He could hear the water running in the room next door as Capo got ready for the day ahead.

Martin finished the last of the coffee and thought about ordering more. He was living on coffee and cigarettes, and had lost eight pounds since starting this tour. His cheekbones stood out like a fashion model's, and he looked like a man visited nightly by an incubus, a man expiring of a surfeit of passion.

Which was almost the truth. He could hardly bear to be around Ashley, for fear of what his expression might reveal, but when he was away from her it was worse, as he was tortured by his ignorance of what she might be doing.

His only consolation was that he wasn't away from her much.

A waiter knocked and went past Martin into the bedroom with a tray at seven-thirty. At eight o'clock, he heard her on the phone with one of her cronies in the Justice Department, and at eight-thirty she appeared, wearing jeans and an oxford cloth blouse.

"Good morning," she said, coming through the connecting door.

"Hi."

"Has Meg been in yet?"

Martin shook his head.

"Dad must still be having breakfast. Did you eat?"

"Coffee."

She surveyed him disapprovingly. "You should eat more. You're getting thin, and I think we're responsible. The schedule we're forcing you to keep would run anyone into malnutrition."

"You're keeping the same schedule," he pointed out to her.

"But I get a regular infusion of pastrami sandwiches," she said, and he smiled.

"Holding out on me, huh?"

"Could be."

"If I find out you're hitting those greasy spoons with anyone but me . . ." He let the threat hang in the air, and she grinned.

"Let me order you up some breakfast," she said, reaching for the phone extension on the TV table.

"I don't want anything, really."

"Stubborn, eh?"

"It will just go to waste."

"What will the police commissioner say when we return a skeleton to his ranks?"

The mention of the end of his tour brought sobering thoughts for them both.

"Ten more days," Martin said.

Ashley nodded slowly.

"Then I go back to Philly," he added.

She nodded again, not looking at him.

"What happens to you?" he asked softly.

"I keep on with . . . this," she said, gesturing around her.

"And with Jim Dillon?" he said, looking into her eyes.

She was silent.

"What happened to him, Ashley?" Martin called her that only when they were alone together.

"We had . . . an argument."

He saw that she wasn't going to be more specific, so he prodded, "What about?"

"Just a difference of opinion." She was having trouble holding his gaze; she was a lousy liar.

"Must have been a major one."

"You could say that."

"Ashley, was the argument about me?"

There was no mistaking the flush that spread up from her neck to her cheeks.

"Why do you ask that?" she murmured.

"The way he looked at me when he left the boat the night of the auction," Martin replied.

"How did he look at you?"

"Like he wanted to kill me."

"All right, yes. The argument was about you," she conceded uncomfortably.

"What did he say?"

"He wanted me to call the police department and request that you be replaced," Ashley responded.

"Why?"

"He thought there was something between us," she answered. "I told him that we were friends, but he couldn't understand that. He was jealous."

"Is he that insecure?" Martin asked.

"He never was before," she replied.

"You never gave him reason."

"I didn't give him reason this time."

"Yes, you did," Martin told her in a low tone, taking a step closer to her.

She closed her eyes. "Tim, please."

"You know you did," he said huskily.

She didn't answer, her mouth working.

"Are we just going to go on this way?" he said, pressing her. "I'm about ready to jump out of my skin all the time, we're tiptoeing past each other like a couple of burglars, and when I think of leaving and never seeing you again . . ."

"Shh." She put her finger to his lips, and he kissed it.

She moved her hand and touched his face, running her index finger over the hard line of his jaw.

"It's like a miracle to be able to touch you, after wanting it for so long," she whispered.

"You could always touch me," he said, taking her hand and placing it against the pulse in his throat. "Any time."

"If only it were that easy," she murmured, her eyes filling.

"Why should it be hard?"

"You'll lose your job if your captain finds out you were doing anything more than guarding me," she said.

"What have I done?"

"Oh, Tim, don't be naive. This wasn't supposed to happen, and you know it."

"What does that mean? Your daddy won't like it?"

Her hand fell away.

"Is that it?" Martin insisted.

"If you really believe that, then you don't know me at all," Ashley replied.

"Then what? Why is it so impossible? Damn it, Ashley, why are you looking at me like that?"

"Do you think I don't know the contempt you feel for

all of us?" she said quietly. "I've felt it myself, seeing us through your eyes. You think we're all rich parasites who've never done a day's work, and you think my father is about as qualified to be president as you are to teach at the Sorbonne."

"That has nothing to do with you."

"Of course it does! This is what I am. I come from the Fair family, and I *want* my father to be president! He may not be perfect, but he's better than anybody else who's running now, and he'll do the best job he possibly can."

"Ashley, this isn't about your father. Don't confuse the issue." He took her chin in his hand and forced her to meet his eyes. "Can you face the idea of never seeing me again after I'm through here?"

She bit her lip, her eyes searching his.

He reached for her and pulled her into his arms. When he kissed her, the satisfaction was so intense for both of them that they remained for a long time locked in a fierce embrace, like teenagers who are loath to lose contact for fear the magic may never happen again.

When Martin finally lifted his head, Ashley locked her arms around his waist and buried her face against his shoulder.

"Come down to my room with me," he said huskily.

"What room?" she whispered, luxuriating in the feel of his hard body under her hands.

"Where I shower and change. It's empty."

She stepped back from him and looked up into his face. He was regarding her with an intensity that told her he was feeling exactly what she was.

She nodded.

"I'll go," he murmured. "Come after me in five minutes."

He left without looking back at her. Ashley stood rooted, her heart pounding, wanting to race after him but forcing herself to remain until he was gone.

She was in love with him, but she didn't want to be. It was all wrong, they would never be able to make a future together, but she had never felt anything as powerful as the need to follow him and be with him. It overrode everything else.

When she had waited long enough she slipped down the hall, as furtive as a thief, and when Martin heard her footfall he opened the door and let her in. As soon as she entered, he closed the door and locked it firmly behind her.

They fell into each other's arms. Ashley found herself pulling at her shirt and his almost in a frenzy, trying to undress both of them at the same time. He kept kissing her, as if he could never get enough of her mouth, and they were half undressed when the phone rang on the table beside the bed.

"Ignore it," Ashley whispered urgently.

But he was still a cop. He set her aside and picked up the receiver, saying into it breathlessly, "Yeah?"

He listened, said, "Got it," and hung up the phone.

"Capo," he said tersely. "I'm needed downstairs."

Ashley sagged visibly in frustration.

"I'll go," Martin said, picking up his shirt from the floor and shrugging into it. He buttoned it rapidly, but Ashley noticed he was not as controlled as he seemed; his fingers were having a lot of trouble.

"Don't go," she moaned.

"Have to. You slip out after I'm gone." He made for the door.

"Is that all?" Ashley demanded, bewildered. "You have nothing else to say to me?"

"If you don't know how I feel by now, you never will," he replied, and left.

Ashley went over to the bed and sagged onto its edge. Slowly, she put her blouse back on and straightened her clothes, absorbed in thought.

He had made himself clear, and the next move was hers.

After a while, she got up and went back to the suite. Meg arrived shortly after she did and strolled into the room.

She took one look at Ashley's expression and said, "What?"

"Come inside with me," Ashley replied quickly, and fled into her bedroom.

Meg followed Ashley into the bedroom and closed the door behind them.

"What was that all about?" Meg asked.

"I've just been with Martin. We were . . . uh . . . if the phone hadn't rung, we'd be in bed together right now."

Meg looked stunned. "He's on duty," was all she could say.

"We were . . . I don't know what we were," Ashley said, hardly listening. "We were talking beforehand, and we made . . . a confession? An admission? Can't I express myself in anything but legal terms? Meg, I'm very confused about this."

"That much I gathered," Meg said flatly.

"Oh, God, what am I going to do?" Ashley moaned.

"I want him so much I have to restrain myself every minute from following him around in a trance. It can't work, but that doesn't seem to matter. Why doesn't that seem to matter?"

"All right, calm down," Meg said, glancing at the door as if wondering if they could be overheard.

"He's only a little less conservative than Birch Bayh and thinks my job serves only to put lifelong felons back on the streets to continue their criminal careers," Ashley went on. "He has a fine disdain for my family and friends and would probably be happiest going back in time to the Eisenhower administration. How can I possibly become involved with somebody like that?"

"Because you're crazy about him," Meg said.

"I did leave out that one point," Ashley agreed miserably.

"It's an important one."

"I spend almost all of my free time fantasizing about him making love to me."

"I see."

"Do you think it could be just a superficial physical attraction?" Ashley asked, almost hopefully.

"I seriously doubt it, Ash. You're not the superficial type, and neither is he."

"But every time I see him I want to take him by the hand and lead him to the nearest bed. That doesn't strike me as a particularly mature attitude."

"You're just in love, Ash. That's the way it feels."

"Did you ever notice his hands?" Ashley asked dreamily.

"No."

"The backs of his hands have these big veins, and there's downy black hair on his wrists."

"Oh."

"I keep picturing those hands all over me."

"I don't know if I'm old enough to listen to this," Meg said jokingly, raising her brows.

"And did you ever see anyone look sexier smoking a cigarette?"

"Keith Carradine in *Choose Me*?" Meg suggested.

Ashley wasn't listening. "I don't like cigarettes," she ranted. "I hate smoking. I never would go into a restaurant unless it had a nonsmoking area. Now I don't even care. In fact, I'm growing fond of that tobacco smell because it reminds me of him."

"Humphrey Bogart in *Key Largo*," Meg said.

"What?"

"Somebody who looked sexier smoking a cigarette."

"I thought you were going to take this seriously."

"Well, you asked." She thought a moment and added, "Harrison Ford in *Hanover Street*."

"I'm sorry I brought it up. With your encyclopedic knowledge of movies, we could be here all day." She paused and said thoughtfully, "Do you know what the worst part of it is?"

"What's the worst part?" Meg asked sympathetically, sitting next to Ashley on the bed.

"Despite his infuriating attitudes, I need him desperately, and I know that if I were ever in trouble, he'd be there for me. That quiet strength of his is very reassuring."

Meg nodded.

"But I'm scared. I don't know what's happening to

me. I'm usually not combative, but I've been so edgy lately, first fighting with Jim and now this. . . . I wanted to punch him when he walked out on me just now. The frustration was just incredible."

"If you're getting emotional, it's probably a good sign," Meg interrupted her. "You were always too restrained, Ashley. This man is finally shaking you up."

"This man is driving me insane."

"I think I know what your problem is," Meg said. "You've led a very sheltered life and have never really gotten to know anyone outside your own rarefied circle. Now you find yourself falling for a very different kind of man, and it's unsettling."

"Tell me about it."

"You have a choice, you know. You can let him go back to Philadelphia when he's finished here and end the relationship before anything really happens."

Ashley put both hands over her mouth and shook her head, her eyes wide.

"Then you'd better learn to accept him," Meg said.

"It's not a question of accepting him. I do. His values are sound, and I understand why he feels the way he does. I'm actually proud of his convictions. But he's so rigid."

"What do you mean?"

"Well, I introduced him to Carlo on the yacht the night of the auction. And I know if Carlo hadn't left as quickly as he did, Tim would have been horribly rude to him."

"That's not so surprising. I've come close to being horribly rude to Carlo myself. What happened, did Carlo make a pass at him?"

"Not exactly. He made some remark about Tim being attractive or something. You should have seen the look on Tim's face."

"I can imagine. But did you really think that somebody like Tim would take that sort of thing easily?"

"I guess I thought that he would be sophisticated enough to laugh it off."

Meg shook her head. "You don't want 'sophisticated,' Ash. You've been drowning in sophisticated all your life. Tim is straightforward and solid and decent, and if you're honest with yourself you'll admit that's a large part of what you find so compelling about him. Aside from his hands, of course."

"But if he can't deal with Carlo, how can he possibly be with me? You know what my life is like. Carlo is the least of it. How could Tim handle the people I meet in my career, the clients I represent?"

"Are you sure you're giving him enough credit? I suspect he's capable of compromise, and if he wants you, as I think he does, he'll meet you somewhere in the middle."

"And what about my family? Can you imagine Sylvia's reaction to all of this?"

"Since when have you ever cared what Sylvia thought?"

"My father cares what she thinks. I really don't want to cause an uproar."

"You may have to do just that. Don't you think it's time you stopped playing good little Ashley and did something you wanted to do, did something for yourself, regardless of your image or what the rest of the world might say?"

Ashley sat thinking for a long moment, and then said, as a slow smile spread across her face, "Maybe you're right."

"What are you going to tell Tim?"

"Nothing, for the moment. I need time to think about how to handle things with Jim, my family, everyone."

"Why don't you just get Jim on the phone and tell him you're throwing him over for Tim Martin because Tim has sexier hands? It makes sense to me."

Ashley smiled thinly. "Very funny. Jim is not so easy to get rid of, as you may have noticed in the past. He's mad right now, but he'll get over it and turn up again. He won't want to miss out on the publicity connected with the rest of the campaign, and he knows Tim's assignment will be over soon." She sighed and surveyed Meg objectively. "Now that I've bored you with my problems, how are you? I must say you're looking very chipper this morning."

"I am chipper. Peter stayed with me last night."

"You mean here?"

"Yup."

"And I missed him!"

"He left very early this morning for a meeting."

"Was it wonderful?"

"It was."

"Well, I'm very happy for you."

"You don't look very happy for me."

"That's because I just remembered that luncheon this afternoon. Could we say I came down with something rather suddenly? Something serious."

"Whooping cough?"

"Only kids get that."

"Oh. Diphtheria?"

"There's a vaccine for that now."

"Then I guess you'll have to go."

Ashley nodded glumly and stood, stretching.

"What should I say to Tim on my way out?" Meg asked.

"'Bye, Tim.'"

"Okay," Meg agreed, smiling. "It's all up to you." She left the bedroom and pulled the door closed behind her.

Ransom studied the diagrams on the computer screen before him and took a final drag on his cigarette. Then he shut off the machine and stubbed out the smoke in the same motion, relaxing back into the cushions of the sofa in his apartment.

It had to be Millvale, which was only a few days away. He had examined and discarded the other possibilities for various reasons. Fair's murder would take place in the Millvale Hotel ballroom.

Ransom was satisfied; it was the best choice. He'd analyzed the detailed architectural plans of the hotel and the structures on either side of it, which included all passageways, fire exits, and utility doors. There was an apartment building next to the hotel, which made access easy. He was an expert at slipping past doormen. Once inside, he could take the staircase to the roof, cross onto the hotel's fire escape, and break in through a window leading to a service hallway on the second floor.

It was all there in the information he'd pirated from Meg's computer. Lucky for him she was so thorough.

It should be a snap, he thought; he'd gone through

similar scenarios dozens of times, with less preparation. Meg was making it very easy for him.

Meg. He didn't want to think about her, but she kept creeping into his consciousness, disturbing his concentration. He'd told her he was going away on a business trip to leave himself open for the hit, but she didn't think he was departing until the next morning.

He sat up suddenly and sneezed loudly, his eyes watering. He went into the kitchen and swallowed a handful of tablets with a glass of water. Goddamn cold. He had no tolerance for illness, especially his own. He was accustomed to his body's perfect obedience, and when it revolted he felt like killing it. He would have done so if it hadn't meant killing himself in the process.

The doorbell rang, and he glanced toward the computer immediately. There was only one person it could be. With the hit so close, he couldn't afford another visit to Meg's room, so he had brought her to the apartment a couple of times. Now she knew where he lived.

Better that it was ending soon. This was getting out of hand.

"Just a minute," he called as he unplugged the computer and lugged it to his bedroom closet, where he dropped it into its original packing box and closed the lid. He returned to the living room and grabbed the software, tossing it all on the closet floor and kicking it behind his row of shoes, under a folded blanket. He slammed the door closed and parked a straight chair directly in front of it, on which he piled his briefcase and coat.

If she tried to get into the closet, he would have enough warning to intervene and stop her.

He ran to the door and opened it to find Meg standing on the threshold, holding a covered cardboard container.

"Surprise," she said. "What took you so long?"

"I was in the bathroom."

She brushed past him into the living room. "I knew you weren't feeling well, so I thought you might like this for lunch."

"What is it?" he asked, viewing her present suspiciously.

"Chicken soup." She took off the cover, and the pungent aroma escaped into the room.

"Why?"

She turned to stare at him. "Hasn't anyone ever brought you chicken soup when you were sick?"

"No," he replied honestly.

Her brows knit as she went into the kitchen and dished up the steaming soup. "What about your mother when you were a little kid?" she asked.

He sighed. "There was no mother when I was a little kid."

"What do you mean? You told me your parents were dead, but they must have been alive once. Did your mother die when you were born, or very young?"

He shook his head.

"How come you have no pictures of them around here, mementos or snapshots, things like that?" she asked.

"I told you my parents were dead to forestall your questions in the beginning. It's not the sort of thing you want to get into right away; it creates the wrong impression."

She turned and faced him. "Well?"

"I have no family, and never did." Surely it couldn't hurt to give her just this little part of himself, let her know something that was actually true, and that explained so much.

"None at all? You've never been married, no kids? You never talk about yourself."

"I'm alone. I was abandoned as an infant, raised in orphanages."

"Really?"

Ransom shrugged. "Why is that so surprising? It happens."

"I'm surprised because it happened to me, too," Meg said, rattling spoons.

Now she had his full attention. "What do you mean? You've told me about your relatives."

"My parents adopted me when I was a baby. In the biological sense, I have no family either."

"I didn't know that."

"Two lost souls, eh?" she said lightly, handing him a full bowl of the soup.

Ransom watched her eat, ignoring his portion. She must have shared his own fundamental sense of rootlessness and rejection, but unlike him she had made something of herself, something good that people respected.

He had lost his appetite.

"Aren't you going to have any of that?" she asked him. "I made it myself, specially."

"Maybe later," he said, putting down the bowl. "Right now I'd rather have you."

She smiled and came to him willingly, as she always did.

She didn't know it, but he had told her a basic truth.

He would rather have her, permanently, than do anything else.

CHAPTER
Seven

I T WAS raining lightly when Fair's group hit Millvale, Pennsylvania, on the last leg of the senator's junket.

Martin was nervous about the tour's final fund-raiser. He and Capo usually visited the sites of major events beforehand, and they saw immediately that the Hotel Millvale's ballroom was too vast to supervise adequately, with a great many narrow, interlocking hallways leading up to it.

Peter Ransom had come to the same conclusion. He'd checked out the ballroom and the adjacent apartment building and was convinced he had made the right choice.

On the afternoon of the dinner, Ransom packed an overnight case in his apartment and put his passport and other necessary papers in the zipper portion of the bag. He removed all traces of personal occupancy from the rooms, shipping the clothes and dishes, even the computer, to goodwill with no sender's address. He dumped the leftover toiletries into plastic bags and put them into the car, then wiped the place clean of prints, doing a final check to make sure that everything that might be traced to him was gone.

As he left and locked the door, he didn't look behind him. The place where he had lived for almost two months was no longer functional and therefore of no further interest to him.

The gun he would use that evening was concealed inside his jacket. It was a lightweight Luger equipped with telescopic sights and silencer. He had bought it from his usual source, a dealer in illegal weapons, for about three times what he normally paid, but it was perfect for the job. The serial number was filed off and its foreign manufacture made it ideal, difficult to trace. Even better than that, it was impeccably accurate. He had practiced with it at a local target range until he could use it in the dark.

When he left the apartment, he drove the gray Mercedes to a suburban Philadelphia shopping mall he had selected for its wealthy ambience and parked the car near a dumpster. He left the sedan there, wedged between the Jaguars and Volvos and Audis, where it probably would not be noticed for days, possibly weeks. He threw the plastic bags into the vast metal rubbish container, mixing them with the mall refuse that he knew would be picked up later that day, and dropped the apartment and car keys through a sewer grating on his way out to the street.

Then, wearing dark glasses and nondescript work clothes, he took a Greyhound bus to Millvale.

*   *   *

Meg had reserved the bridal suite in the Millvale Hotel for the senator, and at seven o'clock his party assembled there, outfitted for the occasion. The women wore cocktail dresses, and the men, including the two cops, wore three-piece suits.

Ashley, in a pearl-gray sheath that matched her eyes, was noticeably fidgety. She kept glancing in the mirror and adjusting the sequined shoulders of her dress. Meg, in deep rose-pink, came up behind her and said, "If you tug at those pads any more, you're going to look like Joan Crawford."

"I feel like Joan Crawford. What's that movie where she's going to a party full of Nazis?"

"She's doing that in about ten movies. These people are not Nazis, Ash. They all like your father a lot and they all want to give him tons of money."

"I guess I'm just running out of gas." Ashley sighed. "I'm glad this is the last major event." She glanced in the mirror and met Martin's gaze. She looked away.

"He never takes his eyes off you," Meg said to her in a low tone. "Has he said anything else about the two of you?"

Ashley shook her head. "And he won't. He tried once, and that's enough." She knew instinctively that his pride would prevent him from trying again.

The situation was in her hands.

"What are you going to do?"

"I'm going to get through tonight first," Ashley replied. "You know, it's a big hurdle for us. Lots of press coverage, the grand finale. One thing at a time."

Meg didn't push her. Instead she sniffed the air and

said, "That's your usual scent, isn't it? What happened to Carlo's?"

"I sent it back to him, told him I was allergic to it."

"You liar!" Meg said, laughing.

"I was not lying. Every time I smelled it, I remembered Tim's meeting with Carlo on the yacht and broke out in hives."

"Speaking of breaking out, have you heard from Jim?"

"He called this morning and offered to escort me tonight if I promised never to see Tim again after his assignment ended."

"I can imagine what you replied to that."

Ashley smiled thinly. "You don't see Jim here, do you?"

"I'm sorry, Ash."

"Don't be. It had to happen. You were right. It wasn't fair of me to string him along just because I wanted an acceptable escort. And I'm not about to call anyone else, either. I'm a big girl, and I can do this alone. You're going stag too, right?"

Meg nodded. "Peter won't be back until tomorrow or Saturday at the earliest."

There was a burst of laughter from the senator's corner. Ashley and Meg exchanged glances. Fair was sporting a red cummerbund, and his mood was jaunty. Too jaunty. He tended to get very up for events like the one they were about to attend, and the more up he was, the less he worried about security.

Martin stepped forward abruptly and broke through Fair's circle of advisers.

"Senator," he said, "stay inside the ballroom. Don't

go into any of the hallways; they're too enclosed. And if you go to the bathroom, take me or Sergeant Capo with you."

Joseph Fair nodded indulgently, undaunted, and returned to his conversation.

Capo looked at Martin and shrugged slightly. Martin stared back at him expressionlessly.

Tim's worried, Ashley thought. She knew that blank blue stare, and how furiously his mind was working behind it. She moved to her father's side and tapped him on the shoulder.

"Dad?"

He turned and looked down at her.

"Please listen to Lieutenant Martin. He really has your best interest at heart."

Fair smiled and bent to kiss her cheek. "Don't you worry, honey, I'll be fine."

That wasn't exactly what Ashley wanted to hear, but it would have to do.

"Well, folks, I think it's about that time," announced Roger Damico.

"I agree," said Joe Fair.

They all filed out toward the elevators.

Ransom loitered behind the cab stand in the thin rain, watching the apartment building next door to the Millvale Hotel. The doorman lounged inside the glass-fronted lobby, looking bored. People went in and out occasionally, exchanging pleasantries with the man but never providing enough of a distraction to allow Ransom to slip past.

Ransom shifted his feet. He was getting wet waiting

for the right opportunity, and time was passing quickly. Too quickly. It was already seven-fifteen, and the senator would be entering the ballroom any minute now.

Finally, at seven-twenty, an old lady tottered to the front entrance and required the doorman's assistance to inflate her umbrella and negotiate the stairs to the street. As soon as the doorman's back was turned, Ransom sprinted for the steps and shot through the double doors like a gazelle. He crossed the main lobby and headed for the back stairway, which, according to the plans he had memorized, led directly to the roof.

It all worked like an incantation until he got to the roof door, which was locked. He whipped off his jacket and wrapped it around his gun, to cushion the sound even more than the silencer would, and shot off the bolt. It hit the floor with a clatter and he kicked it aside, pushing the door open and emerging onto the roof.

It was raining even harder now, but he no longer felt the discomfort; his whole being was concentrated on accomplishing his goal. The two buildings abutted with an alley between them, in the manner of structures in cities; Millvale was an old town and predated modern fire codes. There was an opening to cross of about four feet, and he glanced down at the ground once before backing up to take a running leap and hurdle the gap like a long jumper.

He hit the roof of the hotel on a roll and then sprang up, catlike, glancing around immediately. The landscape was deserted, as he'd expected, but he still shook his head wonderingly. Why didn't these people protect themselves better? Was it so difficult to station a guard on the roof? Men like Fair made themselves sitting prey

for somebody like him, because they believed themselves invulnerable and resisted security measures. Ransom had seen it so many times, and he hoped they never
changed.

They made his job so easy.

He paused for a breather, wiping the rain from his
eyes. The fire escape was hooked over the edge of the
roof like a swimming-pool ladder. He walked over to it
and took the first step, looking down the side of the
building to count the windows and locate the second
floor. The service hallway should be just inside the window on the east side of the building, where he was.

He climbed down the ladder, listening to the street
noise get louder as he descended. Car doors were slamming as people arrived for the dinner, and snatches of
conversation drifted up to him from the walkway. He
was far enough back not to be seen, and he concentrated
on getting into the building.

He knelt in front of the selected window and took out
the fiber tape he'd brought with him, taping the glass
with long strips that converged in the center like the
spokes of a wheel. When the job was done, he traced
the diagram with a diamond-tipped knife, then aimed a
precise kick at the middle of the pane. The glass cracked
inward but did not shatter, the pieces held together by
the tape. The technique avoided the mess and noise of a
broken window.

It was a trick he'd learned in Vietnam, and it had
never failed him yet.

He picked apart the pie-shaped pieces, wrapping them
in his jacket, and squeezed through the opening he'd
created, dropping onto the wooden floor of a hallway

that smelled of age and disinfectant. Once inside the building, he leaned against the wall and closed his eyes, clearing his mind for the task ahead.

The hard part was over; all he had to do now was find the right opportunity, aim, and fire.

Downstairs, they were checking invitations, the security people flanking the great man, fanning through the crowd, believing they could protect him.

And here he sat, with murder on his mind, and a gun.

Ransom wondered briefly where Meg was, how close to Fair, and then forced himself to think about his next steps. He looked for the closet door he knew should be there, and found it. He removed the black knit hat he wore to extinguish his blond hair and keep it dry, and pushed aside cans of floor wax and semigloss paint to bury the hat with his jacket at the back of a shelf.

By the time they found the clothes—if they ever did—he'd be sunning himself on a Caribbean beach.

At the end of the hall was a larger door that opened into the second-floor corridor, which was flanked by guest rooms. He took out his pocket comb and mirror, combed his hair, and straightened the pullover sweater he was wearing over his shirt. The sweater was not wet, and his pants were thin enough to have dried very quickly.

He could pass for a hotel guest who'd been inside all night. He opened the door a crack and then emerged into an empty hallway.

All was silence.

He passed the elevator bank and walked to the stairwell, listening to the sounds of the preparations taking place below him, and settled in to wait.

The crush in the ballroom was indescribable. Martin knew that Fair thrived on such mass adulation, and tried to keep him in hand, but the senator was soon roaming indiscriminately, the two cops trailing him feverishly. Martin felt relieved when Fair finally sat down to dinner, and he and Capo stood on the sidelines, flanking the dais, as the guests ate the chicken and then applauded the senator's speech.

Ashley looked pale and small beside her father. Her stepmother, on Fair's other side, seemed almost florid by comparison.

Martin wanted Ashley so much that the longing was akin to pain. But *she* had to decide; it was out of his control now. She knew how he felt. If he thought he could bend that fragile body to his will, he would do it, but he knew that her resolution was as firm as his. He watched her, wearing her public face, and wondered what she was really thinking.

When the senator got up to go, the crowd flowed around him, and Martin and Capo sprang into action again. They followed Fair at a discreet distance, and Martin paused once to look around, then turned back to Fair. The senator was caught up in conversation and didn't seem to realize where he was going. Martin saw him greet someone at the entrance to a back corridor and then move forward again. He passed into the hall, disregarding Martin's earlier warning, and Martin ran after him, swearing under his breath, trying to close the distance between them without alarming anyone.

But he was too late. Afterward, it would seem to Martin that it had all happened in slow motion, and in silence. He saw a man rise behind Fair, saw the gun, the snub nose of the silencer. Martin charged toward the senator instantly, shoving people roughly out of his way, shouting for Capo.

Martin heard the whisk-thud of the silencer before he could reach Fair, and the sound went through him like a sliver of ice. He saw the senator drop, grabbing for Meg Drummond next to him, a scarlet flower blossoming in the center of his chest. The second shot caught Capo as he lunged in front of the falling man, trying to shield Fair with his body. Martin screamed Ashley's name as a third shot grazed her arm, stunning her. She looked around, bewildered, and turned toward the gunman as he reversed direction and melted into a hole in the crowd.

Then the film speeded up, and the sound came in suddenly, like a raised volume on a television set. Screams filled Martin's ears as he ran after the gray sweater he had seen disappearing into the sea of humanity. He broke through the knot of people and into the empty hallway, then raced up the staircase. The blank guest-room doors yielded nothing, so he dashed for the service door. He yanked it open and saw the gaping window, ran to it, and looked down. The fire escape and street were deserted, but he could see blurred footprints in the muddy grass below.

The gunman had already fled on foot.

There was no point in continuing the chase. The trail

was already cold. Martin turned and raced back down to the lobby.

"Call for an ambulance!" he shouted to the desk clerk, who stared at him in fear, alarmed by the growing confusion as the hysterical crowd began to pour out of the ballroom.

Martin ripped his badge from his pocket and shoved it under the clerk's nose.

"I'm a police officer. There's been an accident. Call for an ambulance right now," he said in as calm a tone as he could muster.

Convinced, the man lifted the receiver on the desk phone. Martin ran back into the ballroom, fighting his way through the pushing, yelling crowd to Ashley.

He'd been gone less than a minute.

She was on her knees next to her father, the blood from her abraded arm running onto her dress and pooling on the floor. Capo sprawled like a crumpled handkerchief next to them, bleeding from an abdominal wound. He appeared to be unconscious, his face heavily dewed with perspiration. Meg Drummond was holding his head in her lap and crying. Other people from the senator's group were trying to take charge of the situation, but chaos still reigned.

Martin knew at a glance that the senator was dead. His skin was like wax, and there was too much blood for him to have survived its loss. The cop felt for a pulse in the older man's throat, then bent his head to listen to his chest.

All was silence. Life had departed forever from Ashley's father.

Sylvia Fair saw the expression on Martin's face and began to sob helplessly.

Damico led her away as Martin raised Ashley to her feet. She seemed to be in shock; she stared at him stupidly.

"We have to get my father to a doctor," she said, struggling to turn back to the body.

"Ashley, he's gone. I'm sorry," Martin said gently, pulling her into his arms.

She moaned and sagged against him, closing her eyes, her body stiff with denial.

Photographers were closing in on them through the melee, flashbulbs creating small explosions of light. Reporters circled madly, firing questions with the rapidity of a ticker-tape machine.

"Stay here," Martin said, putting Ashley away from him.

She clung. "Don't leave me," she whispered.

"I'll be right back. I have to check on Capo."

"Anthony," Ashley murmured. Her gaze followed Martin as he shoved past a couple of microphones to reach Meg, who looked up at him with drowned, tragic eyes, incapable of speech.

Martin knelt next to the prone man and felt for the pulse in his wrist, which fluttered against his fingers, faint but steady. He took off his jacket and draped it over his friend's still form.

Meg's expression was beseeching.

"He's hanging in there," Martin said to her, trying to communicate a confidence he didn't feel.

Meg sobbed with relief, mopping Capo's brow with what looked like a strip of her petticoat. A larger piece of the same material was wadded up at Capo's waistline to stanch the flow of blood.

"His wife," Meg murmured, swallowing.

"I'll take care of it. Keep him warm, and don't let anyone move him. Help is on the way."

Meg nodded, looking down at her charge. Easygoing Tony, she thought, her comical nemesis, always ready with a teasing remark. She blinked rapidly as the tears began to well up once more. Where the hell was that ambulance?

When Martin approached Ashley again, it was clear that reality was setting in with terrible finality.

"Tim," she gasped, her face white. "Tell me. Is Anthony . . . ?"

"He's alive," Martin replied grimly.

"Thank God." She wove unsteadily for a moment.

He reached for her, and she fell against him as if he were the only solidity in a quaking world.

"Take it easy," Martin said. "You're okay. I'm with you."

"Get me out of here," she pleaded.

He glanced around, sizing up the situation, and then scooped her into his arms. He carried her rapidly through the crowd as Ashley buried her face against his shoulder, hiding from the press and shutting out the madness that surrounded them. Newsmen and photographers dashed past, running into the ballroom, paying no attention to Martin and his anonymous burden.

Once in the lobby, Martin set Ashley down on one of the sofas in the reception area. She hugged her torso with her arms, shivering, as he got down on one knee in front of her on the marble floor.

He searched her face as she gazed back at him unseeingly, her eyes still filled with the images of the horror in the ballroom.

"Ashley, look at me," he said in a strong tone, commanding her attention.

Her eyes focused, fixed on him.

"Are you listening?"

"I'm listening," she murmured.

"Did you see him?"

"Him?" she repeated stupidly.

"The man who shot your father, Ashley. Did you see what he looked like?"

She nodded, dazed.

"Are you sure?"

"Yes."

"Describe him to me."

"He was tall, maybe a little shorter than you are, with blond hair, fair skin. Not bad looking, actually." She shuddered at the incongruity of it.

"What was he wearing? A gray sweater?"

"Yes, with darker slacks, I think. Did you see him too?"

"Not as well as you did." Martin looked away from her, thinking. "If he wasn't disguised, he didn't expect to be seen," he added softly. "How old would you say he was?"

"Mid-thirties, maybe. Not a kid, but still young."

"Ashley, try to remember. I know it happened fast, but is there anything else you can tell me about him?"

She closed her eyes, forcing herself to relive those terrible seconds that took her father's life.

"His eyes were light, I think. Dark eyes look different

from a distance; they don't reflect the light as much. I'd say his eyes were blue or green, something pale. And that's more likely with blond hair anyway, isn't it?"

"Yes, it is. Good girl. I'll get a sketch artist to do some renderings for you, and we'll try to pin this guy down." He inched forward slightly and took both her hands in his.

"Now, Ashley, this is very important. Don't tell anyone but the police that you saw his face, that you know what he looks like. I don't care who it is. Tell no one. Do you understand me?"

She nodded solemnly, her eyes huge.

Martin was satisfied. He didn't want to take a chance on someone leaking the information that she could identify the killer. As long as the gunman didn't know he'd been seen, she should be safe.

He took her face between his hands and kissed her forehead lightly. "I'm going to bandage that arm. I'll be right back."

Ashley glanced down at the flap of flesh hanging loosely from her forearm, now oozing a thin trickle of blood. She had forgotten the wound; shock had nullified the pain.

Martin returned from the men's room and bound the cut with his wet handkerchief. The bullet had just grazed her, but the skirt of her dress, her stockings, and shoes were gory with a combination of her blood and her father's.

"Now, I have to leave you for a little while to make some calls. Will you be all right?" he said.

She nodded. "Take care of my father's . . . my father." She closed her eyes again, pressing her lips together.

Martin went back to the desk, which was now swamped with reporters vying for the house telephones. The bank of pay phones was also tied up, the center of a confusing babble of voices.

Martin grabbed the nearest desk phone out of the hand of the reporter holding it.

"Hey!" the man yelled, turning to confront Martin, who held up his shield.

"Police, buddy," he said. "Clear out."

"Wait a minute, I've got a deadline! You can't just—"

"Yes, I can," Martin replied, already punching buttons. "Unless you want to get your ass arrested for obstructing a police officer in the performance of his duty."

The reporter impugned Martin's ancestry, added something about the First Amendment, and then dashed madly for the pay phones to wait his turn.

Martin contacted the Millvale police, who had already dispatched several cars to the scene, and then called Captain Gerald Rourke in Philadelphia.

Rourke answered his own phone, unusual in itself.

"Yeah?" Rourke barked.

"Gerry, this is Martin."

"I heard," Rourke said.

"What the hell? It just happened!"

"Never mind that. Is it true he's dead?"

"Yeah, and Capo's down. I don't know how bad. Gutshot."

Rourke swore expressively. "And the Fair girl? She was hit too, wasn't she?"

"It's minor. She'll be all right." Ambulance sirens shrieked in the distance, coming closer.

Rourke sighed. "Okay. Tell me about it."

Martin described what had happened as briefly as possible, keeping editorial commentary to a minimum.

"Okay," Rourke said when Martin was finished. "That fits with what I heard. You tried, but the guy wouldn't listen to you. He was well known for that. Short of holding his hand, I don't see what you could have done. It wasn't your fault."

"I wish I felt that way," Martin said expressionlessly.

"Hey, I don't want to hear that. There'll be an IA investigation, but you'll be cleared. Everybody knew how Fair was. He had to be badgered into taking you and Capo on in the first place, and you have witnesses who heard you telling him what to do earlier tonight. He didn't follow your instructions, and that's all there is to it."

Martin was silent.

"Did you hear me, son?" Rourke demanded.

"I heard you."

"How's the girl?"

"Shaky."

"I'll bet."

"I think she'll be okay. She's stronger than she looks."

"And the wife?"

"One of the aides took her away. It wouldn't surprise me if she lost it; she's not wrapped too tight anyway."

There was a commotion at the front door of the hotel as the paramedics arrived with stretchers.

"Got to go and see about Capo. The medics are here," Martin said into the phone.

"All right."

"Gerry, please call Lorraine and . . . tell her gently, okay? Be optimistic. Tony's alive, and we all know how tough he is. That sort of thing."

"I'll call her," Rourke replied, and his tone was more compassionate than Martin had ever heard it. "Don't worry."

"Thanks."

"Keep in touch," Rourke advised him, and hung up.

Martin set the receiver in its cradle and turned back to deal with the aftermath of tragedy.

Ransom sprawled on the motel bed, fresh perspiration mingling with that which had already dried on his body. His adrenal glands were still pumping so hard that he could feel his pulse banging in his throat. He made a conscious effort to calm down, closing his eyes and relaxing his limbs. He began to tremble as his body cooled, and he pulled the threadbare spread on the bed up to his chin. He was still fully dressed, the gun concealed at his waist. He knew he would feel better if he took a hot shower, but the bathroom seemed too far away.

The water probably wouldn't be hot in this fleabag anyway, he thought. If there was water at all. Through the grimy window with its plastic curtain he could see the motel's neon sign, with two letters blacked out, announcing "Vacancies."

He had jogged the two miles from downtown Millvale to the Blue Star Motel in order to avoid using a traceable cab. He had never intended going back to the apartment, even though Meg believed he was away on a business trip.

Meg, he thought despairingly. She was the reason he had blown it, blown it sky high.

He'd had the senator in his sights, a drilled shot, when she moved between him and his target, a rosy smudge on the magnified, computerized crosshairs.

And he had hesitated, pulled back.

He could not take the chance of hitting Meg.

Then she had moved out of range, and the senator was in position again. But the timing was off; he had missed his chance. With his trained reflexes he was able to act anyway, getting off three shots, but there was a rhythm involved in the act, as in dancing, and he remained out of step. He was exposed too long in the crowd, and the shots weren't clean. Fair was dead, he'd accomplished that much, but he'd heard on the motel clerk's portable radio that both a cop and the daughter were wounded, the cop critically.

It was a sloppy job, and his trademark was precision. He had never injured anyone else but the target before, and he had never left such a mess.

He mopped his face with the sleeve of his sweater, then pulled it off over his head and dried his hair. At least nobody had seen him; none of the reports mentioned it. But he had made a mistake, and he didn't like it.

He didn't like the reason for it.

He hadn't realized how emotionally involved he was with Meg until she had drifted across his gunsights like a deep-pink sunset cloud. His trigger finger had frozen, then erupted into delayed action, and now he had a bloodbath on his hands.

Look for the woman, he thought, rolling over and

turning his face into the lumpy, foul-smelling pillow. The French proverb was correct. Meg had wormed her way into his life, not with the bold tactics others had used on him to no avail, but with a tenderness and concern that eventually left him defenseless.

Ramsom sat up abruptly, rubbing his eyes, suddenly composed enough to take charge again. He stripped off his clothes and stepped into the tepid shower, doing the best he could with the drizzle of water, ratty washcloth, and discolored sliver of soap.

He had to get out of the country, but before he could do that he had to get out of this bedbug paradise.

And he had to forget Meg Drummond.

The rest of the night was a blur for Martin. He rode in the ambulance with Ashley and her father's body; her stepmother had collapsed and was under sedation.

Meg went with Capo in the paramedics' van and to meet Lorraine Capo at the hospital.

The admissions area was swarming with reporters and federal agents by the time they arrived. The press had not been officially informed that the senator was dead, so his stretcher was whisked inside through a service entrance in order to dodge reporters.

Ashley was treated in emergency, where Martin left her in order to go with Capo, who was admitted to intensive care.

Lorraine was waiting for him there.

"Timmy," Lorraine said as he embraced her. She was trying not to cry.

"He's going to be all right, Lori, I know it," Martin

said, hugging her tightly. His expression was one of abject misery.

"I always thought that as long as he was with you, nothing would happen to him," Lorraine said as he released her.

Meg saw that this made Martin feel worse, if that was possible, and she said quickly, "Mrs. Capo, I'm Meg Drummond. Your husband regained consciousness on the ride over here. I'm sure that must be a very good sign."

Lorraine took Meg's hand and said, "Call me Lori. Mrs. Capo is my mother-in-law. Tony told me all about you. He got quite a kick out of some of the things you said." Lorraine smiled bravely.

"The kick was more than mutual, Lori," Meg replied, her throat tightening.

A doctor in surgical greens appeared and informed them that Sergeant Capo would be undergoing surgery immediately to repair a perforated intestine. The intern was reluctant to give an opinion, but when he mentioned that Capo would need several units of blood, Martin volunteered to be the donor.

He left the two women together and shortly afterward wound up in a pale-green cubicle screened off by a canvas drape. He had nothing to do for the next thirty minutes but stare at the ceiling and flex his hand as his blood ran through a plastic tube and into a plastic bag on a stand next to his cot. This gave him too much time to relive the evening's events in detail, and he was very glad to see the nurse come back to remove the needle from his arm. She taped the incision and handed him a paper cup of orange juice. He bolted the juice and dropped the cup in the trash on his way into the hall.

He found that Capo was still in surgery, and he went looking for Ashley. It was now two in the morning, and the overworked night-staff people were not at their most helpful, but he finally found her installed in a private room on the women's medical ward, guarded by a federal agent.

Martin displayed his badge for the man. "I'm Lieutenant Martin of the Philly P.D.," he said to the fed, whose plastic lapel badge proclaimed that he was Special Agent Thomas Forsyth.

Forsyth looked unimpressed.

"I'd like to speak to Miss Fair," Martin added.

"She's asleep," replied the fed, who made it clear that he was now in charge of the situation. "She's spending the night here for observation. No visitors."

"She'll see me."

"I guess I haven't made myself clear," Forsyth said. "Nobody gets in, and that's final."

"Look, I brought her here—" Martin began, but Forsyth cut him off in midsentence.

"Yeah, I heard all about it," Forsyth said sarcastically. "You were assigned to guard her and her old man, and you did such a great job that Fair's dead and she's flat on her back in the hospital with a bullet wound. If I were you, buddy. . . ."

Martin punched him so hard that he flew across the corridor and smashed into the opposite wall. He slid along it senselessly and then crumpled to the floor.

"You're not me, buddy," Martin muttered savagely as he bent to see if Forsyth was still breathing. Satisfied that he was, Martin looked up and down the deserted corridor and then hoisted the unconscious man onto his shoulder in a fireman's carry. He tried several doorknobs with his one free hand and finally dumped his burden on the floor of a linen closet and slammed the door closed.

Rubbing his sore knuckles on his shirtfront, he slipped into Ashley's room.

She was lying in the bed, dozing, her face turned toward the window. He could just make out the contours of her body under the sheet in the dimly lit room.

She looked around when she heard him come in, peering at his dark shadow backlit by the light in the corridor.

"Tim?" she said, recognizing his outline.

"Yeah."

"I thought I was dreaming." She held out her hands, and he came to her side to take them in his.

"I was so afraid they wouldn't let you in," she murmured. "I heard the doctor tell that federal man . . ."

"Shh," Martin said, holding her fingers to his lips. "Forget about him. I'm here." He let her go long enough to pull a chair up to her bed and then leaned over her again, saying anxiously, "Are you all right?"

"Oh, yes, I'm fine. The bullet just grazed my arm. The doctor insisted I spend the night, and I just didn't have the strength to fight with him. They're going to release me in the morning."

"Good."

"I've been so lonely, waiting for you," she whispered.

These were the words he had longed to hear, but he would never have wished for these circumstances to elicit them.

"I was donating blood for Capo," he explained.

"How is he?"

"They're operating on him now."

Ashley looked at him in silence until he bent his head and said in a choking voice, "I'm sorry."

She reached up to touch his hair. "It wasn't your fault, Tim. I know how hard you tried with my father, but he would never listen to you. Or anyone else, for that matter. It isn't possible to protect someone who won't cooperate. He always thought nothing could hurt him." Her voice broke. "He was wrong."

The door swung open, and a nurse entered with a hypodermic. "Here's your sedative, Miss Fair," she announced.

"Oh, please, I don't want that," Ashley said wearily. "I really don't need it."

"Doctor's orders," the nurse replied firmly. She snapped on the bed lamp and looked at Martin with a puzzled expression. "Are you the guard's replacement?"

"Yes, ma'am," Martin answered, standing, looking warningly at Ashley.

"Nurse," Ashley said quickly, "could you check with the doctor and see if I can have something to settle my stomach? I'm feeling a little nauseous."

"All right, Miss Fair," the nurse said. "I'll be back in a minute." She turned to go, then paused to say to Martin, "Aren't you supposed to be outside the room?" She marched off, her nylon uniform swishing officiously.

"Tim, how did you get rid of that guard?" Ashley hissed as soon as the nurse was out of earshot.

"I sent him for a break," Martin replied.

Ashley eyed him suspiciously.

Martin shrugged. "He wouldn't let me in to see you, so I punched him," he said like a fourth-grader confessing to a snowball fight.

"Is he all right?" she asked, alarmed.

"I knocked him out and left him to sleep it off in a linen closet across the hall."

She put her hand over her mouth, and it was a tense moment before he realized that she was laughing.

"What am I going to do with you?" she asked fondly.

"At another time, I'd give you an answer to that question," he said seriously.

The nurse returned, and Martin didn't wait for her to take issue with his presence again.

"I'll be back," he said to Ashley, and went into the hall as the nurse prepared to administer the injection.

He was met by an FBI section chief who informed him that his lack of cooperation with the federal authorities had been noted and that he had two minutes to exit the building or federal assault charges would be filed against him.

He checked with Lorraine Capo on his way out and found that her husband was in recovery and holding his own.

Meg had already left the hospital to take charge of the staff people and pick up the pieces.

As Martin walked past the admitting desk, he saw Agent Forsyth holding an ice pack to his swollen jaw.

Martin kept walking.

There were three messages from Captain Rourke when he returned to the Millvale Hotel at 4:15 A.M. The local police had long since cleared the ballroom and cordoned off the murder scene, but patrolmen still milled about the lobby, conversing on walkie-talkies.

Martin got the house key from the desk clerk, who recognized him, and went up to Ashley's suite, walking through the sitting area and going into her bedroom.

He was the only one of the group at the hotel; everybody else was either at the hospital or in the hospital.

The senator's aides and advisers and hangers-on had all dispersed, to regroup, rethink, and ultimately fasten their political ambitions to somebody else.

Martin tossed the messages into the wastebasket and undressed rapidly, climbing into Ashley's bed.

The sheets smelled like her, and, thus comforted, he fell asleep.

The ringing phone woke him less than three hours later at seven-fifteen.

"What are you doing in the Fair girl's room?" Rourke barked.

"She's in the hospital. The bed was empty. I felt like a change from the sofa in the sitting room, okay?" Martin responded hoarsely, peering at the clock in disbelief. It seemed as if he'd been asleep for about ten minutes.

"What the hell is going on down there?" Rourke demanded. "I just got a call from some fed who wants to roast you on a spit."

"I had a little trouble with one of them last night," Martin told him, yawning until his jaw creaked.

"So I gathered. It sounds like it was more than a little trouble. Let me have your version."

"I came to the hospital with Capo and the Fair girl, and then later when I went to check on her they had this agent stationed outside her room and he wouldn't let me in to see that she was okay."

"And?" Rourke prompted him.

"And so I decked him and hid him in a closet."

There was a long sigh from the other end of the line. "I suppose it was out of the question for you to take his word for it that the girl was all right?"

"She was my responsibility, and I wanted to see for myself."

"Couldn't you have handled it a little more diplomatically?" Rourke said, exasperated.

"I wasn't feeling very diplomatic," Martin answered testily.

"Okay, okay, forget about that. Get over to the local FBI office downtown first thing this morning and straighten it out. They want a statement on exactly what you saw last night when the senator got it. They're taking over the case."

Martin sat up in bed. "What about me?"

"You're out of it."

"Wait a minute . . ." Martin began tensely.

"Forget it," Rourke broke in brusquely, losing patience. "That's all she wrote."

"I see. One try, I blow it, and it's over? No chance to follow through and get the bastard who did it?"

"It's not like that, Tim. You didn't blow anything. I told you in the beginning that if anything happened, the feds would take over. It's procedure."

"Don't give me procedure, Gerry. I know when I'm being dumped for dead weight."

"And you don't give me any lip," Rourke replied. "Do what I told you and then go to the hospital and

check on Capo. I want a report by five P.M. today, and I
want your carcass back in my office by tomorrow."

The phone went dead in Martin's ear.

He slammed the receiver into its cradle and lay still
for several moments, thinking, before he got up to
dress.

Meg returned to the hospital a few hours later and
was in the waiting room, nursing a lukewarm cup of
coffee, when Lorraine Capo joined her.

"Tony's in and out. The doctor says it will be a little
while before he's completely awake."

Meg nodded. Their common tragedy had made them
instant friends.

"He also told me the senator's daughter's going
home," Lorraine added.

"Good." Meg stood and stretched. "I'd like to make a
phone call," she said.

"Go ahead," Lorraine answered. "I'm just going to be
marking time until Tony wakes up again anyway."

Meg walked down the hall to the wall of public
phones. She had changed to slacks and a sweater, but
she realized, almost laughing, that she was still wearing
the peau de soie slippers that had matched her pink
dress.

She needed to talk to Peter. She wasn't sure if he was
still out of town, but he must have heard about the senator and perhaps had tried to contact her.

Maybe his office knew something.

She dialed the number on his business card and heard
a series of bell-like tones.

"The number you have reached is no longer in service," a mechanical voice said. "Please check the listing with your local directory."

Meg broke the connection and tried again. Same response.

That was odd. Could his office have moved during the last couple of days? She dialed Ransom's home number and, instead of getting his answering machine, she got the sound of incessant ringing until she hung up.

Coincidence? Ransom might have forgotten to put the machine on when he left home for his trip, but she had never known it to be disconnected.

Meg turned away from the telephone with a troubled expression. She was walking slowly back to the waiting room when Lorraine intercepted her.

"Tony's awake, and he wants to talk to you," she said.

Meg followed the other woman to Capo's room. He smiled weakly at his wife, but his expression changed when he saw Meg.

"Make it fast. Don't tire him out," a nurse said as she pulled back the curtain around his bed. In her hand she held a basin that contained a stained, discarded dressing.

"Boyfriend," Capo said thickly, looking at Meg.

The two women exchanged glances.

"Where . . . is he?" Capo added.

"What is he saying?" Lorraine asked.

Meg shrugged.

"New boyfriend, flowers. Where is he . . . now?" Capo insisted.

"He's out of town," Meg answered, catching on.

"Tell Martin," Capo whispered.

"Why?" Meg asked.

"Tell Tim," Capo repeated.

"Tell him what?" Meg asked.

Capo's eyes closed.

"That's it, ladies," the nurse said, ushering them briskly back into the hall.

"What do you suppose he meant?" Meg asked Capo's wife.

"He's delirious," Lorraine replied. "Don't pay any attention. He doesn't know what he's saying."

Meg wasn't so sure.

By the time Martin got to the hospital later that day, Ashley had been discharged. He found out that Capo's condition had improved slightly and talked to Lorraine, who told him that Meg had gone back to the hotel to pack before going on to campaign headquarters. Martin returned to the hotel also, and discovered that both women were already gone. The suites were empty, and no one would tell him a thing.

The message was clear. The FBI was now in charge, and he was, indeed, out of it.

Martin disregarded that message and drove his unmarked department car to the Fair estate on the outskirts of Harrisburg. He was stopped at the gate for a repeat performance of the scene outside Ashley's hospital room, but this time he managed to elicit the information that Miss Fair was at the house and convinced the agent to call her.

The fed was an inexperienced kid and obviously afraid to do the wrong thing by turning Martin, a Philadelphia police lieutenant, away without checking.

"The maid said Miss Fair would like you to come up to the house, Lieutenant Martin," the kid said, hanging up the gate phone in surprise and turning back to Martin.

"Thanks." Martin got back into his car and the fed escorted him up the long, winding drive, bordered on either side by elm trees, to the front of the house. It was a huge brick colonial with a mansard roof and enameled double doors. A uniformed maid admitted them. The fed stepped back as Martin followed her through a marble-floored entry hall and into a walnut-paneled study on the left.

Ashley was there, with her mother and a college-age stepbrother Martin recognized from pictures.

James Dillon was also present.

"What is he doing here?" Dillon said bitterly as Martin entered the room and Ashley came forward to greet him.

She was wearing a navy dress that made her look sapling slender, and her hair was drawn back behind her ears. A white bandage encircled her right forearm.

"I asked him here," Ashley replied quickly.

"Hasn't he done enough?" Dillon demanded of her. He turned to Martin. "The senator is dead because of you. Do we all have to be reminded of that?"

Martin's fists balled at his sides, and he took a step forward.

Ashley moved in front of him.

"My father is dead because he disobeyed Lieutenant Martin's direct orders," she said fiercely to Dillon. "If Dad had done as he was told, he would be alive right now." Her face contorted, and she put her hand to her mouth.

Dillon looked from her to Martin, then turned away and strode from the room. The others moved to Ashley as if to comfort her, but she composed herself and said quietly, "I'd like to be alone with Lieutenant Martin, if you don't mind. Would you please excuse us?"

Her tone was polite, but there was no mistaking the undercurrent of authority. She spoke with the expectation of being obeyed, out of long habit, and they responded to her as if to royalty, withdrawing with murmured replies.

The instant they were alone, Ashley rushed into Martin's arms.

"Where were you?" she whispered desperately. "Where did you go? I needed you."

"I didn't know where you went when you left the hospital," he replied, closing his eyes and burying his mouth in her fragrant hair. "I just took a chance and came here."

"I left a message for you with one of those agents."

"I never got it," Martin said, suspecting what had happened to it.

"How is Anthony?" she asked, clinging to him, rubbing her cheek on the lapel of his jacket.

"Hanging on. A little better, actually. His wife was with him all night." He held her off and looked into her face. "Did you talk to the FBI, tell them what you know?"

She nodded.

"But you didn't talk to anyone else about it?"

"No." She looked up at him. "Can you stay for the funeral?"

"I have to be back in Philly tomorrow."

She searched his face. "I'm being selfish, I know, but your presence would have made it so much easier to bear." Her eyes filled, and Martin drew her close, overcome by the scent and feel of her. He knew the timing was all wrong, he knew everything was all wrong, but he simply couldn't hold back another second. The fear he'd felt when he saw the gunman aiming at her, his frustration at their separation, overwhelmed him and he kissed her.

Ashley's mouth opened under his, sweet beyond imagining. She responded avidly, giving vent to frustrated desire, affirming the life she'd come close to losing. His lips moved wildly to her throat, her hair, and she yielded, matching him caress for caress until he was breathing harshly and she could hardly stand without his assistance.

"Stay with me," she said against his mouth. "Please stay with me here, now. Don't leave me again."

He looked down at her. "No more doubts, Ashley? I've been waiting for you to tell me what you want."

"Oh, Tim, forgive me," she murmured, turning her head to kiss his cheek. "I was acting like a child, worrying about trifles. This is what counts, what we feel for each other."

"Yes, yes."

"Everything else is unimportant, darling, I know that now. Last night put things in perspective for me. All I want is you."

They heard voices in the hall, and Ashley drew back.

He followed after her blindly, his mouth moving inside the neckline of her dress.

"Will you stay?" she whispered, reaching up to cover his seeking lips with her hand.

He nodded, not trusting his voice.

She released him and pressed a button on an intercom sitting on her father's desk.

"Elsie, can you come to the study, please?" she said into it.

Martin heard a faint response.

"Go upstairs with Elsie, and I'll get rid of the others," she told Martin, turning to him again and kissing him lightly. "I'll join you as soon as I can."

Seconds later, the maid knocked on the door.

"Elsie, please take Lieutenant Martin up to the green sitting room," Ashley said.

The maid, who was well trained, responded with impassive politeness, leading the way.

As Martin passed Ashley, she murmured, "I won't be long."

Martin followed the maid up a grand curving staircase to the second floor. They went down a wide corridor flanked by doors on either side and carpeted with Oriental rugs. At the end of the hall, the maid turned the handle of a white-paneled door edged with gilt.

"Please wait in here," she said, and turned away.

Martin entered, looking around at the room, which seemed like a set piece in a museum. A pale-green Aubusson rug complemented the leaf-green flowered wallpaper and cream-yellow silk drapes. He sat gingerly on the edge of a brocade love seat, wondering what he was doing in this mansion and if he had really just embraced the daughter of the house.

He felt like a sharecropper come to receive his percentage from the landed gentry.

But he could still taste Ashley's kisses on his mouth, and so he waited.

CHAPTER
Eight

ASHLEY WALKED into the living room, where her stepmother and stepbrother were talking in subdued tones. They both looked up as she entered.

"You'll have to go without me this afternoon," Ashley said. "I'd like to stay here, if you don't mind. We won't be finalizing the funeral arrangements until tomorrow, so I don't think my presence today is necessary."

Her two companions exchanged glances.

"Ashley, James has left," her stepmother said in a puzzled tone. The older woman looked drained by her recent ordeal; she was carefully made up, as always, but cosmetics could not conceal her pallor or the contrasting dark shadows under her eyes.

"I see," Ashley said neutrally.

"I'm sure he understands that you're upset," Sylvia continued uncertainly.

"Ash, this policeman," her son Charles interrupted, glancing at his mother.

"What about him?" Ashley said, looking from one to

the other challengingly, daring them to take issue with Martin's presence.

"Ashley, what is he doing here? The federal authorities have taken over. He's off the case," Sylvia said.

"He is here as my guest," Ashley said.

"Your guest? What does that mean?" Sylvia demanded.

"Do you need a definition, Sylvia? There's a dictionary over there on the shelf behind the desk."

"I don't think you need to take that tone with my mother," Charles said stiffly. "She's just had a terrible shock, suffered an awful experience, and . . ."

"Tell me all about it, junior. I was there," Ashley said to him sarcastically.

"There's no need to do this," Sylvia interjected. "I was merely inquiring about the propriety of having that man here."

"Propriety? Is Miss Manners standing behind the drapes, taking notes?" Ashley snapped.

"Ashley, that cop was supposed to be guarding my father, and my father is dead," Charles announced with that juvenile pomposity that always made Ashley want to smack him. "Do you really think you should be entertaining him in this house after that? Personally, I can't believe he had the nerve to come here."

Ashley whirled on him immediately and said crisply, "Oh, stuff it, Charles."

Sylvia stared, amazed, and Charles looked dumbfounded. What on earth had gotten into sedate, controlled Ashley, who had handled even her father's assassination with minimal loss of composure? Now she was going to make a scene over this?

"You don't have a clue as to what happened in Millvale," Ashley continued, still addressing the boy. "As I recall, you were disporting yourself at a fraternity mixer last night while 'that cop' was risking his life to protect a public figure who resisted every effort to ensure his own safety. And as to whom I should be 'entertaining' in this house, I think I'm a better judge of that than you are, since I was living right here with our mutual father before your mother, much less you, ever crossed his line of vision."

Sylvia gasped aloud.

"Furthermore," Ashley said in conclusion, "as I'm sure you're aware, Dad's will gives me a life estate in this house. So both of you are here on sufferance, not by invitation."

The silence in the parlor was like a thunderclap.

"Now, if you'll excuse me," Ashley said coolly, "I'll say good-bye. Please leave word with Elsie if you need to contact me about the plans for Dad's service."

Ashley swept from the room, leaving Sylvia and her son to stare after her in shock.

In the hall she ran into the maid, an unflappable woman in her fifties with iron-gray hair and the serious demeanor of an expatriate nun.

"Elsie," Ashley said, "I don't want to be disturbed this afternoon for any reason. I will not be receiving visitors, and please take messages if anyone calls."

"Yes, ma'am."

Ashley almost ran up the stairs, feeling guilty for asking the maid to handle her condolence calls. But the urge to be with Martin dominated everything else. The night without him had been awful; the thought of a future without him was even worse. Life was too short; her father's had already ended, and she was determined to make the most of hers.

No one was going to keep her away from Tim today.

She entered the green room to find him looking out the window at the lush, rolling lawn.

He turned and faced her as she locked the door.

"I feel like I don't belong here," he said, gesturing helplessly at the elaborate furnishings.

"Do you feel like you belong with me?" Ashley asked softly, going to him and putting her arms around his waist.

He pulled her close and said, "I guess the others were as thrilled with my visit as Dillon, huh?"

"*I'm* thrilled with your visit. Forget the others. Forget everyone but you and me."

He didn't need to hear any more. When he kissed Ashley, her mouth opened under his in tender welcome.

She felt warm and alive and seductive in his arms. He preferred to go slow and be gentle; he wanted everything to be perfect for her. But it had seemed like forever since he had desired a woman so urgently and so completely.

"I need . . ." he said against her mouth.

"I know what you need," she whispered back. "I need it too."

He bent his head and ran his lips along the line of her throat as she sighed deeply, sinking her fingers into the wealth of hair at the nape of his neck. Ashley arched her back and bent like a bow over his supporting arm as he lowered his mouth to her breasts, nuzzling them through the thin cloth of her dress. She held still as he ran her

zipper down its track. Then she shrugged her shoulders
to let the rustling silk fall in a puddle to the carpet.

Underneath she was wearing a camisole and pants.
Martin reached for the little pearl buttons on the sheer
bodice, but his large fingers felt like sausages and made
no progress with the tiny, elusive fasteners. As impa-
tient as he, Ashley slid her smaller hand under his and
tugged hard, sending a spray of buttons flying to the
floor.

Martin pushed the covering material aside quickly,
separating it to reveal her breasts, small and rounded,
perfectly shaped, with dusky satin nipples. He had one
in his mouth almost before he'd seen it, covering her
other breast with his free hand.

Ashley gasped at the contact and swayed unsteadily
as he bent and slipped his arm under her knees, raising
his head to negotiate their passage as he carried her
through the sitting-room door and into the adjacent bedroom.

He brought her to the four-poster and set her on the
bed, releasing her just long enough to yank off his
jacket and tie. When he joined her, she pulled him down
with her and they sprawled full length on the lace coverlet.

He kissed her again, lingeringly, and then turned his
attention once more to her breasts. He laved the pouting
nipples with his tongue until they were drenched and
swollen and sensitized to a point just below pain. Ashley lay supine, pinned by his weight, her eyes slitted
and her breath coming in increasingly short bursts.
When Martin moved his head to plant a row of kisses on
the soft flesh of her shoulder, she hooked her arms

around his neck and sat up, pressing her lips to the pounding pulse in his throat.

"Take off your shirt," she murmured. "I want to see you again."

He tilted his head back to expose his skin to her exploring mouth, running his fingers down the satiny expanse of her naked back, too absorbed in touching her to free his hands and obey.

"I'll do it," she added. "I'm a little better with buttons than you are." She undid the shirt and pulled it off him, then hugged him tightly, rubbing her cheek on his chest, enjoying the feel of his smooth skin roughened by the thatch of black hair.

"Oh, you're beautiful," she murmured, overcome with longing. "I remembered how beautiful you are."

He tugged on her hair to make her look up at him.

"Ashley, I have to tell you . . . I have to say . . ." he began huskily, then stopped abruptly as words failed him.

She put her finger to his lips.

"Don't talk," she told him softly. "I feel the same way you feel. Just love me, darling. That says it all."

He was eager to comply, pressing her back into the bed and taking off the rest of her clothes. When she was nude, he stared down at her, then slowly traced the firm line of her waist and hips with the back of his hand.

"Your skin is like milk, so perfectly white all over, not a mark," he murmured in wonderment. "I'm almost afraid to touch you."

"Touch me," Ashley replied huskily, taking his hand and placing it on the mound of light brown hair at the apex of her legs.

He turned his hand, slipping it between her thighs, and she moaned aloud and returned the pressure when he felt her readiness.

Martin made a sound deep in his throat and bent swiftly, wrapping his arms around Ashley's hips and lifting her off the bed. When his mouth made contact with her, she gasped at the sudden sensation of wet heat, then went limp with pleasure. She bit her lip, incapable of speech, until the need to have him with her, in her, became insupportable, and she clawed at his shoulders, forcing him to raise his head.

"Please," she said, the throaty voice hardly recognizable as her own. "Now, Tim, please."

He stood quickly and unbuckled his belt, taking off the rest of his clothes as she watched him expectantly, her expression besotted, almost drugged. When he finally moved over her, she clutched him desperately, sighing with satisfaction as he covered her slight body with his larger, harder one.

Ashley closed her eyes luxuriously. This was the way a man was supposed to feel, taut and muscular and enveloping.

Martin pushed himself up with one arm and pulled her into the cradle of his hips. She traced his spine with her thumbs; it was slick with sweat and as rigid as steel.

He looked down into her eyes as he entered her, and they both gasped aloud with the sensation.

Martin pressed his flushed, hot face into the hollow of her shoulder, and she kissed the side of his neck, tasting the musk and salt of his perspiration.

He pulled back slightly as she locked her legs tightly across his lower back.

"I love you, Tim," she whispered, and then gave herself up to a world of sensation.

Martin awoke around sunset. Ashley was curled into his side fast asleep, her cooling skin still dewed with their lovemaking. He needed a cigarette desperately, but his jacket was crumpled on the floor by the foot of the bed and he didn't want to disturb her to get it. So he watched the slanting reddish rays of the sun coming through the drapes until the light faded to gray and Ashley stirred against him. She blinked, looked around, and then stared up into his face.

"It is you," she whispered.

He smiled down at her.

"You're really here."

"I really am."

She turned slightly, trailing her nails across his chest and kissing his shoulder. "I was afraid I was dreaming."

"It's no dream."

"It used to be. I thought about this all the time," Ashley said, settling against his shoulder.

"Me too," he replied, kissing the top of her head. "I never believed it would happen."

"I was afraid it never would." Ashley sighed, closing her eyes.

"How do you feel?"

"Happy. So happy."

Martin was silent, stroking her bare arm. His fingers touched the small bandage a couple of inches above her wrist.

She moved to look at him. "Does it seem wrong to be so happy when my father was just killed?"

"I don't know. I do know that nothing we do or refrain from doing will ever bring him back."

"It's very strange, really, but I have never felt so alive," she murmured.

He set her aside and climbed out of the bed to get his jacket. "It's not so strange," he replied, locating his cigarettes and extracting one from the pack. "Survival syndrome. I experienced it in Vietnam. You saw someone killed, you're glad it wasn't you, and you want to affirm the life you still have." He sat next to her and struck a match, lighting his cigarette.

"Is that where you got this?" she asked, touching the ridge of scar tissue on his right thigh. "Vietnam?"

He nodded. "Mortar shell."

"You must have been very young."

"Eighteen at the time of the Tet offensive."

"Just a kid."

"We were all kids. All kids, and scared to death."

"You still like that music, from the sixties."

"It's about the only good memory I have of that time."

"The sixties are coming back in a big way now, movies and television shows set during that period. How do you feel about all of them?"

"I don't watch them. As far as I'm concerned, the sixties can stay dead. The war and the riots, the assassination of the Kennedys and Martin Luther King . . ." He stopped, realizing what he had said.

"It's all right, go on," Ashley said quietly.

"I didn't mean to remind you of your father."

"I understand. You were talking about the past." She

paused thoughtfully. "So I guess that makes you about thirty-eight now, right?" she said.

"Thirty-nine in about two months," he said, exhaling a stream of smoke.

"When you graduated from high school, I was in fourth grade."

"I think it's a little late to tell me I'm too old for you," he observed dryly.

"I wouldn't consider it. But how come no silver in that beautiful black hair? I thought the Celts were world famous for their premature gray."

"If you keep working me over like you just did, I'll be completely white in no time."

"That's not funny," she said archly, trying not to laugh as she registered his teasing expression. "I think you would look very distinguished with a little frosting at the temples."

"I'll talk to my genes and see what we can do about it."

"What about your mother? Is she dark like you?"

He shook his head. "Blond."

"My color?"

"No, strawberry. Freckles. My brother looks like her."

"Where does she live now?"

"With my sister. They have a two-family house in Abington. She baby-sits for Maureen's kids a lot."

"Do you see much of them?"

He shrugged. "Holidays." He looked down at her. "Am I being interrogated? I feel like I should have a strong white light shining in my face."

"I just want to know all about you."

"You do. I think you knew all about me the first time you looked at me."

She smiled. "Not quite. But I did think you were very cute."

"Cute?" He raised his brows.

"All right. Devastatingly, overwhelmingly sexy."

"That's better."

"And what did you think of me?"

"Fishing for compliments?"

"I just gave you one."

He fixed her with his blue stare and said flatly, "The first time I saw you, I thought I was in serious trouble."

"Why?" she murmured, watching his face and thinking that he had little gift for small talk; he was blunt. Whereas she enjoyed listening to amusing chatter from other people, she found his directness refreshing and endearing.

"I knew I would have to spend a lot of time with you," he said. "I felt . . ."

"What?" she prodded.

"Drawn to you. Very powerfully. And with Dillon on the scene and the whole situation, it just seemed . . . hopeless."

"It wasn't," Ashley said softly. "Here we are."

He didn't answer.

She watched his movements as he smoked, and added languidly, "I love your hands. I told Meg that I was having erotic fantasies about your hands. I'm sure she thought I was deranged."

"Do lady lawyers have fantasies like that?"

"This one does." She sat up and studied his face in

the dim light. "Do you remember that weekend I spent on the family yacht just before the auction?"

He nodded.

"I tormented myself the whole time you were gone. I had visions of you sleeping with a parade of gorgeous creatures during your nights away from me."

"I went to Capo's house for dinner and played with his kid's trains," Martin said, laughing.

"Well, I didn't know!" Ashley shook her hair back from her face impatiently, remembering her anguish. "I even thought you might call Carmen Hughes."

"Now *that* might not have been a bad idea," Martin said, smiling slyly. He dragged deeply on his cigarette.

Ashley punched him playfully. "So you haven't forgotten her!"

"How could I forget a body like that?"

"I beg your pardon. You practically broke your leg trying to get away from her, Lieutenant."

"Then why did you think I would call her?"

"Jealousy, I suppose. I certainly knew she would be receptive. I guess I was paranoid."

"Sounds like it." He stubbed out his cigarette in the bedside tray and pulled her down next to him. "I was the one with reason to be jealous, watching you with Dillon all the time. It drove me wild." He buried his nose in her hair, inhaling its fragrance.

"It's over with Jim, you know that," Ashley said. "But he's still a friend, and I guess I should have expected him to show up here when he heard what happened." She pressed her lips together in distaste. "I'm so sorry about what he said to you."

"Forget it. And don't worry about that Hughes dame. I like my women a little less . . ."

"Forward?" Ashley suggested after a pause. "Obvious?"

He grinned.

"I know your style," Ashley said, reaching up to trace his lips with a delicate fingertip. "You like to take a ladylike type and break her down in bed."

"How did you ever guess?" he muttered, lowering himself on top of her.

She wound her bare legs around his hips. "After this afternoon, it wasn't difficult." She kissed him lingeringly. "I can't imagine being with anyone else but you now. I feel like I've been branded, marked indelibly for life."

"You have," he said huskily. He lifted her to meet his thrust, and she arched like a cat to receive him.

"Enough talk," he murmured.

Ashley could not disagree.

About an hour later, Ashley rolled over and said, "I'm starving."

"What a surprise. How long since your last meal this time?"

She propped her elbows on his chest and stared down into his face. "Can you honestly tell me you're not hungry?"

He lifted his head and kissed her lightly. "I can honestly tell you that I am."

"Good. I'll call down to Elsie for a snack."

He watched as she got out of bed and wrapped the

sheet around her. She went to a phone on a small gilt table and pressed a button.

"Elsie, could you bring a tray of sandwiches and a pot of coffee up to the green suite for me?" she said into the receiver.

Martin observed as Ashley listened to the response.

"Yes," she said. "Fifteen minutes would be just fine. Thank you, Elsie."

"So that's how you do it, huh?" Martin said admiringly from the bed. "So easy."

"Do what?"

Martin ignored the question. "Do you think Elsie could come to my apartment?" he asked ingenuously. "She could make herself very useful; there's quite a lot to do. Actually I could use a whole team of Elsies, one to cook the meals, one to wash my dirty gym clothes, maybe even one to go to the record store and get me some new tapes when I don't have the time for it."

Ashley came back to the bed and sat next to him. "All right, all right, I get the idea." She took his hand and held it to her cheek. "It really bothers you, doesn't it? The difference between us."

He withdrew his hand; she didn't try to hold it. "Ashley," he said, "at my place when you want a sandwich you get up and make one. And if there's no stuff in the refrigerator or there's no bread, or it's moldy, or the cheese is bad, you go down to the deli. If the deli's closed or it's too cold out or you forgot to cash a check, you do without the sandwich. I'm just not used to this."

"It doesn't have to affect us," she said quietly. "I don't live like this all the time. I have my own apartment in Georgetown. I work. This is my father's life-style, not mine."

"But you fall right into it when you're here, and you did grow up with it."

"Are you going to punish me for that now?" she asked, frowning at the unfairness of it.

"Baby, I don't want to punish you," he said, touching her hair. "It just disturbs me. I can't help it; I can't see where this is going to go."

"This?"

"Us," he replied.

She dropped the sheet and crawled into his arms. "It will go wherever we want it to go, won't it? *We're* in control, not the rest of the world."

"I'm afraid that's where you're wrong," he murmured, his fingers trailing down her arm.

"What do you mean?" she asked anxiously.

He could see that he was upsetting her, and she had been through enough in the past couple of days. He released her and got up, looking around for his clothes. He rescued his wrinkled pants from the floor where they had landed in a heap.

"I think I'll take a shower before the food comes," he said. "I've got to get on the road soon. The bathroom's through there, isn't it?"

Ashley nodded, her expression withdrawn.

"Be right back," he said, and left her alone. She heard the water begin to run next door seconds later. Her eyes roamed the familiar room, then settled on the patterned rug morosely.

Physically she was relaxed and sated, deliciously comfortable, with a subtle edge that subconsciously waited for Martin again. Now that she had experienced him, the thought of doing so again made her weak with anticipation. She was hooked; satisfaction of her desire for him had not cloyed, but rather whetted, her appetite for more of the same. In that respect, her time with him had been all she could have wanted.

But still her mind was racing with unsettling thoughts, not only about her father's recent death but about the man whose bed she had just left.

It was certainly curious. Out of all the men she had met in her life, she wound up falling for a macho cop who thought her family was effete and indulged, who actually objected to servants and mansions and yachts. Everyone else she knew would have taken those things for granted, or else been impressed by such evidence of wealth. Not Martin. His sense of fairness, or decency, or whatever it was, objected to the excesses of the haves in a world of have-nots. Whereas she could understand his attitude, and even respected him for it, she was terribly afraid that in the end it would take him away from her. She could not change what she was, where she came from and what she had been, and she feared that a part of him would always resent her background.

The water shut off as she stood and slipped into Martin's shirt, buttoning it up the front on the wrong side and rolling the sleeves to her elbows.

When he stepped into the room, he was wearing his pants, barefoot, and toweling his damp hair. He stopped and surveyed her appreciatively from head to foot.

"You look better in that than I ever did," he said.

"On second thought, I'll change to my dress. Elsie overlooks a lot, but I don't want to push it."

"What do you imagine she thinks we've being doing up here?" Martin asked her, smiling.

"She won't have to guess if I answer the door in your shirt," Ashley replied dryly.

She retrieved her dress and slipped into it. When she returned to him, he dropped his towel and zipped the dress up the back. Then he put his arms around her waist from behind.

Ashley turned her head to look up at him. His hair was curling in glistening ringlets, and his lavish eyelashes were still clumped and beaded with water.

"Mmm, you smell so good," she said, resting her head back against his bare shoulder.

"I found some regular soap in the closet. There was a dish of seashell-shaped things in the shower, but they kept squirting out of my hands. Smelled a little swishy, too."

"Regular soap?" she asked.

"Yeah, you know. A bar, in a wrapper, the kind you buy in a supermarket. No fancy stuff."

"That's my man," Ashley said fondly. "No fancy stuff."

There was a knock at the door.

"Elsie?" Martin said in a dramatic stage whisper. "I sure hope it's not a raid."

Ashley threw him a dirty look as she opened the door and took the tray from the maid. She set it on the nightstand next to the bed and poured coffee from the silver server into ivory china cups with a deep-blue intaglio border.

"Here you go," she said, handing a cup to Martin.

He sipped from it, watching her over its rim. "Ashley, we have to talk about your father."

She closed her eyes, then bent briskly to unwrap a sandwich. "Can't I just be happy a little while longer?" she asked distantly, not looking at him.

"I'm sorry, but you must know this. I'm going to see Rourke tomorrow to get reinstated on the case."

Ashley's hand paused with half of the chicken sandwich partway to her mouth. "What do you mean? The federal people have taken it over, haven't they?"

"That doesn't matter."

"I think it may matter to them," Ashley said quietly, her eyes on his face. She was losing her appetite.

Martin put down his cup and came to her, taking her by the shoulders and turning her to face him.

"Ashley, listen to me. It was my case. I was assigned to protect your father, and now he's dead. Capo was seriously injured and almost died. You may not like what Dillon said earlier today, but there is some truth in it. I'm not letting them take this case away from me."

"I don't think you'll have anything to say about it," Ashley replied, alarmed by his tone.

"I'm going to get the guy who did this personally," Martin concluded almost to himself, as if she hadn't spoken.

Ashley didn't respond. She looked away, her whole being flooding with fear.

He took her by the chin and turned her to face him. "What?" he asked softly.

"I'm afraid for you. My father is already dead. I couldn't bear to lose you too. Not now."

He pulled her into his arms. "You're not going to lose

me. A dozen crooks behind bars at this very moment thought they had my name on a bullet. I'm lucky. I've always been lucky."

Ashley was silent, her eyes filling with tears. He sounded just like her father.

"Will you change your plans and stay the night?" she whispered, clinging to him, blinking rapidly to dispel the tears before he saw them. "Please?"

Martin hesitated. He wanted to get things straightened out with Rourke as soon as possible, but the invitation to spend the night with her was far too alluring to refuse. And he could sense how much she needed him.

"All right," he said. "I'll drive back to the city in the morning."

Ashley curled her arms around his neck and held him as tightly as she could.

For the moment, she would have to be satisfied with that.

Ransom sat in the airport lounge, waiting for his flight. It was the middle of the night, and the other travelers were scattered about the waiting area, napping or reading. He consulted the schedule monitor again, and it showed that his plane to Switzerland was still on time.

There were several hideouts he used after a hit; he changed them frequently for variety as well as safety. This time he was going to Lucerne, to ski in the mountains where there was snow year round and to check personally on his bank account in town.

He wanted to make certain that his clients had paid promptly and in full.

He propped his feet on his overnight case and unzipped his jacket restlessly. He had ditched the clothes he'd worn in Millvale and changed after his unsatisfactory motel shower, but he still felt grimy and unsettled. He was waiting for the letdown, the sense of peace and relief that usually followed a successful hit, but it would not come.

Meg weighed heavily on his mind.

He couldn't dismiss her, as he had all the others. Several times he'd found himself thinking that in six months or a year, after the furor had died down, he could find her again. He would invent some explanation for his disappearance and pick up where they had left off, try to become what she thought he was.

Ransom shifted in the stiff-backed chair and took out his cigarettes, shaking one loose from the pack. He knew, of course, that such an idea was insane. He could never reenter the lives of those he had used for a hit and left behind; to them he had to be dead. But he kept teasing himself with the possibility, even though he was aware that the issue was academic: Meg wouldn't love him if she knew the truth.

Ransom registered the No Smoking sign over his head and dropped his unused cigarette into a standing ashtray next to him in disgust. He didn't want to attract attention, so he wasn't going to violate any rules.

He looked around the lounge in boredom.

The lone ticket agent behind the airlines desk was watching a black-and-white portable television. The airwaves were filled with stories about the assassination, and Ransom had heard the same facts parroted over and over again during the trip to the airport on the cab radio. Now an announcer concluded a recap of the senator's life and accomplishments by saying, "This exemplary public servant will be sorely missed. And of course the hunt is still on for Fair's assassin, and that search has taken a turn for the better in recent hours. It has been reported that the senator's daughter, Ashley Fair, is an eyewitness with a complete description of the man who so brutally ended her father's life. The authorities are pursuing all avenues . . ."

Ransom straightened, his feet dropping from the bag to the floor. He picked up the satchel and stood in one smooth movement. His expression had not changed, but his mind was racing.

So the daughter had seen him; the cops must have let that slip. He had known that he was in view too long, but thought that for once in his solitary, friendless life, luck had been with him.

He wasn't going to Switzerland or anywhere else. The first rule of his business was to leave no witnesses to identify him in court. The police might have a description or a sketch, but if they didn't have a warm body to sit in the big chair and tell a jury he was the killer, the whole picture changed.

He had to silence Ashley Fair. Her father's murder was a capital crime with a prominent, wealthy, and politically connected victim. The case would receive priority attention; the FBI would never stop looking for him.

Ransom shoved his unused boarding pass into his pocket and strode toward the terminal door.

When Ashley awoke in the morning and found Martin gone, she was disappointed but not surprised.

He had left no note, and she hadn't expected one.

She went back to her own room to shower and dress. She was contemplating going downstairs to face her stepmother over the breakfast table when the telephone rang.

It was Meg.

"How are you?" Ashley asked quickly. She felt a sudden stab of remorse about spending the night in her lover's arms. Meg had spent it doing her job, certainly a better memorial to the senator than his daughter's behavior.

Martin made Ashley forget everything.

"All right," Meg said. She sounded tired.

"How's Tony?"

"Better. They've taken him off the critical list, and he's been moved from intensive care to a private room. His wife called me just a few minutes ago."

"What does his doctor say?"

"His doctor is so afraid of a malpractice suit that he won't say grass is green. I don't know who to dismember first, that closemouthed quack or the people who colorized *Casablanca*."

"But if they took him off the critical list, that should be good news, shouldn't it?"

"I'm sure it is, but you wouldn't know it from the medical staff. When I was there, they were all creeping around like moles from the Pentagon. But Lorraine was reassured; she's gone home to see the kids. Her mother stayed with them while she was at the hospital."

"Meg, please send out the word to make sure Tony has everything he needs. Bill it all to me."

"I will. Don't give it a second thought," Meg said. "I'll take care of everything."

"Do you think if I called Tony I would get through? These gorillas here won't let me move, but I'd like to talk to him. Is he up to a phone conversation?"

"Maybe a short one. It's worth a try."

"Okay, I'll call." Ashley sighed. "How are things with the staff there?"

"You can imagine," Meg replied shortly. "Everybody's just stunned or crying, staring into space."

"I can't cry," Ashley said dully. "I don't know why, but I can't."

"Shock," Meg said.

"Is the press giving you a hard time?" Ashley asked.

"Roger's trying to handle them, but you wouldn't believe how boorish they can be. The biggest request is for pictures and old bios. It's gruesome."

Ashley swallowed, unable to reply.

There was a silence before Meg said in a controlled voice, "Have they set the funeral arrangements yet?"

"They'll be finalized today," Ashley said. "I was just about to go down and get the details from Sylvia."

"I guess you're letting her run the show, huh?" Meg said sympathetically, aware of the situation.

"I don't care what kind of a service they plan," Ashley said wearily. "The man is dead. What does it matter?" She bit her lip hard, fighting tears.

"I know how you feel," Meg murmured.

"Do you think you could come out to the house soon?" Ashley inquired, feeling childish for asking. "I could certainly use the moral support."

"I'll get there as soon as I can," Meg promised. "I want to wait until I'm sure everything is under control here."

"Are you really okay, Meg?" Ashley asked. "You've been a rock through all of this."

"I guess I'm numb," Meg replied. "It hasn't really sunk in yet. The loss, I mean."

"No, it hasn't," Ashley agreed quietly.

"Have you heard from Tim?" Meg asked.

"I talked to him," Ashley replied briefly. Somehow it was too soon to share the details of the previous night with anyone. She wanted some time to keep them to herself, as if she were hoarding a secret treasure.

"How is he?"

"All right. You know . . . he never talks much."

"I heard they took him off the case," Meg said.

"He wants to fight that."

"I kind of figured he would."

"Did Peter get back from his trip?" Ashley asked. "He must have been frantic when he heard the news."

There was a pause at the other end of the line. "I haven't been able to get in touch with him," Meg finally said.

"What do you mean?"

"I tried his office and his apartment and, oh, it's a long story, but I'm certain I'll hear from him soon."

"I'm sure he's concerned about you," Ashley observed, wondering why Meg sounded so bewildered about it. After all, how many places could the man be?

There was a knock at Ashley's door. She said "Hang on a minute" to Meg and covered the mouthpiece of the phone with her hand.

"Come in," she called to the person in the hall.

Elsie opened the door and, seeing that Ashley was on the phone, retreated.

"Elsie, wait," Ashley called after her. Into the phone

she said, "Meg, I have to go. I'll be in touch. And thanks for everything."

Meg said good-bye and Ashley hung up. She looked inquiringly at Elsie.

"Mrs. Fair would like to see you, ma'am," Elsie said politely. "She's waiting downstairs in the dining room."

"All right, Elsie, tell her I'll be right there."

"She sent all the senator's people away. She said she wanted to talk to you privately."

Ashley nodded.

"There are four federal marshals downstairs in the library, and a bunch of FBI people outside all around the grounds," Elsie added in a lower tone.

Ashley sighed. That was to be expected.

"Shall I have the cook prepare your breakfast now?" Elsie asked, folding her hands.

"You can tell Mary I'll stay, but not to make anything special. I'll have whatever is already out on the buffet for the others."

Elsie nodded.

"And please straighten up the green suite also, change the bed linen, clear away the dishes," Ashley added.

"Yes, ma'am." Elsie stood in the same spot, watching her.

"What is it, Elsie?" Ashley asked impatiently.

"Miss Fair, I was wondering . . . and well, some of the other staff people were too. . . ."

"Yes?" Ashley prompted her.

"What's going to happen to our jobs now?" Elsie finished in a rush. "I mean, with the senator gone, and Mrs. Fair in charge . . ."

Ashley waited.

Elsie hesitated, obviously distressed.

"Mrs. Fair is not in charge of this house," Ashley said firmly. "It was left to me in my father's will, to be run perpetually from a trust set aside for that purpose. You can tell everyone from me that you will all be kept on in your present positions. No one need worry. Please reassure anyone who is concerned that nothing will change."

"Yes, ma'am, I will," Elsie said gratefully, obviously relieved. She left, and Ashley stood slowly, her mind racing with thoughts of her father and the changes his death would bring to her life and the lives of everyone who had surrounded him during the campaign.

His death. She could hardly bear to consider it. The nightmarish vision of his shooting had replayed itself in her dreams until she thought she would never be able to close her eyes without seeing it.

Ashley put her hands to her temples and squared her shoulders resolutely.

She would think about it later, when she could stand it. One thing at a time, she recited to herself. First she would deal with Sylvia, then with the household, and then she would relive every moment of her night with Martin, savoring every detail.

That would sustain her through this difficult period until she saw him again.

CHAPTER
Nine

ASHLEY DESCENDED the main staircase and crossed the entry hall into the formal dining room at the front of the house. She preferred the smaller breakfast room off the kitchen, but Sylvia always dined in state, even at eight in the morning.

Her stepmother was seated at the head of the table, and Ashley was not surprised to see that she had company. There was no sign of Charles, but Sylvia's other children, Cynthia and little Joe, were there.

"Good morning, Sylvia, kids," Ashley said levelly, going to the buffet and helping herself to a cup of coffee.

Sylvia eyed her without responding. The older woman looked no better than she had the day before; her eyes were ringed with deeper circles and her lack of color was alarming.

"Where's Charles?" Ashley asked.

"I sent him to the townhouse," Sylvia replied crisply. "You made it clear that we were no longer welcome here, so I wanted him to get everything ready. Elsie is packing for me right now." Sylvia raised her cup to her lips. Her hand was trembling badly.

Cynthia, a sensitive twelve-year-old, was staring at Ashley, her expression confused and sad.

"Sylvia," Ashley said gently, "I admit I was annoyed yesterday and spoke sharply, but I never meant to imply that you should leave. Of course, you may stay as long as you like, you and the children. I was merely saying that Lieutenant Martin was my guest and should be treated as such, with respect, that's all."

"Is he still here?" Sylvia asked.

"No. He left early this morning."

"So. You spent the night following your father's death with him. That's in questionable taste, you must agree."

"Sylvia, it's a situation you could not possibly understand, so don't try."

"I understand a daughter who is too busy cavorting with her new lover to take an interest in her father's funeral arrangements," Sylvia snapped, casting a glance at Cynthia. She was obviously wondering if this conversation should take place in front of her daughter, but was too angry to restrain herself.

Ashley hung on to her temper with an effort. "Sylvia, we're both under a strain, and I'm sure you don't mean to be as rude as you sound. Anything that you arranged for the funeral is fine with me. My father exists in my memory now, and fancy eulogies and flowers won't alter my recollection."

Sylvia smiled bitterly. "Nicely put. You're so good with words, aren't you? Such a lawyer, right to the end."

Ashley fell silent. Sylvia had clearly stored up some

resentment there, and Ashley was nonplussed. Sylvia had always seemed content with her charities and her children, the family from which Ashley had constantly felt excluded.

"And now you've forsaken Jim Dillon, whom you've known for years, and if I may say so treated very cavalierly, to take up with this . . . cop," Sylvia said. "And a useless one at that. He didn't fulfill his function and prevent Joe's murder, did he?" Her face crumpled and her eyes grew wet as she remembered the tragedy.

Ashley looked at the kids, who were glancing from their mother to her like spectators at a tennis match.

"Why don't we continue this in the library?" Ashley said softly to Sylvia. "I'll call Elsie to serve Cindy and Joe, and we can talk."

Sylvia made no objection, and by the time the two women were settled with a tray in the adjoining room, Ashley had herself under firm control.

"Sylvia," Ashley began, "Lieutenant Martin did everything possible to keep Dad safe. I was there most of the time; you weren't. You'll have to take my word for that."

"Oh, you'd say anything to defend your boyfriend," Sylvia answered bitterly.

Ashley realized that discussing the subject was useless. She wasn't going to get into the issue of Martin's competence again. She had witnessed what happened in Millvale, and she knew he was blameless. Grief looked for a scapegoat, and Sylvia could not accept that the unthinkable had happened. She wanted to point an accusing finger at somebody, and the cop assigned to the case was the most convenient target.

"Have you considered the possibility that this oh-so-wonderful policeman may be after your money?" Sylvia demanded.

Ashley stared back at her, stunned. Then she started to laugh. She couldn't help it.

"I don't find that concept particularly amusing," Sylvia said to her stiffly.

"If you knew Tim at all, you would realize how ridiculous that question is," Ashley said, still smiling.

"Why ridiculous? Cops are not known for their lavish earning potential, and you have just inherited all this," Sylvia said, making a sweeping gesture to include the house.

"Tim considers 'all this' to be the chief barrier to our relationship," Ashley informed her.

"'Relationship'? I suspected it was something more than comforting the bereaved. I suppose from your last remark that he wishes you were poor?"

"I think he would like it a lot better if we were more evenly matched in the monetary department, yes."

"You're a fool if you believe that. Other people envy us, and some of them will try to take advantage."

"Not Tim. I think I know him better than you do."

"He looks like a gigolo to me."

Ashley stared at her, openmouthed. "A gigolo?"

"Why not?"

"A gigolo cop?" Ashley said. She couldn't believe it. She felt laughter bubbling up again, but suppressed it.

"He has the look, the manner," Sylvia said. "I've watched him. So handsome . . . and that intensity. It works on women like a magnet."

"Sylvia, Tim is a lieutenant on the Philadelphia police

force. Cops work for a living; they work hard. Gigolos hang out in casinos and service rich women."

"He's servicing a rich woman. He did so last night. And you're very vulnerable right now. We all are."

Ashley bit back the angry words springing to her lips. It had been a mistake to even discuss Tim with Sylvia, but maybe the older woman really was trying to give her good advice.

"Look, Sylvia, I know what I'm doing, and I have every intention of behaving sensibly. Can we change the subject and talk about the practicalities now?"

Sylvia was silent for a moment, and then said shortly, "Fine."

"I will be staying here until after the funeral, when I plan to return to my apartment," Ashley informed her. "My father left you the town house and the place in Bar Harbor, as well as the cabin at Bear Trail Lake. You said you'll be at the town house for now, is that right?"

"Yes. I may sell the cabin. I really haven't had the time to consider what's best. Joe rarely used it in recent years, and I have no interest in hunting."

"I see. Well, I told Elsie to assure the staff here that they would all be kept on in their jobs. I plan to keep the house open, and you and the kids can use it whenever you want."

"Thank you," Sylvia said grudgingly.

"Sylvia, I want to make this as easy on both of us as possible. Now, why don't you tell me about the funeral plans?"

A truce effected, her stepmother nodded and proceeded to do just that. It was an hour before Ashley was finished with the conversation, and then she went looking for her stepsiblings, of whom she was fond. They were stunned and bewildered by their father's violent passing, bereft of his presence when they were too young to understand the forces that had taken him away.

Ashley found Cynthia in the kitchen with Elsie, helping the older woman put away the breakfast dishes in the pantry.

"Cindy, how are you feeling?" Ashley asked her, taking the child aside as Elsie made a tactful departure.

Cynthia shrugged, her eyes on the floor.

"You can tell me," Ashley said gently.

"I miss my dad," Cynthia mumbled.

"I know," Ashley said. "I miss him too."

"He's not coming back."

Ashley shook her head, wishing that she could contradict that statement.

"Ash, what happened?" Cynthia asked.

Ashley didn't answer immediately, wondering what Sylvia had told the girl.

"They're trying to keep me away from the news," Cindy said, "but I know Dad was shot with a gun."

Ashley nodded.

"Who did it?"

"We don't know."

"Are the police looking for him?"

"Oh, yes. They'll find him, too."

"They don't always find assassins, I know. I read about it in school. Sometimes the police don't get them."

"The police are looking very hard, Cyn, I promise."

"Why would somebody shoot Daddy?" Cynthia asked, her adolescent face crumbling.

Ashley hugged her close. "I don't know, baby. There are sick people in the world. Maybe somebody who didn't like what he was trying to do for our country, maybe somebody who's just insane and doesn't have a real reason. It's hard to understand something like this; even adults have a lot of trouble with it."

"Mommy says we have to remember what a good man he was and keep him in our hearts forever."

Ashley's eyes began to sting. "Your mother is absolutely right. And we all have to do our very best to help her now, because she's very upset."

Cynthia drew back to look at her stepsister. "Aren't you very upset, Ash?"

Ashley sighed, then nodded.

"Then don't we have to help you too?"

"We all have to help each other; it's the only way we can get through this. Will you give me your word that you'll mind your mother, and if you need anything you'll let me know?"

Cynthia nodded.

"Good girl," Ashley said, kissing her. "Now, where is Joey. I want to talk to him too."

"He's upstairs in Mom's bedroom, playing with the thunderbikes Mom bought him."

Ashley kissed Cynthia and then went up to the second floor to look for the little boy. She found him on the floor where Cindy had said he'd be, assembling plastic motocross bikes from a kit.

"Hi, Joe," Ashley said, crouching on the rug next to him.

He looked up at her, and she saw the telltale tracks of tears on his face.

For some reason, that released the flood that had been blocked up inside of Ashley. She gathered the boy into her arms, and with that solid little body cradled next to hers, she cried and cried.

Martin drove back to Philadelphia from the Fair estate in record time. His thoughts were filled with images of Ashley and their lovemaking, but as he got closer to the city, his concentration shifted to Rourke and the coming confrontation.

He was still wearing the clothes he'd worn to see Ashley, but he went straight to the precinct house, not stopping off at his place to change. The police station looked the same as it always had, but Martin felt that he'd altered immeasurably since he was last in it. He walked through the corridor outside Rourke's office, oblivious to the pea-green institutional walls, the notices tacked to bulletin boards, the soft-drink and coffee machines one of which predictably bore a hand-lettered Out of Order sign.

Heads turned as he passed, but no one spoke to him.

He knocked on Rourke's door.

"Yeah," Rourke barked from inside.

Martin went into the office.

Rourke was on the phone. He looked up when Martin entered the room, then said into the phone, "I'll get back to you."

He hung up, staring at his visitor.

Martin faced him across the desk.

"You look like hell," Rourke greeted him.

Martin said nothing.

"You been getting any sleep?"

"Some."

"You got skinny, too. It's all those smokes, kid. Give the cigarettes a rest; you'll live longer. I gave 'em up four years ago, and look at me. Never felt better."

Martin stared at the wall behind Rourke's head. This was all he needed now, a health lecture.

"How's Capo?" Rourke asked.

"He's going to make it." Martin paused and added shortly, "No thanks to me."

Rourke held up his hand. "We've been through this already. I don't want to hear that."

"I still feel like I screwed up. Fair was my responsibility, and he's dead."

Rourke shook his head. "Internal Affairs already knows the senator disobeyed your instructions. He didn't stick to procedure. They're aware of exactly what happened."

"I thought IA would be involved."

"You'll have to talk to them, but it'll be routine. They know there's only so much you can do in a situation like that." Rourke got up from his chair and walked around his desk, putting his hand on the younger man's shoulder. "Don't take it on, Tim, or you'll never get over it. You're a veteran, you've been through things like this before. Put it behind you."

"I never saw anyone I was protecting get murdered right in front of my eyes. I felt . . . helpless."

"Yeah, I know. Cops hate helpless. But you've got to let these things slide. Neither one of us expected this to happen."

"I want to go after the guy, Gerry. It was my show. I deserve the chance."

Rourke stared at him. "The feds have it now."

"Then give me a leave of absence. Starting now."

"Tim, you know how long it takes to get a leave approved around here. You'd be in a rocking chair before it came through. And anyway, I think you should stay clear of this until the IA investigation is over and you're pronounced clean."

"Gerry, it's my case, and they're pushing me out of it."

"It's not your case anymore, I already told you that."

"So I'm just supposed to fade into the woodwork? I have nothing to say about it?"

"For Christ's sake, Tim, let the feds have it. The damn thing's getting worse every minute. That was the Bureau on the phone when you came in here."

"And?"

"It's hit the media that the daughter saw the shooter."

Martin went white. "What?" he whispered.

"Yeah, I know, it's bad."

"I told her not to tell anyone she saw the guy," Martin murmured, stunned. "She promised me she wouldn't."

"I knew you would have told her to keep her mouth shut," Rourke said. "I checked into it, and it seems the girl was sedated in the hospital. I guess she was confused by the drug, half asleep maybe, and she mumbled something to a nurse, who then leaked it to the papers."

Martin swore under his breath.

"It seemed fishy to me too, so I . . ." Rourke said.

He stopped in amazement as Martin pushed past him roughly.

"Where the hell do you think you're going?" Rourke demanded, blocking his path.

"Get out of my way," Martin said, dodging.

"Don't give me that," Rourke barked. "I'm still your superior in this department, and you'll answer a direct question, boyo, or I'll have the desk sergeant detain you at the door."

Martin paused in flight and sighed. He knew Rourke would do it, and a hassle would only delay him further.

"I'm going back to the Fair house," he said. "The gunman will be after the girl as soon as he finds out she saw him."

"That's not your problem now!" Rourke shouted, as if increased volume would get the message across. "You're off the case!"

"Gerry, he'll kill her," Martin said, trying to remain calm. If Rourke stopped him, he'd be no good to Ashley or anyone else.

"You don't know that."

"Don't bullshit me, Gerry. We both know what's going to happen. This guy is a pro. He was in and out of that hotel in Millvale like a bolt of lightning. He'll track her down and eliminate the witness."

"She has the FBI to protect her."

"Oh, screw the FBI!" Martin exploded. "She needs me."

Rourke stared at him, his watery blue eyes widening. "She needs you," he repeated slowly. "Would you mind telling me how you came to that startling conclusion?"

Martin didn't answer.

"Timmy, talk to me. What's going on here?"

Martin still avoided his eyes and did not reply.

"Are you sleeping with this Fair girl?" Rourke demanded, getting the drift.

Martin looked at him then.

"You were always a great one for the ladies, Tim, I know that. I've heard all the love-'em-and-leave-'em stories circulating through this department, but up till now you always managed to keep it separate from business. Now, tell me, are you getting it on with the late senator's daughter?"

Martin stared him down, his eyes blazing angrily.

"Oh, I see. Like that, is it?" Rourke said softly. "Not just a tumble, then. Are you in love with her?"

Martin's mouth became a hard line.

"I lost my psychic abilities when I was promoted to captain," Rourke said harshly. "And I'm not invading your precious privacy, because this is involved with your job and therefore my concern. Answer the question. Now."

"Yes. I'm in love with her."

Rourke closed his eyes. "Sweet leaping Jesus. I thought I'd heard everything, but this has to be it. Timmy, what is the matter with you? I knew you were working too hard; I thought this assignment would give you a break. Instead you go soft on me."

"I haven't gone soft, and we're wasting time. The killer is probably tracking Ashley as we speak. Can I go now?"

"Stick your feet to the floor, son. I'm talking to you," Rourke replied flatly.

Martin stayed where he was.

"Tim," Rourke said in an approximation of a reasonable tone, "this girl is rich as Cleopatra. Her whole family is rolling in dough. Her father was running for president, for God's sake. You're a cop. How are you going to fit into that?"

"You let me worry about it," Martin replied shortly.

"Do you mind if I do worry about it, since I consider myself your friend as well as your boss?"

Martin sighed deeply and shifted his weight like a schoolboy called on the carpet by the principal. He could almost feel time passing, time that would bring the assassin closer to Ashley, and here he was, trapped with Gerald Rourke, dispenser of wisdom.

"Tim, you're a good-looking guy, single. I understand how it is," Rourke said. "And God knows the girl's a knockout; I've seen the pictures. If I were twenty years younger and in your situation, I'd be tempted myself. But it's the circumstances that throw people together. She's depending on you now. She's scared and upset, and she wants someone to lean on through this. You're handy, and she sees you in the role of ally and defender. Isn't that right?"

"You seem to be doing all the talking," Martin replied lifelessly, eyeing his boss levelly.

"But what if you're just a diversion in this crisis?" Rourke continued, ignoring the younger man's tone. "If you have nothing in common with her, it can't last for the long haul. I know you, and you don't risk your feelings lightly. You'll be left out in the cold if her usual type looks good to her again once this thing is over. Have you thought of that?"

Martin didn't answer, but his expression indicated that he had thought of that. Often.

"What will you do then?" Rourke demanded.

"I'll deal with that when the time comes, but right

now I'm more interested in saving her life. Will you let me out of here so I can do that, Gerry?"

"I can't cover for you if you leave now," Rourke said flatly. "Your career in the department will be over."

Martin ripped his shield from his pocket and tossed it on Rourke's desk. "So it's over."

Rourke shook his head sadly. "You're going to take this on as a civilian?"

"You leave me no choice."

"Vigilantes are heroes only in the movies, Tim. In real life, they wind up in jail."

"I'll take that chance."

Martin moved toward the door, and Rourke called after him, "Tim, remember your dad."

Martin paused and said sarcastically, "Are we going to have old home week now, too?"

"Remember all the time you've put in already," Rourke continued, undaunted. "Are you going to give that up for some high-society dame who could be moving on to a new man next month? Please, think about it."

"I don't have to think," Martin said tightly, turning back to him. "I lost Maryann because of this job, and I am not going to let it jeopardize Ashley's life. I'm going. You can't stop a private citizen from taking a trip."

"Want to bet?" Rourke asked softly.

"Then I'm asking you, as a favor, not to do it. Let me go."

Rourke thought a long moment, searching the younger man's face, and then stepped aside.

Martin brushed past him through the door, and Rourke heard his running footsteps travel down the hall.

The police captain reached down to his desk and picked up Martin's shield, turning it over and over in his hand.

Ashley picked up the phone in the library and, like magic, an agent appeared at her side.

"I'm afraid you can't make any telephone calls out of the house, Miss Fair," he said politely.

"I'm just calling the hospital to speak to Sergeant Capo, the policeman injured when my father was . . . killed."

"I'm sorry," he said.

Ashley bit her lip. "Look, Agent . . ." she glanced at his tag, "Agent Marks, your people spirited me out of the hospital before I could visit him, and I haven't been in touch with him directly since. He almost lost his life trying to protect the senator, and I think the very least he deserves is to speak to me on the phone. Now, can you arrange that or not?"

"Please wait here and please don't use the phone until I return," Marks said evenly, and disappeared.

Yes, sir, Ashley thought to herself, saluting mentally.

Marks came back several minutes later and said, "You can call, but I'll remain with you."

"Fine," Ashley said, willing to accept any terms that would allow her to make the call. She got the number from the operator and was put through to Capo's room.

The agent stood by listening, his face impassive.

A woman's voice answered, "Hello?"

"Mrs. Capo?"

"Yes?"

"This is Ashley Fair."

"Oh, uh, hello," Lorraine Capo said, taken by surprise.

"I'm very sorry that I haven't called before now, but I've been caught up in the federal security net, and it's proving difficult to do much of anything."

The agent did not react to this.

"I understand," Lorraine said.

"I wanted to visit your husband when he was first hurt, but I was taken away from the hospital early next morning and didn't have the chance."

"Yes, I know. Meg Drummond told me."

"I want you to know how much I appreciate his efforts on my behalf and my father's," Ashley said.

"He was just doing his job," Lorraine said.

"He did it very well. May I speak to him, by any chance?"

"I'm sorry, Miss Fair, he's asleep. They're keeping him knocked out most of the time. I'll be sure to tell him you called, though."

"Thank you."

Lorraine hesitated and then said, "Miss Fair, is Tim Martin okay?"

Ashley realized that Lorraine Capo must know something of her relationship with Martin, so she replied, "He's fine."

"He's taking all of this very hard."

"Yes, I know."

"You'll look out for him, won't you? Don't let him get into trouble with the Philly brass."

"I'll do my best."

:"Thanks. And Miss Fair, I'm sorry about your father."

"I know you are. Please give my message to Tony."

"I will. Good-bye."

"Good-bye."

Ashley hung up the phone and glanced at Agent Marks.

"All done," she said crisply.

She walked out of the room, and he followed, right on her heels.

It was midafternoon by the time Meg finished at campaign headquarters. She left, lugging her most essential papers in her briefcase, and went out to the parking lot. It was a sunny, warm day, the weather contrasting sharply with her mood.

As she got closer to her car, she saw that a man was leaning against it.

He straightened as he saw her, and she began to run.

"Peter!" she cried. "Where on earth have you been?"

CHAPTER
Ten

RANSOM GRABBED her up and held her tightly, his eyes closing. He'd thought he would never see her again, and although necessity compelled him to change his plans, he was not sorry about this aspect of his misfortune.

He had missed her.

"Are you all right?" he asked. "I heard about the senator. It was all over the news." He deliberately held her against his shoulder and talked into her ear; he knew he would not be able to meet her eyes as he said those words.

"I'm fine."

"I tried to get in touch with you the night it happened, but the cops had all the lines at the hotel tied up. They weren't putting any civilians through."

"I know, it was chaos." She paused and then added, "I really don't want to talk about it, okay? Between the questions from cops and reporters, I'm all talked out, and I'd just like to be with you and forget it for a while."

"All right," he said. "But I'm so glad you weren't hurt." He had made sure of that, at his own expense.

"Peter, I tried to reach you, but I couldn't," Meg said, her voice muffled by his jacket. "I called your office, and a recorded announcement answered saying that the number was no longer in service."

"It was changed. I should have told you about it. I'll give you the new one later," Ransom replied, holding her away from him to look down into her face.

"But why didn't the announcement say that the number had been changed? They do that first and then give you the new one."

"How should I know, Meg? It sounds like the phone company made a mistake."

"And your answering machine wasn't on. The phone just rang and rang."

"I must have forgotten to put it on. I left in kind of a hurry. I was late getting out and didn't want to miss my plane."

"But . . ." Meg said, her brow furrowing.

He put his hand over her mouth. "Are you going to ask me a million questions or are we going to get out of this parking lot and make up for lost time?"

Meg fell silent, putting aside her confusion for the moment. Whatever had happened, he was back now, and she was too happy about that to conduct an inquisition at the moment.

"Where do you want to go?" she asked. "Do you want to drive back to your apartment?"

"No, that's too far. I can't wait that long to be with you. Let's just get a hotel room."

"Here in town?"

"Let's drive out into the country, okay? An inn. There's a bunch of them around here."

"All right. Where's your car?"

"I had some trouble with it. When I got back from my trip, it wouldn't start. I had it towed from the airport to an auto-repair place. It's being fixed now."

"So how did you get here?"

"I booked a one-way rental, dropped it off in town. I'm afraid our only transportation is your chariot here."

"That's okay, no problem. None of the tires appear to be flat at the moment."

"Where were you going when you came out just now?" he asked carefully.

"I was going to drive back to the Fair estate."

"Can that wait?"

"Long enough for us to be together, certainly," she whispered, leaning into him.

"Good."

He took her hand and kissed it, then stood aside as she unlocked the door of her car and handed him the keys. He was just turning to get in when a police car screeched in the distance, coming closer to them, siren wailing.

Ransom froze, his head jerked around sharply in the direction of the noise.

"What is it?" Meg asked.

He didn't answer, peering into the distance with an intent expression.

"It's just a squad car chasing somebody in felony shoes," Meg said. "What's the matter with you?"

Ransom looked at her then, and his face visibly relaxed. "Oh, I don't like sirens. I always think an ambulance is coming."

The police car blew past them, screaming shrilly, red and blue light rotating. Meg nudged Ransom, who was still leaning in the door of the car, fixed in the same posture.

"Let's go," she said, and walked around to the passenger side of the car.

Ransom got behind the wheel and started the motor, moving quickly to conceal how much his hands were shaking.

"Are you feeling all right?" Meg asked as he left the lot and pulled out into the stream of traffic. Her voice was concerned.

"Why do you ask?" he said, wondering if he would be able to keep up his act as long as he had to; it was obviously showing signs of falling apart.

"You seem . . . shaky . . . or something. Are you sick?"

"I haven't been feeling well lately. Maybe I'm coming down with a bug."

Meg surveyed him closely. "It's true, you don't look so hot."

"I'm sure I'll be better with you here," he said confidently.

"Why? I'm not an antibiotic."

"You know what I mean."

"Am I to understand that you missed me?" Meg asked.

"You can understand that, yes."

"A lot?"

"A lot," he confirmed.

"How did the trip go?"

"The trip?"

"Your business trip, dummy, the one that took you away in the first place."

"Oh, yeah, it was fine."

"Fine. That's all you can say?"

"I saw a shopping mall, Meg, like a thousand others. They all look the same."

"Then why did you have to go there?"

"I wanted to check the location and traffic pattern in person, talk to the mall manager about the amount of business he did and the draw from the surrounding towns. It was something I really couldn't do over the phone."

"Okay, okay, don't get testy." She slid over next to him and put her hand on his thigh. "Exactly how far is this country inn we've been talking about?"

He pulled a travel brochure from his pocket and handed it to her. "I got this when I returned the car," he said. "There's a place about ten miles from here. Swanleigh."

"Swanleigh? Aren't we grand? Will Queen Elizabeth the First and Leicester be there to greet us?" She examined the pamphlet and began to read aloud, describing the hotel's appointments.

Ransom had consulted a map before he met Meg that day, and found the inn with no trouble. It was located on the end of a country road that fed off a state highway, isolated enough to attract romantics but close enough to the main arteries to attract tourists. The grounds were in full bloom at this time of year, and on weekends the place was usually booked solid.

But for an extra hundred passed over the desk there was always room.

They registered as Mr. and Mrs. Peter Ransom. He didn't care about using the name; once he eliminated the Fair girl, he would be out of the country in a matter of hours.

But he had to find her first.

They were shown to an airy room on the second floor with a splendid view of the gardens below them. Meg went to the bay window, exclaiming over the flowers, but Ransom followed close behind her, circling her waist with his arms.

"Forget the hibiscus," he said. "Concentrate on me."

"With pleasure," Meg replied, spinning around to face him.

When he kissed her, he almost lost his nerve. Was he really about to use her again, this woman who had given him more in the short time he'd known her than anyone else in his life? Why couldn't he just stay here with her, in this blossom-laden paradise, and take his chances? The police weren't magicians, and he had covered his tracks.

Then reason asserted itself, and he knew he couldn't do it. But he could love her one last time.

He undressed her and took her to bed, and Meg sensed the urgency in him, the almost desperate need to imprint her on his mind and body. When they had finished and she turned away, confused, he pulled her back to him, holding her within the curve of his body and drawing her head onto his shoulder.

"Peter, what is it?" she said, looking up at him. "Something's wrong."

"I just missed you, that's all."

Meg subsided uneasily. Something *was* wrong, different, but she couldn't put her finger on it.

He drew the sheet down from her shoulders and stroked her naked back. "How is Ashley now?" he asked.

"Ashley?" Meg said.

"Yeah, she's your friend. I wondered how she was doing."

"About how you'd expect, I guess."

"Is she still at the estate in Harrisburg?"

"Last I checked, but I imagine the federal people will be moving her soon."

"Why?"

"She saw the assassin; it was on the news. I think they'll want to protect her."

"Where do you think they'll take her?"

"I don't know. Bear Trail Lake, maybe. The senator's family has a hunting cabin there, but it was never used much. Very few people know about it. And it's in the woods, difficult to get to. You can hide out there easily enough."

Ransom listened, his mind racing. He remembered the cabin from the information in Meg's computer. He had destroyed all the disks he'd copied before he left his apartment, but he'd studied them so often while planning the hit that he almost had their contents memorized. He visualized the plans for the cabin, its location, the surrounding terrain. It was perfect.

Meg was right. He knew cops and how they thought, and the feds were just souped-up cops who made some more money than the average flatfoot.

They would take Ashley to Bear Trail Lake.

He slid his legs over the side of the bed and stood up to put on his pants.

"Where are you going?" Meg asked.

"Downstairs to order dinner."

"You can do that over the phone."

"I want to get something really special to surprise you."

"Come back to bed and surprise me here. I'm sure there are a few things left we haven't tried."

In spite of his situation, he had to smile. Meg. This was the last he would ever see of her.

"Indulge me, please," he said to her. "I want to talk to the chef. This restaurant is famous in the county. I'd also like to select the wine personally. It won't take long."

"Oh, all right," she said sleepily, rolling over in the bed to face the wall and yawning. "I'll take a nap until you get back."

"Do that," he said, slipping into his shirt. He opened the door into the hall and tossed his jacket on the carpet, then came back to sit next to Meg on the bed.

"You still here?" Meg said teasingly, turning to look at him.

"Kiss me," he said, gathering her into his arms.

"I just did. Many times."

"Kiss me again."

Meg complied, and then he held her tightly, his eyes shut, his anguished expression concealed from her as he buried his face in her soft hair.

"Peter, are you sure everything is all right?" she asked again.

"Everything's fine. Take your nap. I'll be right back." He forced himself to go into the hall without looking back, and then picked up his jacket and marched to the elevator, his heart pounding.

It must be done, he told himself. I must leave her now.

When he stepped off the elevator into the lobby, he went straight to the desk clerk who had registered them.

"I've been called away on business," he said to the man. "I'll be leaving now, but my wife will stay on in the room."

"Oh, what a shame," the man said sympathetically. "I'm sure Mrs. Ransom will be very disappointed."

"I want to leave the car for my wife, so I'll need to rent a car this afternoon."

"We have a standing contract with the Avis in Hunterdon, a few miles away. We can make the arrangements over the phone, and then our driver can take you to pick up the car."

"That will be fine."

"Would you like me to call them now?"

"Please. I'm in a hurry."

Ransom watched the man pick up the receiver and begin to punch the buttons on the phone.

Meg woke about an hour later and realized that Ransom had not returned. Thinking that he had decided to take a walk and let her sleep, she showered and dressed, then read a fashion magazine. Then she did her nails.

When two hours had passed, she called down to the desk.

"This is Mrs. Ransom in two-fourteen," she said to

the clerk. "My husband and I just came in a couple of hours ago."

"Yes, Mrs. Ransom."

"I can't seem to find my husband. Have you seen him?"

There was a long pause at the other end of the line, and then the man said, "There must be some misunderstanding, Mrs. Ransom. Your husband checked out about three o'clock. He said you would be staying on for a while."

Meg's fingers curled so tightly around the receiver that her knuckles whitened. "Did he say anything else?" she said in a taut, barely controlled voice.

"Just that he wanted to rent a car. Our driver took him into town to the Avis there." The clerk hesitated and then said, "Is there a problem, Mrs. Ransom?"

"No, no, we just got our wires crossed, that's all. Thank you."

Meg hung up the phone, feeling faint.

She had made a terrible, dreadful mistake.

Calm down, she instructed herself. Think. Think hard.

Fragments of ideas chased themselves through her head. What could she check? Who did she know who knew him? Calling the business was no good; she'd just get the recorded announcement again. She suddenly seized on the idea of Ransom's doorman, Julio, a young Filipino who knew her from her visits to Ransom's apartment.

It was just before five; he would probably still be on duty.

She followed the procedure for making long-distance

calls on the hotel phone and called Philadelphia information, getting the number of Ransom's building. Then she dialed that, her heart banging like a hammer on an anvil in her chest.

"Hello. Stratford House," a male voice answered with a faint Spanish accent.

"I'm calling for Julio, the doorman," Meg said.

"This is Julio."

Thank God. "Julio, this is Margaret Drummond, Mr. Ransom's friend. I've been there several times with Mr. Ransom. The last time I visited him, all three of us talked about the racetrack in Manila, remember?"

"Sure, I remember you," Julio said, but his tone was cautious. He had been a doorman too long.

"Julio, I'm concerned about Mr. Ransom. I haven't seen him for a while and I'm afraid something may have happened to him. Can you remember the last time you saw him?"

There was a silence while Julio thought about it. "I haven't seen him for a couple of days, maybe. I can't remember exactly."

"Think, Julio. Last Thursday, the day Senator Fair was killed, did you see him then?"

"I think he left here right after noon that day."

When he was supposedly away already, according to what he had told Meg.

"Did he have anything with him?"

"Overnight bag."

Meg considered that, then said, "Julio, how long has Mr. Ransom lived at the Stratford House?"

"He moved in about six weeks ago."

Just around the time I met him, Meg thought.

"Miss Drummond, what's going on here?" Julio said. "You're asking a lot of questions, and I don't want to get into trouble. The residents don't like me poking into their private business."

"I understand that, Julio, but this is vitally important. Just a few questions more. Did you notice what kind of hours Mr. Ransom kept? Did he go to the office the same time every day, that sort of thing?"

"Nah, he kept odd hours. He came and went all different times, day and night. I filled in on the night shift a couple of times. I saw him go out two or three in the the morning, come back at dawn."

"Did you ever see him bringing things in or out?"

"What kind of things?" Julio asked suspiciously.

"Anything. Boxes, cartons."

"Well, he had a couple of big boxes of clothes packed up for the Salvation Army last week. I helped him carry them outside for the pickup by the truck."

Getting rid of his wardrobe? Meg wondered. Why?

"Did he ever have anything delivered?"

"Some computer stuff once."

"Computer stuff?" Meg said faintly.

"Yeah, I knew what it was from the apple on the box. That's what they call them, right? Apples?"

"Right," Meg echoed, swallowing. Oh, God.

"Miss Drummond, you there?" Julio said.

"I'm here. Julio, I don't suppose you could unlock Mr. Ransom's door, check the apartment for me."

"No, ma'am," Julio said firmly. "I've got the master key, but the super needs a court order to go into one of the apartments without the tenant's permission."

"I see. Well, thank you, Julio. You've been very helpful."

"Miss Drummond, you won't say anything about this to anybody, will you? I already told you too much."

"I won't say anything, Julio. Thanks again. Goodbye."

Meg severed the connection, then dialed the number of the Fair estate outside of Harrisburg.

A man's voice answered.

Meg hesitated. Elsie or one of the other female house staff usually answered the phone.

"Who is this?" the man demanded.

"This is Margaret Drummond, the late senator's personal assistant. Who are you?"

"This is Special Agent Forsyth of the FBI," the man replied.

Meg thought that over for a second. The Bureau must have descended on the homestead with a vengeance once they realized that Ashley was virtually alone there, and could identify the killer.

"May I speak to Miss Fair, please?" Meg said.

"I'm sorry, I'm not authorized to give any phone clearances," Forsyth replied.

Meg had a choice to make. She could confess what she was thinking to this unknown agent over the phone, or she could go to the estate and talk to Ashley herself.

She opted for the latter course of action, primarily because she didn't want to cast suspicion on Ransom needlessly. He had definitely been up to something, but she wasn't sure it had anything to do with the senator's death. Maybe he was just a nosy reporter looking for a campaign scoop, and his report back to his newspaper or magazine had coincided with the assassination. Such a cover could explain a lot of what had happened, including her hunch that he had raided her computer.

"May I speak to the senior house maid, Elsie Jenkins?" Meg asked Forsyth. "She knows my voice and can identify me."

"Hold on, please."

These people are always so polite, Meg thought impatiently.

There was a long pause, and then Elsie came on the line.

"Hello, Miss Drummond, is that you?"

She sounded upset.

"Yes, Elsie, it's me. What's going on there?"

"I can't tell you about that, Miss Drummond."

"Well, is Miss Fair there?"

"I can't tell you that, either."

Meg could picture Forsyth standing next to the diminutive maid, towering over her and scaring her to death.

"All right." Meg sighed. "I will be there in about two hours. Will you tell the agents that so they can alert the men at the entrance to let me on the grounds? I don't feel like having another conversation like this one at the gate."

"Yes, ma'am," Elsie said meekly.

Meg hung up. She had to get to Ashley as soon as possible.

Martin got off the shuttle and headed immediately for the car-rental desk at the airport. He was now technically unemployed, but he shamelessly displayed his police ID to the clerk when signing the rental contract, thinking that all his credit cards would probably be revoked once Big Brother discovered his recently acquired welfare status.

He was on the road in minutes, headed back to the house in Harrisburg.

"I don't see why I have to leave this house," Ashley said to Agent Forsyth. "Can't you protect me here?"

"This house is too well known. The killer may come here," Forsyth replied.

They were standing by the fireplace in the library, and Forsyth was explaining why she had to be removed to the hunting cabin until the assassin was caught.

"Mr. Forsyth, you have turned this place into a fortress. If he can get in here, he's supernatural."

"Nonetheless, we feel that you would be safer at a more remote location."

There was no point in arguing with this man, Ashley thought. He listened to what she had to say, courteously, and then repeated his position as if he hadn't heard her.

It was like talking to a computer.

"The funeral is tomorrow," Ashley pointed out to him.

"You won't be attending the funeral."

"But it's my father—"

"It's your life," the FBI agent interrupted her. "Everyone will understand."

Ashley gave in, defeated. "All right, I'll go. But I'll have to leave a message about where I am for someone who might be coming back here to see me."

"No messages," Forsyth said. "Just pack a bag. We'll be ready to leave in fifteen minutes."

"But I want Lieutenant Martin to be able to reach me," Ashley said quickly, before she realized with horror that Forsyth knew Tim. All too well.

"Martin? Is that the cop who was assigned to this case before we came in? He was at the hospital when you were brought there."

Ashley was silent. The damage had been done.

"You're not going to be leaving word for that guy about anything," Forsyth said grimly, and strode away.

Ashley went upstairs to get her things.

She tried to see Elsie alone, but an agent was with them the whole time she was packing.

Forsyth met them in the hall.

"Sir, what shall I do with Miss Drummond when she arrives?" Elsie asked, following Ashley and the FBI men down the stairs.

"You can let her in, but say nothing about Miss Fair's situation. No speculation on her destination, especially."

"I don't know anything about it, so how could I speculate?" Elsie replied, meeting Ashley's eyes.

"Fine," Forsyth replied. He signaled to two more of his men, and they escorted Ashley out to the waiting car.

Elsie watched them go from the front bay window, her expression bleak.

When Meg arrived an hour later, the man at the gate let her go up to the house, and Elsie greeted her at the door.

"Miss Fair is gone," Elsie said. "They took her away."

"Where did they take her?" Meg asked, about ready to burst into tears of frustration.

"I don't know. They told me not to talk about it."

"Was it Bear Trail Lake?"

"They never said so," Elsie replied carefully.

"What does that mean?"

"Well, Miss Fair took her Aran sweater. She mentioned it particularly and asked me to fold it for her. She never takes that anywhere except to Bear Trail."

"She was sending you a message."

"I think so."

Meg fell into a chair in the entry hall.

"Well, Elsie, what do we do now?"

CHAPTER
Eleven

A S SOON as Martin approached the gate of the Fair estate, he knew that Ashley was not there. The same FBI sentry was still in the guardhouse at the foot of the hill, and there were agents about on the grounds for appearance's sake, but the whole place had the air of an abandoned camp.

The maid, Elsie, admitted him, and he wasn't surprised when Meg Drummond greeted him inside.

"Where is she?" Martin demanded without preliminary.

"The federal people took her away. They felt it wasn't safe for her to be here since it was on the news that she saw the killer."

"I heard it," he said tersely, looking around. He could see through the door at the end of the hall to the kitchen, where two agents lounged against the banquette, watching him from a distance. They clearly knew who he was, but did not seem disposed to interfere. They must have been assigned to guard the house, and, like robots programmed for a certain task, that's all they were going to do.

"How many did they leave behind?" he asked Meg, nodding to the federal men.

She shrugged. "There's more outside."

"How many went with Ashley?"

"Four, I think. Forsyth and three others. I know that they took two cars."

"Okay, where did they take her?" he asked.

Elsie and Meg exchanged glances.

"We could only make a guess," Meg said.

"Forsyth told us not to say anything," Elsie chimed in weakly.

"Tell me," Martin said.

Meg bit her lip. "I don't know. The rest of the family is at the town house with Sylvia. They can't make any decisions . . ."

Martin seized her by the shoulders. "You have to tell me. You know she would want me to know."

"She asked if she could leave word for you, and they forbade it. Tim, don't put me in this position. She's really scared, and so am I. You're not being fair."

"He's going to kill her if you don't tell me where she is."

Meg felt a chill. All of her doubts about Ransom, which she had managed to suppress since arriving at the house, returned. And Capo had asked her about him, too, she remembered, at the hospital.

The boyfriend with the flowers.

Martin surveyed her with intense blue eyes, waiting.

Even if Ransom was not involved, did she really want

to take the chance that Martin might have been able to help Ashley, and didn't, because she wouldn't tell him where her friend was?

She looked at Elsie, who nodded.

Meg made her decision. She trusted Tim Martin; he wasn't an alarmist and he knew what he was doing. If he believed that Ashley was in immediate danger, there was good reason for it.

"They took her to the senator's hunting cabin at Bear Trail Lake, about twenty miles from here," Meg said quickly.

At her side, Elsie sighed audibly, then walked away.

"And?" Martin said.

"It's a one-room cabin, much easier to guard than this huge place. It's not well known; only the senator's intimates are aware that it exists. I guess they didn't think the killer would know about it."

"He'll know. How do I get there?"

Meg told him, praying that she wasn't sending him to create worse trouble than they already had.

"Do you have a floor plan for it, some kind of blueprint?" he asked, pocketing his scribbled directions.

Meg thought a minute, then left the room, returning with a manila folder, which she handed to him.

"It was built twenty-five years ago. Those are the specs," she said. "You're not going alone, are you?"

Martin ignored her, already headed for the door. "Capo okay?" he called over his shoulder.

"He's much better. He asked for you and said to tell you—"

The door slammed on her words.

Meg didn't move, absorbed in her private thoughts.

Should she have told him about her suspicions concerning Ransom? She could hardly bring herself to consider them, much less discuss them with an itchy cop in love with Ransom's potential victim. But her conscience bothered her.

Something was wrong with Ransom's presence in her life, that much she knew, and she still hadn't told Martin about it.

Was it because to do so would have been to face the fact that her lover had been using her? Was she still denying that on some level, despite the mounting evidence to suggest it? Was she protecting him, though she wasn't sure he deserved it?

Meg went to the window and watched unhappily as Martin got into his car.

She had never felt more miserable and confused and scared in her life.

"The men in the kitchen are asking for coffee," Elsie said, coming up behind her.

"I'll make it," Meg replied automatically, glad of something to do.

"That's my job," Elsie volunteered.

"Go ahead and finish polishing the silver," Meg told her. "You can supervise those two new girls. I'm not sure they know what they're supposed to be doing."

"Yes, ma'am," Elsie said, and walked ahead of her into the vast kitchen, where the two agents Martin had seen were now seated in the breakfast nook, going over some papers.

Meg put on the coffee and then chatted with the two men, who were young and clearly bored. Another agent came in through the back door just as the coffee machine was steaming to a conclusion. He had a sheet of paper in his hand.

"We just got this from headquarters," he said, handing it to his colleague. "According to the Fair girl, this is the perp."

Meg got cups from the glass-fronted cabinets and went to the refrigerator for cream.

"A guilty face if I ever saw one," the recipient said.

Meg passed behind his shoulder to look at the picture, then dropped the container of cream to the floor. It shattered noisily, causing Elsie to splatter polish on Sylvia Fair's ornate silver teapot.

"Lady, you all right?" the closest agent said quickly, grabbing Meg's elbow as she appeared about to fall.

With a sudden burst of clarity, she heard herself telling Ransom about the Bear Trail Lake cabin. She saw herself in the Swanleigh bed with him, bathed in afterglow, telling him exactly where to find the woman he was planning to kill.

Just as he had killed her father.

"Sit down," she gasped.

He guided her into a seat, and when she could talk again she said, "Let me see that, please," pointing to the sketch he still held.

He surrendered it, and she studied it closely, her face a mask. So it was true—what she had not been able to bring herself to believe, even though she had known it in her heart.

"What's the matter, lady? You don't know this guy, do you?" the agent said.

"No, I don't know him," Meg replied quietly. "I never knew him at all."

She waited until they were drinking coffee and absorbed in conversation, and then she snatched up her car keys and ran out the front door before anyone could question her further.

Ransom sat on the roof of the senator's cabin, waiting for the federal cars to arrive.

Darkness had fallen, and the trees around him were swaying in a slight breeze. Night sounds abounded, and he was almost enjoying the tranquility of the setting as he prepared his ambush.

His friend the arms dealer had put him in touch with a local colleague who had supplied Ransom with grenades and a rare, expensive, U.S. Army rocket launcher, with two shells, the cost of which had emptied Ransom's domestic bank account. But there was plenty more money waiting for him in Europe, and he wouldn't get a chance to spend any of it if he didn't follow through on this mission.

He had also made some arrangements by Telex with his bank in Switzerland, in case this didn't work out the way he had planned.

He was ready.

He peered into the darkness, feeling the heady adrenaline rush he had often experienced in Vietnam, when he waited, at night and similarly equipped, for the enemy to appear.

He heard the crunching of gravel on the dirt road in the distance, and soon the two dark sedans came around a bend in the road. Ransom knelt and hoisted the launcher to his shoulder, taking from his belt the same

Luger that had killed Senator Fair, trying to determine which of the cars was Ashley's.

He didn't have long to wonder. The doors of both cars opened at the same time and the four agents emerged to flank Ashley, two on either side of her.

Ransom sighted her and was about to drill a bullet through her heart when, purely by chance, the agent nearest her glanced up and saw him on the roof.

The agent threw Ashley to the ground, and Ransom's bullet went astray, kicking up dirt. With his instantaneous reflexes, Ransom fell flat on his stomach and lobbed one of the shells at each of the cars, exploding them to prevent escape. Then he pulled a grenade from his belt and flung the live round into the path of the running agents, who were trying to drag Ashley into the house.

The grenade exploded and two of the agents fell dead. Ransom drew down on a third and shot him, then aimed at the last, who was crawling to the Fair girl as he pulled his gun, shielding her with his body and firing rapidly at the roof.

Ransom tried for the girl again, but the agent was well trained, keeping her behind him as he returned fire. Frustrated that the girl was still on her feet, Ransom jumped down from the roof and ran around the corner of the cabin.

He would have to take them out inside the house.

By the time Martin found the dirt road leading to the senator's cabin, it was fully dark. He was lost anyway, so he set out on foot with only a flashlight for guidance.

It took him about twenty minutes to locate the lake, and ten more to find the cabin.

He found it because the burning cars were torches to point the way. As he got closer, the smell of their incineration was overwhelming and the smoke stung his eyes.

He stumbled over the first body about thirty feet from the house. He recognized the dead agent, and his companion, sprawled nearby on a carpet of pine needles. The sight wasn't pretty.

Martin glanced up at the cabin, which was blank and silent and told him nothing.

An ambush, he thought. The killer had been waiting for them and probably had Ashley in the house.

Martin had memorized the layout of the cabin, and he crept to the back window, which looked into the living room.

He recognized the blond man holding Ashley, with his arm around her throat, from her description. The blond held a gun on Forsyth, who was backed to the far wall.

Standoff. It wouldn't last long.

The fact that he was using a gun told Martin that the killer was out of heavy-duty ammunition; there was only so much one man could purchase under the table, even with the best connections, or carry with him in one shot.

Martin felt a delicious, cold fury stealing through his veins. The bastard, blindsiding them like this, with an arsenal at his command. It was a miracle Ashley was still alive. Anger made him want to charge the house and take his chances. But he forced himself to think calmly, remembering that his caution could save Ashley's life.

There was a catwalk about the living room where the air-conditioning system had been installed years after the cabin was built. It had a trapdoor that opened into the main room, right where the gunman was standing.

It was his only chance. Wishing that he were a flyweight who would make little noise, Martin stood on the railing of the back porch and hoisted himself to the roof, feeling in the dark for the hinge on the door, hoping that it hadn't rusted shut. His fingers found it, and he heaved the door upward.

The door opened and Martin dropped onto Ransom in one smooth motion, knocking him to the ground. The gun shot out of his hands, and Ashley, stumbling from her abrupt release, scrambled for it wildly. She seized it and turned, confronting the struggling men, who were wrestling on the floor.

"Shoot!" Martin shouted.

Ashley hesitated, along with Forsyth, each of them trying to get a clear shot.

Suddenly Martin broke free of Ransom, rolling away from him, and Ashley and Forsyth both fired at the same time. The noise was deafening.

As the pungent smell of cordite filled the room, Ransom went limp. Forsyth walked over to him and poked.

"Done," he said with satisfaction. "Or almost. Still breathing, but not for long."

Martin sat up and looked at Ashley, who was paralyzed, the gun welded to her hands.

"Good girl," he said.

She dropped the gun to the floor and walked to him in a daze. He embraced her.

Forsyth approached Martin and said grudgingly, "You did good." He extended his hand.

Martin shook it, holding Ashley with his other arm.

The outer door burst open and a group of feds rushed in, stopping short when they saw the scene.

"About time you guys arrived," Martin said.

CHAPTER
Twelve

"HOW ARE you feeling?" Martin said to Ashley, handing her a cup of coffee through the car door.

"Whipped," she replied. She was huddled on the back seat of one of the federal sedans the second group of agents had brought, wearing Martin's jacket. The woods, usually so quiet, had erupted into life, with flashing lights and walkie-talkies and a fire engine dousing the blazing cars, not to mention a constant stream of vehicles trundling up and down the dirt road.

"Take a nap," Martin advised her. "I'm going to be talking to these people for a while."

Take a nap, Ashley thought incredulously. With all this relentless commotion?

Shortly thereafter, she fell asleep.

Martin walked back to the group of officials just as Meg's car careened to a halt on the lawn. Two feds intervened to stop her as she emerged from it, and Martin called to them to let her pass.

"What's going on?" he said to her as she ran up to him.

"Where is he?" she demanded.

"Who?"

"The . . ." She stopped. "The man you were looking for. Is he dead?"

"Close to it. He's inside. The medics are with him. Why?"

"I have to see him. I . . . know him. He's the one, the one who was sending me the flowers." She closed her eyes, stumbling on the last few words.

Martin understood instantly.

"Are you sure you want to see him?" he asked quietly.

She nodded. "Is Ashley all right?" she asked.

"She's fine." He looked down at her. "Ready to go?"

"Yes."

He shepherded her inside the cabin.

Ransom was lying on the floor where he had fallen, covered by a blue ambulance blanket. Two paramedics stood nearby, their white uniforms a stark contrast to the dark suits of the agents in the room.

"Aren't you going to take him to a hospital?" Martin asked them in an undertone.

"No point," one of them replied, shrugging, and turned away.

Meg knelt on the pine-board floor and took Ransom's flaccid hand in hers. Blood was puddled under his back and beneath his head.

His lashes fluttered, then lifted. She looked into his hazel eyes.

"Why?" she said, when she was sure he had recognized her.

"Money," he murmured. "Fair, and others. My job."

"You used me," she said accusingly, her voice breaking.

"At first," came the whispered reply. "Not now. Wish . . . had been different."

"You're lying," Meg said despairingly, but wanting to believe.

A faint smile touched his lips. "Why . . . lie?" he said. "Dying."

"No, you're not. Don't give up," she said fiercely, holding his hand to her cheek. "We'll get lawyers. I know the best."

"Ashley?" he whispered, still smiling.

Meg didn't know what to say.

His fingers curved, touched her mouth, then his eyes closed. His head moved ever so slightly back and forth.

"Over," he said faintly.

"Don't say that," she moaned.

His eyes opened again. "Telegram," he said, coughing. A thin trickle of watery blood escaped his lips, and Meg wiped it away with her fingers. "Pocket," he added.

It was a moment before she understood that he meant his jacket pocket. She removed a slip of yellow paper from it and saw that she held a copy of a telegram he had sent to the Bank of Lucerne earlier that day.

It gave access to all the funds in a numbered account to her.

The sum was staggering. He must have realized that

he might not survive his attempt on Ashley's life, and he had done this in case he didn't make it.

"I don't want your money," she cried, looking away.

"Take it. All . . . have to give." His voice was growing softer, more breathy, and his hand was cold.

"You gave me much more than that," Meg whispered.

His eyes flooded with tears, his first since childhood.

"Meg," he said to her as he died.

Meg sobbed her grief aloud as she was led away, past the sedan in which Ashley slept, to her own car. She collapsed into the back seat, where she stared sightlessly ahead, unresponsive to anyone who spoke to her.

After a while, one of the agents drove her home.

When Ashley awoke, it was morning, and she was in the guest-room bed in the Harrisburg house, still fully dressed. She stumbled out into the hallway, where she was confronted by two more men in the regulation dark suits.

She felt as though she had been living in the FBI training barracks for a week.

"Where's Lieutenant Martin?" she said to them.

One of the men shrugged. "He just carried you up to bed and then took off," he replied.

"Did he say anything?"

"No, ma'am, he just left."

Ashley burst into tears.

The two agents exchanged glances, astonished.

Ashley turned and ran back into the bedroom, slamming the door behind her.

"Do you believe that dame?" the one agent said to the

other. "After all she went through last night, she didn't shed one tear, and *now* she's crying."

"Women," his companion said.

A day later, Rourke looked up as the door opened, then stood as a young woman entered his office. She was wearing a pale-blue linen suit with white shoes and purse and white wrist-length gloves.

It had been a long time since he had seen a woman in gloves like that. When she extended her hand, he took it.

"Captain Rourke, I'm Ashley Fair," she said. "Thank you for agreeing to see me."

"Have a seat, Miss Fair," he said, sitting when she did.

She crossed trim legs, agleam with expensive hose, and met his gaze squarely. Luminous pearls glowed at her ears and throat.

"What can I do for you?" Rourke asked.

"I'm trying to locate Lieutenant Martin," she said to him.

Rouke stared at her. "Ma'am?" he said.

"I'm trying to locate Lieutenant Martin," she repeated, thinking that he had misunderstood. "I got his apartment address from Sergeant Capo, but Tim isn't there. I thought you might be able to help me. Is he on assignment or something?"

Rourke blinked. "Miss Fair, Tim Martin is no longer with the Philadelphia Metropolitan Police. He quit the day he went looking for Ransom against my orders. I haven't seen him since. I thought he was with you."

It was Ashley's turn to stare. She was silent for several moments, then said softly, "He left after he rescued me at my father's cabin. I woke up in my house and he was gone, no note, no message, nothing. I waited until I realized that he wasn't going to call me, and then I came here." She stopped and then added, "I had no idea he had left his job."

"Why do you want to see him?" Rourke asked bluntly.

"I love him, Captain," Ashley said simply. "I've only just begun to realize that he probably doesn't believe that."

Rourke met her gaze, then looked away. He had seen her pictures, but in person her impact was considerable; she had much of her old man's charm. Rourke could understand what had grabbed Martin, made him risk so much, and at the same time he felt a twinge of envy for the younger man for having won a woman like this.

"I think he has some idea that he won't fit into your life now that the crisis is over and you're safe," Rourke finally said, sighing. "I think that because I helped to give him that idea."

"I see," Ashley said slowly. She stood. "Captain Rourke, I must find him. Do you have any suggestion where I might start?"

Rourke thought about it. "When Tim was a kid, his father used to take him and his brother and sister to a summer house on the Jersey shore every year. Mike finally bought the place after his father died, for his own kids. He lets Tim use it for vacations or just when he wants to get away. I'd bet money Tim's there."

"Do you have the address?" Ashley asked.

Rourke held up a stained finger and consulted a notebook on his desk. He gave her the information, and she turned to go.

"Miss Fair?" Rourke called after her. "Good luck. I think that I misjudged you."

"We're all guilty of that sometimes, Captain," Ashley said quietly, and left.

Rourke turned in his swivel chair, thought for a moment, and then grinned.

Martin was sitting on the back porch of his brother's beach house, staring out at the inlet and smoking, when he heard a knock on the front screen. He got up, stubbing out his cigarette, and padded barefoot to the door.

He halted when he saw Ashley.

"Hi," she said. "May I come in?"

Martin stepped aside to let her pass. He was naked to the waist, wearing a threadbare pair of denim cutoffs and the red-gold blush of a new tan.

"Taking a vacation?" Ashley asked, looking around the room, which was furnished with rattan and bright printed curtains, rag rugs.

"Not exactly," Martin replied, deciding not to lie about it. "I'm unemployed."

"So I heard," Ashley said, turning to look at him. "I've just been to see your Captain Rourke. He was most informative. You might have said that you lost your job because of me."

"I didn't lose it. I quit."

"I bet the police would take you back. You're a hero."

Martin snorted. "You're always a hero when the bad guy dies." He paused. "How's Meg?"

"Not good. I still can't believe the assassin was that man she was seeing. I don't know if she'll ever get over it." She stopped, then added, "She really cared for him."

"Yeah," Martin replied thoughtfully, remembering the scene at the cottage. "And I think it was mutual. Strange, huh?"

"Maybe not so strange," Ashley murmured. "People get together under all sorts of circumstances."

She looked at him and he glanced away. She pointed to the porch. "Were you sitting outside?"

He nodded, not meeting her eyes.

"Let's go back there. I'd like to talk to you."

They went out onto the porch, which was really a redwood deck with an aluminum overhang, and Ashley noticed the pile of butts in the large glass ashtray on the railing.

He'd been sitting there smoking for a long time.

Ashley dropped into a canvas chair and Martin sat on the railing, leaning toward her with his forearms on his knees. He was looking at a spot in the air over her left shoulder.

"Tim, why did you leave me like that?" she asked, getting directly to the point. "I woke up and you were gone, and I've heard nothing from you since."

"I was trying to let you off the hook," he said quietly.

"What does that mean?" she asked.

He shrugged. "Look at you," he said, gesturing to her suit, the high heels. "Look at me. It would never work."

"I am looking at you. I'm remembering how it was to touch you, and how your hands and mouth felt on my body," she said softly.

He swallowed hard, his sapphire eyes darkening.

"Did you think that's all it was?" she asked him.

"I thought you were scared and needed somebody," he said. "I was there."

"Jim was there. He was there all the time. I needed you then and I still do."

Martin didn't answer.

Ashley got up and stood next to him. "Tim, listen to me. All of what you saw, the house in Harrisburg, the dinners and galas, it was my father's life, and it's over now. Sylvia can go on with it, but I don't have to anymore. I had left it before when I went to school, and then to work, but I got involved again for Dad's campaign. My obligation to that is finished. I'm a lawyer; I have a job. I'll go back to my apartment in Georgetown and go to work each day like you and everyone else." She moved closer, her breath fanning his cheek. "I can get a different job, whatever it takes. I can move, or you can. We'll work out the details if we want to be together. After all we've been through, do you really want to throw in the towel now?"

He turned and looked down at her.

She reached up to touch his face, her eyes glittering with unshed tears.

"I don't want to miss you all my life," she whispered. "Don't you love me, Tim?"

"God, yes," he said, turning his head to kiss her palm. "Why do you think I was running?"

Ashley closed her eyes, and tears coursed down her face. He pulled her into his arms and felt the wetness on her cheeks against his bare skin.

"Tim, listen to me," she murmured. "I don't care if

you're a cop or a train conductor or a clerk. I just want you."

He kissed her, running his hands up her back under her jacket, unhooking her bra. He turned her in his arms, cupping her breasts in his hands and pressing his mouth to the nape of her neck. Ashley gasped, leaning into him, and then they both jumped at a sudden barrage of whistles and catcalls from a passing speedboat.

"I guess we'd better go inside," Ashley said shakily, stepping away from him.

He picked her up and carried her into the house.

GET
LOVESTRUCK!

AND GET STRIKING ROMANCES
FROM POPULAR LIBRARY'S
BELOVED AUTHORS

*Watch for these exciting
romances in the months to come:*

June 1989
LOVE'S OWN CROWN by Laurie Grant
FAIR GAME by Doreen Owens Malek

July 1989
SHIELD'S LADY by Amanda Glass
BLAZE OF PASSION by Lisa Ann Verge

August 1989
BODY AND SOUL by Sherryl Woods
PROMISE OF SUMMER by Louisa Rawlings

September 1989
STAR STRUCK by Ann Miller
HIDDEN FIRE by Phyllis Herrm

October 1989
FAITH AND HONOR by Robin Maderich
SHADOW DANCE by Susan Andersen

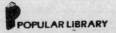